The White Raven Saga: The Price of Fire

Daniel Lucas

The White Raven Saga: The Price of Fire
© 2024 Daniel Lucas
https://www.karlielucas.com/p/daniellucas.html

Cover Design by Karlie Lucas
Maps created by Daniel Lucas

Paperback ISBN-13: 978-1-948028-33-2
Library of Congress Control Number: 2024940321
DragonKey Press
Dallas, Texas USA

PRINTED IN THE UNITED STATES OF AMERICA

DEDICATION

I dedicate this to all the pickled llamas of the world.

Before you sleep, before you eat
Be sure to remember, recite, and repeat
Fire blesses us with warmth and light
It cooks our food to our delight
But fire without wood could not be
For this we must respect and honor the Tree
However, tree would have no strength except for the Earth
Because from her, she gives all the grace of birth
And Water helps Earth not to be barren and dry,
For it blesses us all from the sky
With these four all is well
If one of these were gone, all would fail.

Child's training prayer from the Cathedral of Faith

PROLOGUE

At the far reaches of the endless cosmos, beyond the eternal Void, existed the realm of the Parthenon. Within her everlasting planes, the Deities of Old watched for the chance to increase their influence. The fates of mortal beings and lesser gods were playthings to those that call the Parthenon home. It was their right to move creation as pieces on a game board. Few, mortal or God, understood the meaning of this game. And what a game it was.

Fawdake, Lord of Chaos, lived for it. It thrilled him to no end. Being a master strategist, the lithe God loved thinking on his feet. Adapting to the whimsical, rudderless choices of mortals was a rare treat to the immortal. His counterparts needed order to thrive. But he relished in uncertainty.

His realm, if one called it that, was unique. No worshipers or acolytes adorned the grounds. No altars or prayer benches shimmered in or out of view. He was truly alone. Save for a palace and a garden.

A touch of irritation teased Fawdake this day. Like an itch just out of reach. The very air grated against him. Something in existence had changed. A game move he did not instigate. A mental darkness seeped into the immortal the closer he got to his garden.

A hurricane of color, size, and species welcomed the God. The organisms that call the garden home were as eccentric as Fawdake. No mere plants or flowers adorned this landscape. Such things were too pedestrian, too elementary. Nothing stayed still for long. Roses changed to cats. Ivies morphed into marble sculptures. They desired a glance from Fawdake. A mere touch of his gaze to prove their genius.

But such grabs for attention were folly.

The God of Chaos pondered on this irritation plaguing him. He knew the fluid state of the garden normally peaked his interest. Yet, nothing. No thrills or shock. No surprises. Only one word summed up his mood. Yes, the mighty Fawdake, Bringer of Chaos and Destruction, Giver of Life and

Luck, was bored. Bored of the cycle he had kept these innumerable eons. Bored of seeing his fellow Gods getting praised by their creators. Bored of the same cycle.

Fawdake wanted true change. Change in the Parthenon. Change in the worlds.

Casually returning to the palace's main hall, the irony of the one constant in his existence was not lost on him.

As a gift from the beings that gave him life, the Palace Hall was the one thing the God of Chaos could not change. It stayed exactly the same, like an immortal sentry in a place of everlasting variations. Numerous rooms, galleries, and wings populated the eternal structure. Each one showing a world in the known universe. Its levels reached high into the star-blanketed heavens. Its sheer size testified that the responsibility of completing the great plan of life rested solely on Fawdake's shoulders.

Caressing the alabaster and green jade staircase rail, the lithe God chuckled at the oddness of it all. For eternities before time began, his hatred for the unvarying building festered like a septic wound. It was that feeling that drove the hunger to dismantle all order and structure throughout time and space. Morphing a palace was child's play to creating a planet. But, for all his powers and abilities, nothing he did changed the home he once thought of as a prison.

Cresting the last polished stone step, his view filled with items of dire importance. Facing towards the center of the Parthenon sat a crystalline throne. It's back was a good two feet higher than Fawdake if he were standing by it. Opposite the seat of power was a looking glass of pure smooth silver. Its vastness stretched from ceiling to floor. It was here that the Lord of Chaos waxed or waned authority over the universe.

Having reached the throne, and sighing with contentment, the Lord of Chaos felt the itch evaporate. Instead, an all too familiar sensation teased his mind. Another world had come full circle. Smiling, Fawdake flexed his fingers and arms. It was his time to reign over this world.

The seated God flourished his right hand with an air of theatrics. The image of that temporary dominion came into view on the silver display. A malicious smirk passed over the eternal being as he recognized his new toy. His sharp mind churned with ideas of how best to sow change on the main continent of that tiny world. Oh, yes, Fawdake thought as he greedily rubbed his hands together. He remembered the land of Dazmek all too well.

Dazmek, the main continent, surrounded on all sides by numerous chains of islands, was his favorite world by far. Its mortals never ceased to entertain. Even though it was one of the more devote worlds in worship and offerings, a shadowy cancer bubbled just under the surface. And nothing was as it seemed. Fawdake's last visit had thrown the land into such disarray that the Gods of Elemental Order bartered for an extra cycle of their influences to heal its tattered wounds.

Now, it stood ripe and ready for plucking once again.

The seated deity nodded with respect to his fellow Parthenon members. They had made significant improvements since his last visit. Great cities had been erected in the ashes of the Heretic's rebellion. Several of the more powerful clans had been either wiped out completely or rejected by the current government. Roads, trade, and humble hamlets dotted the landscape. Even the most rural of homes had a shrine to one of the Gods. This firm and lasting country stood proud and organized. But, to Fawdake, it was a full course banquet ready to be devoured. Such dedicated efforts just made the act of bringing chaos to the inhabitants of Dazmek all the sweeter.

Leaning back in his seat, Fawdake felt giddy for the first time in an age. A playfully evil plan began to unfold in the Lord of Chaos' mind. His handsome features took on a more sinister tone with each passing second. It was time to shake up this eternal dance routine. And Fawdake had just the idea to do it.

———◆———

The Cathedral of Faith was located in the midlands of Dazmek. It had started out as a simple monastery to a long forgotten god of nature and order. The original converts to this woodland god built on a lush, grassy hill surrounded by dense forests. These pilgrims desired privacy for their sacred rites, and protection from their more bloodthirsty neighbors. This refuge was a perfect place to bask in the glory of their deity. Those seeking to commune with nature, and live a simple humble life, sought the serenity of this haven.

As war and famine had taken hold of Dazmek over the ages, those mud huts failed to provide adequate room for the abused and shunned. Raiders came to pillage the fields and kill the livestock that were so lovingly cared for. The monks of the Forest God had to build thicker walls and stronger houses to protect the holy site. Barns and stables were raised to aid in storing and housing the harvest. Over the long centuries, however; the ideals and beliefs of those first converts morphed into a new faith all together.

Within a mere four generations, a grand city had emerged from such humble beginnings. Spiraling roads circled the hillside. Quarters for tradesmen, homes for members of the Priesthood, and schools for the inhabitants, populated each level of the booming religious center. It became nearly one thousand acres long and wide. A series of thick outer stone walls protected each section of the city from invasion and fire. At the center of this grand metropolis stood, triumphant, the crowning jewel of the Order of the Faithful: The Cathedral.

Four grand towers, connected by massive walls and ramparts, encircled the Cathedral. Each spire was dedicated to an aspect of teaching within the religious sect. Artisans, masons, mages and shamans all aided in the construction of this lighthouse of truth and order. No other city on the continent rivaled its size or splendor. If the Gods based salvation solely on merit, then the workers of this mighty city would gain the highest level of exaltation.

The Bastion of Truth, the oldest of the towers, faced the north. It testified to the masses that all must walk the true course. Its alabaster walls shone as a beacon of hope and righteousness to the faithful parishioners throughout the country. It illuminated as a perfect example of devotion and perseverance in the face of uncertainty. The thirty floors housed not just dorms and classrooms, but a private chapel and sacrament hall. All new to the priesthood received their first ordinances within this tower. After four years of tutelage, most went on to preach and teach to the masses within the city walls.

The School of the World stood to the west. Made of gray stone brick and mortar, it reflected the vows of poverty and the separation from earthly desires expected of the priests. There, traveling monks, missionaries, and scribes learned of the different cultures and societies throughout the lands. The Harvesters Guild even sent their experts in foreign markets to study from her grand masters to ensure honest and true dealings. Even the occasional Blessed One visited from the Desert of Tears to instruct those wanting to bring the good word to the northern nomad tribes.

The Scholars Tower happily positioned itself on the southern point of the wall. Within her peaceful halls, philosophy and church policies were studied, debated, and studied further. Constructed out of red stone, it also housed the largest library in the country. The caretakers and designers, so enamored by hording tomes, decided the eight sub levels, and the first fifteen floors, were needed to house their beloved collections. A strict policy controlled all who entered her doors, for books were seen as sacred and those Inquisitors were fiercely protective of their scrolls and histories.

With the rising of the sun, a roughly-hewn rock tower sat dwarfed by its kin. Here the School of the Paladins resided. They were masters of both War and the Healing Arts. These champions of order were chosen to bring their Lord's guidance and mercy to the most hellish of places. A simple gray stone design spoke to the stoic lifestyle awaiting all who entered. Very few cared to join its ranks. Those who did were used as military forces during war, and law enforcement for the common folk during peace. A small stable and courtyard had been added in recent years to house not just the massive warhorses, but several metal smiths as well.

Beneath this city of order and peace was a dark contrast to the life-giving light that radiated from the hilltop. Damp, ancient catacombs and murky tunnels ran the entire length and breadth of the Cathedral. If there was a physical representation of hell and ruin, this under city was it. The leaky walls were coated in a thick layer of grime and mold. An underground river, once an emergency water source, was only used to give the dead a watery tomb. Transgressors of holy or mortal law were condemned to serve sentences in the nightmarish environment. Their only company was the screams of other inmates, and the fear of Questioners. These were sadistic zealots chosen by the Priesthood to perform interrogations and last rites for such undesirables. One section, in the oldest caves beneath the Bastion of Truth, was reserved for those who dared to blaspheme against all the Gods.

Sadly, one poor soul was locked inside.

The clinking of heavy water droplets on rusted, forgotten metal was always the first thing the condemned prisoner heard when returning to consciousness. This maddening sound kept neither time nor rhythm. The sickly sweet aroma of death soon followed in this assault on the senses. It penetrated everything, even deep within the bedrock foundations. It was the tenth time he had woken in prison since being arrested and beaten. He had hoped the last round of torture had killed him. But he knew the Questioner still wanted to play his twisted game. So, Death's protective oblivion remained out of the inmate's grasp.

Upon finally opening his sweat-stung green eyes, the once powerfully built prisoner squinted. Matted with both blood and dried sweat, his hair and beard had become unruly and grimy. The tunic and pants assigned to him were still soiled from the last occupant. Although there were but four small candles lit, the flickering light tore at his vision. His eyes blinked rapidly to remove the dirt and grime from his eyelids.

Years of military training demanded the prisoner escape. But, such desires were halted by thick wrought iron shackles. His hands were joined together over his head by massive links of chain that connected to the north and south pillars in the room. His feet were similarly joined and equally chained, but were fastened to the eastern and western pillars. Movement was neigh impossible without serious lasting pain.

The hollowed out cell was a mere twelve feet long by ten feet wide. The bedrock ceiling was just nine feet high. Straw and old corn husks had been tossed on the floor to soak up any blood or fluids that would surely come from the inmates. Little room was left after the stone pillars were added to prevent the ceiling from collapsing.

A pale, filthy hand came into the prisoner's view and caressed one of the carved markings on the pillar to the north side of the room. "Beautiful, isn't it?" a husky voice asked in a ravenous tone. "These last three were carved by the leader of my order. This one is my favorite." Upon touching the upside down rune, a dim green light glowed around the tormenter's thin fingers.

A wave of pain and nausea raped through the malnourished inmate, while his body jolted uncontrollably. Thick foam spewed from the prisoner's cracked lips as his eyes rolled back into his head. A small stream of blood trickled down from his nose. Mousy brown hair flopped about wildly as the torment continued.

"Are you ready to begin telling me what I want to know, or will you still act strong and keep your silence?" the Questioner asked in a mocking tone, ending with a small chuckle. Removing his hand from the enchanted rune, the tormentor basked in his work. Yes, such barbaric practices had been disowned by the clergy for years. But the moment some in the Cathedral leadership thought a new Heretic had arrived, they had changed their tune rather quickly.

The condemned man assault, glared just beyond the Questioner at the symbols on the pillars. Each bore the four sacred marks: Kogien, the Fire God of purity and righteous war. Wodras, the Goddess of change and water. Thoprac, the Goddess of craftsmen and the Earth. Zhoutd, the God of structure and wood. Some of the carvings were in the configurations everyone knew, while others were arranged in a slightly perverse fashion.

Once, seeing those symbols had brought comfort and peace to the prisoner. Now they dredged up feelings of foolishness and bitterness. Having finally recovered from the assault, he used the only weapon he had left: Wit. The chained male refused to give his captor any satisfaction. Screaming in pain, or playing along, would not help the prisoner, unless he could break his tormentor's resolve and free himself.

Walking the few paces to the only chair in the room, the Questioner sat, sighing with relief. "How long do you think you can last, *heretic*," the middle-aged priest asked, mocking the bravery of his inmate. "You are not the first to bear this treatment and I pray you are not the last," he commented in a bored yet salivating voice.

The shackled prisoner studied the man before him as his keeper crossed those disgusting sandaled feet. The Questioner wore a filthy gray robe that was bound together with a rope belt. Grime and dried mud caked the bottom two inches, as if he cared not to clean it at all. The man bore no strength of body and seemed weak, almost feeble. His torso was heavy, as if to testify he overly enjoyed fine wine and beer every day. This was no holy man, the prisoner thought. There was not a drop of piety in the Questioner's heart.

For years, the chained man had given much respect to anyone willing to devote themselves to the Gods, regardless of belief. But this human parasite of misery was not the type of acolyte found in any public temple or holy place. The Questioner relished in causing pain and had become intoxicated on the fear of his fellow man.

A cold laugh erupted from the prisoner with the harshest of realizations dawning into an idea. "Do you expect me to return to the fold?" he poised, his powerful, deep voice commanding the room. "Could you and yours accept me back into full fellowship? Could all be forgiven and forgotten? Surely you are not *that* stupid? You make a mockery of your own faith and yet call *me* faithless. You preach not peace and harmony, but seem to bask in torture and agony. Which is worse, Questioner," the prisoner spat with venomous intent, "A man who has no faith or one who lies about it?"

The prisoner knew his questions had hit its intended target. Mocking a belief is one thing, but calling out a hypocrite and unmasking their lies— Well, that was truly painful.

🔥 1 🔥

The residence of the High Priest of the Order of the Faithful was a sight to behold. It took up an entire block in the middle of the city. It rested in the shadow of the Bastion of Truth, facing opposite the Tower's entrance. Usually an inviting place, it was currently covered by a fresh powdering of snow. Fully equipped with a back garden, several bedrooms, and a personal bath house, it was more akin to a manor than a common abode. Very few were ever able to enter the home of the priesthood leader, especially at night. But that freezing, stormy evening was to be an exception.

The second floor library was simply adorned, yet comfortable enough to hold long meetings. Bookshelves lined the walls, with a scriptorium tucked in the back corner so the scribe was able to work in peace during church business. Resting in the center of the room was a large rectangular oak table with six pine chairs encircling it. Darkened over its many years of polishing, it was cleaned and prepared with two candelabras, a pitcher of water, a jug of wine, and three bowls of food. A welcoming site under usual conditions.

Such hospitalities were lost on the lone, brooding figure in the room.

Heavy booted feet stomped the floor in irritation as the fully-armored occupant finished yet another turn around the room. The aged warrior was not accustomed to waiting. The travel armor offered no reprieve for his weary body. Coming to a stop in front of the roaring fire, the iresome Varg rubbed his gloved hands together. He needed to kill the cold and anger controlling his abilities. The military leader's mind had to focus and relax. Traveling in the winter at night was dangerous at the best of times, but such a summons needed to be answered with haste.

Leaning in closer to the hearth, the light of the dancing flames flickered across his breastplate and got lost in the hue. Red was the chosen color of the military. This career soldier had kept it bright and honorable for decades. It inspired greatness, pride, and courage. It was the battle call of

8

Kogien, the God that guarded all fallen warriors. But to an aged veteran such as himself, it tempted memories of lost shield siblings and the heartache of defeat.

A military man since the age of twelve, Varg was not even able to recall his birth name, nor did he care to. He had earned his branding and new name. Family titles and land were coveted by some run-of-the-mill warriors, but such attachments were of no use to an officer. A cut above the average basher, he rose quickly through the ranks with integrity and respect. Always keen on keeping his unit and division honorable, Varg did not revel in bloodshed or wanton violence. Others had gained notoriety in their bloody proficiency on the battlefield. But this man was a surgeon on campaign. Minimal loses and quick victories were his call sign, often ending an engagement by his presence alone.

To some, Varg had the Lord of Chaos' own luck, driving his foes into a fear frenzy. Others saw him as one step below divinity. A living personification of the beliefs and values taught to new recruits at the Red Keep's Battle school. This support and fame earned him the seat on the Council of Four. His shrewdness and ability to hear out the other council members helped him keep his position.

Driving a black iron poker into the fire with force, the weary army leader wished to return to the Red Keep. Since Jaldo's departure, and his promotion as Lord Commander, Varg felt ill at ease. Closing his deep blue eyes, the middle-aged soldier sighed with despair and felt the weight of his years. Each season, less and less young men fill the Firebrand ranks. There was even talk of officers and unit leaders abandoning their posts, only to return home or to join some private army. Something was coming. Varg sensed it would change the very fabric of their army and the nation.

A teasing, playful giggle pulled the Commander from his dark reflecting as Varg turned to his right.

"Calm yourself, Varg. You are making me seasick with your stomping about."

A vision of womanhood appeared, materializing from the dust in the room. She completed her transformation to the right of the table, a few feet from the gawking soldier. Her narrow waist and ample figure caused most men's hearts to race and desire her. But the aged warrior knew she sought no such affections. Long auburn locks cascaded down and stopped shy of the small of her back. A simple forest green dress adorned her curves, with long sleeves that widened as they approached her wrists. Her favorite silver belt and shawl completed the ensemble of serenity and strength, creating a vision of both power and beauty.

In spite of himself, Varg stood taller, almost at attention. His broad shoulders and massive frame often inspired awe, and sometimes fear, in others. Yet he always felt uneasy around the woman currently batting her lashes at him. The Mother Shaman's power was widely respected and feared. He chose to put his faith in his sword arm and his training, not the mystic arts of a bygone age.

"Mother Asiza," he quipped with a bow. "An honor, it is."

Taking a step forward, Asiza opened her arms. "Do you expect me to curtsy, Soldier," she replied with a wink, "or will you give me a hug? After all, we were friends long before we became leaders."

As they embraced, the truthfulness of the comment stung the man more than she realized. They had been childhood friends, even confidants. All that had changed at the bandit rebellion of Shaman Plain. He was present, even led the charge, that resulted in her future husband's death. Of all his sins, that would always be the one that haunted him the most. Their eyes met, both full of pain, lost love, and words never spoken. Varg inhaled to speak, but was interrupted by a new voice entering the room.

"Oh, for the love of *all* the Gods, will you two finally get a room?"

Surprised by the sudden outburst, the couple turned to see a five-foot-two, rail thin young lady entering the room. She wore a peacock feather in her braided, honey-colored hair. With lavender highlighted jerkin and knee high velvet riding boots, this particular pixie was more than met the eye. The youngest head of the Harvesters Guild by twenty years, Yarmilla relished in catching people off guard. She loved nothing more than teasing the two in front of her.

"If you two blush anymore, the room will catch fire," Yarmilla declared with a straight face. Situating herself at the head of the table, the youngest member of the council hungrily reached for the bowl of fruit. She had not eaten all day. Like Varg, she had rushed to the Cathedral. The bowl, however, had other ideas. It glided to the opposite end of the table and rested in front of the Shaman. This bit of magic caused Yarmilla to gasp and pout in a playful manner.

Releasing herself with reluctance from the Lord Commander's embrace, Asiza quipped. "Tisk Tisk. No fruit for you, child, and please do not pout. You are a woman fully grown. Act like it." These two enjoyed each other's company and made it a point to visit on a regular basis. Their bond had been forged in loss and pain, a far cry stronger than Varg and the missing council member.

Varg felt a little like the odd man out as the women continued to banter back and forth. Grabbing a small apple, he took a bite. Leaning against the fireplace mantle, the soldier hoped to get some warmth in his cold armor.

"Well," Yarmilla stated, once the small talk was over. "It seems all we lack is the High Priest. After all, he requested this meeting."

As if summoned by her words, the High Priest, Mathis, shuffled into the room. His ash white robes, offset by his rich ebony skin, barely covered his leather shoes. He came to rest beside Yarmilla's chair, gripping its back for support. The priesthood leader was out of breath. He had run several flights of stairs from the Tower of Truth. Fear gripped the Priest's heart. Fear of what was to come. Fear of an ancient foe back for revenge. "Yes, I did ask you all here," he said panting. "To be honest, I am in desperate need of your help and wisdom."

The tension of the room took on a life all its own as they situated themselves in stunned silence. Yarmilla, with a leg slung over the arm of her chair, commanded the head of the table. Mathis kept his customary chair to the right of Harvester leader. Asiza filled wine goblets and began to disperse them, hoping to ease the heavy cloud of distrust gathering. She, having completed her self-appointed task, sat next to Varg on the left side of the table.

True to form, the Harvester mentally recovered the quickest. Eyeing the Priest with suspicion, the nut-brown-eyed woman began to speak. "So, you need *our* wisdom? Since when did the Cloaked Ones ever seek the wisdom of others?" The irritation in Yarmilla's voice pulled all eyes to her. "You might want to tread carefully, Priest. Mocking any of us is dangerous to your health."

Sighing, Mathis bit back a retort. He never allowed an underling to speak at him in such a manner. She, however, was not one of the several ordained bishops asking for help. He had to keep reminding himself of that. "I never mock, nor do I wish to offend," Mathis answered with a rather guarded tone. "For the first time in a millennia, we have a true Heretic in our halls. By all accounts, this man fears none of the Gods. What's more shocking is that he has spent time in each of the guilds."

The Council members reacted at the same time. Varg's tan face and gray beard hardened from its typical steel-like features to an almost diamond grit. Yarmilla and Asiza looked shocked and pained by the accusation. Anger soon controlled the room, to the surprise of no one. Such accusations were powerful indeed. The citizens still used the tale of the Heretic to scare their children to behave. But if such a person existed, and spent time in any of the guilds, the peace they had fought so hard for would crumble into dust.

The Council of Four guarded their sacred oaths with a passion that few could ever muster, much less sustain. They were the living symbols of their creed. The Fire Brand Army showed the world that might and sheer power ruled all, just as their God purified the universe. The Shamans created the need of all to be in balance with life, in perfect harmony with the Goddess of Earth. Harvesters proved that without sowing there was no reaping, following the dictations of the Female water deity. Priests testified that faith and obedience restored structure and organization, much like their patron God. The thought of a heretic spending time in their guilds, and then willfully committing apostasy, was unthinkable.

Mathis felt the spirit of the meeting change drastically. He knew the others would be outraged by the accusation. Playing to the masses and arousing blind passion were skills he had honed as a minister. As much as he despised preying on their base emotions, he needed the others to feel rather than think. More than that, the High Priest needed them to do the impossible.

"Please steel yourselves and let me explain," the aged priest pleaded with arms outstretched to stem the flow of stinging remarks. "The Order needs information on the man in custody. It appears that each of you personally spent time with him. All we have is a partially removed brand, that of a White Raven. Do you know this clan, Lord Commander?"

The declaration brought a chill to the air that made the frozen storm outside feel warm. Suspicion smeared over the air and polluted the library chamber. Its stench put an edge on the meeting that no one wanted.

Varg leaned back in his chair, pensive. He felt that familiar tightening of his chest returning. Yes, he knew the clan. There had only been one young man in recent memory. Personally, the commander wanted to remove himself from the discussion entirely. Professionally, he knew he had no exit. Was he able to surrender the young man to such a nasty fate again? How was it possible that *he* became a heretic? Sensing an answer due, Varg decided to counter and buy himself some time.

"Yes, I know the clan." Varg began, choosing his words with care. "What right do you and your creed have questioning a branded soldier? According to the edicts, he should have been given to us straight away. More importantly, *Priest*, why was I not informed?!" The last words cracked like a whip through the room, scaring everyone present. They were getting a small taste of the Lord Commander's warrior presence. Even Mathis had the good manners to look ashamed.

"We found him in our tome vault," the older man responded with respect. "He was reading the *Book of the Gods*, apparently looking for an ancient prophecy. How he entered and gained access to that dusty old relic, I do not know. But please, if you know about the man, share. The report stated that he killed three of our Inquisitors in cold blood. Out of respect for you and your guild, I need as much information as you can give. Rushed verdicts often bring guilt to those who pass judgment."

Seeing his opponent retreating with reluctance, the old soldier pressed the advance. "What you ask for is not a simple nor a quick history lesson. But if you indulge me, it might prove enlightening. His story with us begins as most soldiers do, with purification and recruiting."

🔥 2 🔥

The end of the spring harvest meant a brief reprieve for most in the farmlands and vineyards throughout the nation. Celebrations and festivals dotted every side of the Dazmekian landscape. And everyone gathered to bask in the bounty. Every city and township had its form of festivals. The Red Keep was no exception.

The massive spoke-and-hub-designed castle had sections for each of the Fire Brand army divisions. As well as a full medical hospital and housing for the Veritable Mothers and Paladins. The Keep, a smooth, square structure, sat at the center of all activity. Its towers allowed visual access to each of the sections below. It also protected the Inner Circle, who ran the military's day to day operations. A proper city had sprung up around the outer walls over the years. Bearing the same name as the Castle, the city followed the same wheel pattern, with separate sections for inns, craftsmen, the local watch, and homes for those permanently stationed at the Keep.

Traders and craftsmen, from all over, filled the city surrounding the stronghold to capacity. Each hoped to win favor with the Fire Brand Army, and contracts for weapons and armor. Inn keepers had visitors sleeping in stables, so full was the city. Minstrels and storytellers bounced from place to place like bees in a meadow, plying their trades for nobles and commoners alike. The banners and sigils of every clan and house proudly populated the six-sided outer wall of the city. Not only was the end of the harvest celebrated, but the lists for army enlistment were open once again.

Families, rich and poor, converged on the training arena's courtyard in swarms. The massive square, sandstone structure was on the south section of the Red Keep. One of the smallest areas in the castle, it sat nestled between the Battle School on the right and the hospital wing on the left. The military council felt this allowed for a smoother transition for the lads that passed the recruiting process.

Amid all that sand and grit, twelve-year-old young men were tested and tried to see if they were worthy of military life and the treasures it holds. Most came to the Red Keep out of familial obligations. That was how the noble houses gained notoriety and power. Those from farms or poorer families came hoping to secure a future free from the toils of the field and poverty. As well as a chance to move up the social ladders.

The families of the approved recruits received a room in the main castle. It was a way of showing appreciation for their sacrifice. The Lord Commander understood what losing a strong young man meant to a farming family, as he came from one. A special feast was prepared to honor the parents. This gave the Lord Commander the opportunity to thank them personally.

In front of the entry archway, a multitude of writing desks were set up. There, clerks took down the names, clan affiliations, and body types of the young men. After that, the hopefuls were corralled, like sheep in a barn, to the medics stationed within the archway. They needed to ensure that the youth were in a good and healthy state. This stage often sifted most of the lads out. The rigorous training and warrior lifestyle was unforgiving to the unhealthy.

Those that passed the medical inspection were marched under a giant Fire Brand banner hanging on the arena wall. These new recruits were lined up in the arena's circular field, next to a wooden board with their respected sigils placed on a hook. Names were not used in the first week of training so family honor could remain intact.

A stoic gentleman, Striker by name, waited for the medics to complete their duties. His hazel eyes darted this way and that, taking in each lad that entered. He had years of experience chiseled on his face, which showed in his unnatural white hair and stubble. The young men that noticed him instinctively knew he was not one to be trifled with.

With the last candidate joining the group, the medics signaled to Striker that their duties had concluded. The medical personnel gathered up the desks and headed for the Battle School tower to the east of the arena. Since all the reports had to be filed before the next morning, the Red Keep clerks were in for a very busy evening.

Striker saluted the head medic and turned his attention to the waiting group. "Thirty-two of you passed the first test. Now you are *mine*," he barked as he paced up and down the line of hopefuls. "I have trained your brothers, fathers, and grandfathers. I refuse to hear whining about noble blood or family honor. Here, you are all equal. Here, in my arena, you are no one! Your only allegiance is to Kogien, our beloved God, and the Lord Commander. Everything else does not exist until I say it does."

He stopped and faced a particular group of young nobles that he had seen complaining earlier. Due to his years in the service, Striker knew they would be the first to whine about the harshness of training. Pointing at the wooden board, the white-haired man continued. "Behind you, you will see your family sigil and a numbered ring. Find the ring and await further instructions."

Like a flock of birds moving in tandem, the young recruits turned, found their sigils, and sprinted for their rings.

Sixteen iron rings, eight feet in diameter, were embedded in the earth, along with a cloth number staked to the ground. Once satisfied that everyone was accounted for, Striker had the lads remove their boots, tunics, and any jewelry they had with them. A handful of senior trainers entered the arena in time to collect the clothing, personal items, and the stakes. After all was collected, they dumped the items in a pile on the hard dusty ground. Old alliances and ties had to become severed, and new ones strengthened, if the lads were to thrive in their new environment.

Striker sounded the bugle hanging off his belt. He wanted to make sure these recruits followed his next set of instructions to the letter.

"As you can see," the Chief trainer began in a rehearsed voice, "you are not alone in the ring. The lad standing before you is there to test you. The rules are simple. Fight him. Try not to break any bones. And, for the love of the Gods, do not kill him. You can knock him out or grapple him into submission. The winner wins a rest before the next round of testing. Begin!"

Feral battle cries filled the arena while the youth collided in a tangled mess. All pretense and pomp were forgotten in the ring. Here, the lads showed their true colors. Here, they realized the type of men they truly were. One by one, the brawls ended as quickly as they had started. Trainers floated from fight to fight to ensure no one went too far.

By the time the sun reached its noon peak, two sets of combatants remained. The first set fought next to the wooden board. Both young men were evenly matched and trying desperately to finish off the other. The fair-haired one had his tan opponent in an arm bar, while his opponent had him trapped in a pressure point lock. Both grunted with pain and exertion, hoping the other was about to surrender.

With his eyes rolling, Striker called the fight. As the lads released their holds and stood, he congratulated them both on a job well done. Before he was able to pass them off to another trainer, however, a squeal and a hardened thud caught his attention. The white-haired man turned, looking towards the combatants of the last ring with an appeasing eye.

These two fighters were as uneven a match as night and day. Even though all who entered were twelve years of age, body size and strength was never a guaranteed equal. The larger of the two, a lad built like an ox, waited patiently as his adversary lay in the dirt, attempting to catch his breath. The well-built youth paced around the ring at an eased gait, never letting his eyes leave his gasping opponent.

Striker instantly recognized the dirt-covered lad on the ground as Deston. He had seen the scrappy youth running about the Red Keep earlier, claiming he would be a great Cavalier someday. Old Striker had seen his type before. All talk and no real talent. Such future soldiers had little to offer in way of leadership skills, so they were usually used as couriers during campaigns.

Instinctively, Striker's right hand went for his whip. He used the rawhide instrument to instill speed, and a little fear, in the hearts of his charges. As his right hand snapped out and uncoiled the whip, the middle-aged man paused. White scars became pronounced as the larger of the two young men continued to pace. Such scars were prevalent on street kids or slaves. The older man chose not to use his rawhide tool, as it might spur the well-built twelve-year-old to do something stupid. What surprised Striker was the lack of any emotion in the pacing boy's eyes. Usually anger or blood lust filled the eyes of the recruit hopefuls. But this young man looked almost bored as he waited.

As Striker continued to study the young man, Deston grabbed a handful of dirt and slung it at his opponent as he rose. Even though there were few rules in the recruiting process, the instructors looked for speed, skills of strength, and the ability to think on one's feet. Cowardly attempts to win were frowned upon, as it showed a lack of martial brilliance. With lightning speed, the taller recruit darted forward, gripping Deston's right hand, pulling him off his feet. Then, almost at the same time, he cupped Deston's right hip joint with the crook of his right elbow. Rising to his full height, the larger of the two flipped the screeching youth over his shoulders and out of the ring like a sack of grain.

The remaining young men watched in awe as Deston landed in a twisted mess, yet none went to his aid. Each clan wanted the glory and status that came from military service. Only individual achievement mattered in that dusty arena. That was how the Gods judged, and so, too, the Firebrand Army.

Striker's whip cracked in the air, causing all to look at him with rapt attention. "Well, *ladies*," he began as he curled the braided rawhide instrument. "It seems we have stooped so low that childish acts, like dirt throwing, are allowed in *my* arena."

Everyone looked at Deston with disdain. They knew any misdeed or transgression seen by Old Striker ensured a punishment for everyone.

"Now some of you milk drinkers might be allowed to act that way at home with ma and da, but here, I train *men*, and this is *my* house." He concluded with another whip crack to drive the point home.

Thanks to Deston's foolish act, those who had lost their bouts had to de-muck the stables used to house the horses used by visitors . It was a task meant to conclude before the next round of tests. The rest of the young men brought out practice arms and armor from the Arena store room. As both groups completed their allotted chores, Striker called for the roster of applicants. Upon receiving it from a senor trainer, the chief instructor sat by the pile of discarded tunics and pondered how to divide them. He wanted to see what these lads were truly made of and how best to showcase their hidden skills. With luck, by the end of the week, some of the recruits would show true promise. Those who demonstrated martial talents and leadership skills were usually presented with a gold braid, which symbolized rank and prowess.

As the shadows lengthened, Striker called for the youth to return to the proving ground. The ones in the stables had the farthest to run, and all were eager to pay back Deston for his blunder. As they fell into line and stood at attention, Striker changed the location of the family sigils on the board. He wanted some of the better skilled to fight their equals and not have another free pass.

Senior trainers walked down the line, handing out light, boiled leather vests. Meanwhile, the helpers passed out cane swords with wooden shields. Striker, pleased with the new arrangement, turned towards the waiting lads. With a smirk, he instructed them to put on their armor and head to their assigned rings. This round truly separated the skilled from the substandard. Even the senior trainers began to cast wagers on who would win and how badly some would lose. Anticipation crackled on the dry air as the lads walked out to the rings. A blast from Striker's horn signaled the matches to begin.

The sound of canes mercilessly attacking bare skin and leather armor echoed off the stone walls. The young men hungrily attacked each other. Everyone wanted to prove their worth to the whip-wielding instructor. Within minutes, the majority of the matches had been decided, either by knock out or sheer brute strength. To the shock of some of the junior trainers, over half the nobility had been defeated by farm hands or street urchins. Their bodies, accustomed to hard labor, found these exercises easy. While the more pampered boys were ill-equipped for such fights. Five matches were still going by the time the evening torches were lit. Three of them had members of lesser houses pitted against the sons of the Military's inner circle.

Striker wanted to see who of the lesser houses was hungry for redemption and advancement. His eyes, however, kept returning to the large, muscular youth from earlier. He had the lad compete against Finley, the son of the Battle School's Sword Master, just to see how good he really was. The match, it appeared, was a stalemate. Old Striker smiled at the frustration building in the Sword Master's son. Under normal circumstances, the reddish-blond-haired youth should have made easy work out of the lad, due to his familial training. Something in the muscular preteen's stance bothered both Finley and Striker.

As desperation crept into Finley's mind, he began to realize his situation. Every time he attacked, his opponent's shield was somehow there to intercept the blow. It was maddening. Never had he faced an opponent like this. The Sword Master's son had to muster all his training and skill to parry every blow, but the lad knew he was not able to keep this dance up much longer. As Finley slowed his attacks in an attempt to conserve energy, confusion flickered in the jade green eyes of his opponent. Then, out of nowhere Finley's vision became engulfed in a dazzling white light as he felt his body hit the dirt. With a darkness engulfing the white light, none of his limbs answered Finley's mental commands.

Striker, seeing the blow about to land, cringed in anticipation. The young man feinted a stab, and, at the last minute, created a high-sweeping strike that connected with Finley's left temple. As the Sword Master's son dropped like a sack of rocks, Striker barked for all to cease. The senior trainers, confused by the order, cast an inquiring glance at their commanding officer. Ignoring them all, Striker marched up to the jade-eyed youth and demanded to know his name.

The muscled twelve-year-old stood, somewhat awkward, and answered. "Sir, I am Karniel."

The head trainer waved the lad on, as if expecting more. Some clan affiliation or family name, but there was only silence. When nothing followed, the white-haired older man decided to test the lad himself. He hoped to tell which instructor had trained the youth, based on his fighting style. Striker knew each one had a signature, but his hopes were unfounded.

Karniel danced around the arena with Striker, using a grab bag of styles and patterns. The lad combined mace and axe techniques with shield attacks and sword blocks. Striker answered in kind with his own blend of battle-hardened techniques. Each one employed an array of feints, parries, and strategies that, to the naked eye, appeared as two serpentine dragons fighting. Striker's double-edged dagger snaked forward and cut Karniel's shield straps. Before the shield hit the dirt, Karniel's cane connected with a sickening crunch on his foe's ankle. Blood lust, fueled by pain, surged through Striker. Part of him wanted to laugh. He had not felt this alive in years. Another part, however, best left deep and hidden, wanted to end the life of this upstart boy.

Karniel sat low on his heels, knees bent, as he prepared himself for the inevitable death blow that would end the bout. His years on the streets, and his apprenticeship with Master at Arms Captain Zawl, had taught him that any wounded creature was willing to fight to the end if pushed. Karniel watched the whirlpool of emotions agitating in Striker's eyes. Raising his cane sword in a side guard, Karniel steadied his mind to accept any outcome. Striker coiled his body like a snake as he turned his dagger point to Karniel's heart. The two duelists stared at each other, daring the other to attack first.

The tension in the arena hummed as everyone waited on bated breath for a twitch or attack.

A bone horn blast sounded the evening watch to begin as Karniel and Striker charged at each other. The youth attacked with Boar Charging Through Water, as Striker countered with the Serpent's Tongue. Dancing Fans met Antler's in Spring and Falcon's Talons kept Edged Cyclone at bay. Faster and faster they went. Even the senior trainers had a hard time seeing the weapons or who landed hits. After what seemed like an eternity, each combatant held a weapon posed for a kill strike. Striker's dagger point broke the skin by Karniel's jugular. Karniel's broken cane stopped short of pushing Striker's thorax to its breaking point.

Applause erupted from all present, most recruits figuring it was a demonstration. A display of what was achievable in the Fire Brand Army. The noise caused both males to realize just how far they had gone. With both smiling awkwardly, they slowly back away from each other and saluted. A medic rushed to tend Striker's ankle. A look of pride and admiration filled the old man's eyes as he commented on the fight.

"Boy, I haven't felt that much excitement in years. By the Gods, who trained you?"

Karniel gave a sheepish grin and looked down at his feet. "A Watch Captain called Zawl took me in and trained me as an apprentice of sorts."

Whistling in shock, Striker remembered the tough-as-iron Captain. Few were ever able to best him in single combat. Striker had heard rumors that Zawl had taken in a street boy, but had dismissed them as pure gossip. "Well, son, I can't wait to see what you do tomorrow," the instructor stated before a medic carted him off to the medical wing.

With that, the lads were escorted to a small bunk house built into the archway. Here, they were given a change of clothes and allowed to bathe. Battle School cooks provided a light supper of soup and hard bread. As the young men ate, the subject of family bonds and clan history surfaced. For the most part, it was an enjoyable experience, save for some of the noble blood making a fuss. They demanded to be served first and to be given the best portions. The kitchen staff ignored the brash demands of the spoiled youth. One young man did receive a smack with a wooden ladle for attempting to grab more than his share of bread. Soon, silence ruled the bunkhouse as the lads ate with vigor. After second and third helpings, and all the dishes returned to the kitchen, sleep overpowered the hopeful recruits.

As dreams filled their minds, nothing could have prepared them for what was in store the next day.

✋ 3 ✋

Striker roared in pain as the medic set his broken ankle. One of the visiting Veritable Mothers, Katril, had administered a tonic to ease the pain when he was first brought into the hospital wing. But the wound was too much for the medicine. Striker's body was now paying the debt his ego had accrued earlier. The ankle was quite swollen and shattered in two places.

Oil lamps flickered and swayed in their rope hangers as Katril barged into the room. "What in the name of all the Saints are you doing to that man's ankle?" she demanded, using her most authoritative voice.

"If you want to be upset, woman," the seasoned medic retorted with a snarl, "be mad at this straw-brained idiot! He's the one who thought it prudent to fight on a broken ankle!"

The medic chunked the remaining wrapping cloth in his bag and stormed out of the room, slamming the door behind him. It always irritated him when soldiers thought with their egos instead of their minds. They always then demanded to go back into the fray. Prudence and soldiering never seemed to go hand in hand.

"Well that just proves my point exactly. Men should never do medicine," Katril stated as she turned to sit on the cot next to Striker.

The two had struck an instant friendship when Katril first arrived at the Keep. With a mix of Shaman and Cathedral teachings, the all-female order tended to the broken, homeless, and forgotten throughout the country. The Fire Brand Army welcomed a small number of the more resilient Veritable Mothers to help the newest recruits transition from home life to military service. Katril often pondered how their mutual respect became an odd courtship over the last five years. Like most in the order, she came from a troubled home and tended not to get attached to men, especially soldiers.

Her mother died in child birth, leaving her alone with a very abusive father. His drunken tirades and gambling kept him away from their cottage most of the time. During those episodes, the young Katril cooked, cleaned, and learned to manage their small farm. One day, while tending the herbs by the back door, she heard her father offer her up as payment on a loan of money. The debt collector, a local brothel owner, agreed to wipe the debt, if Katril would arrive at his home by sunset. Fear and tears poured from the eleven-year-old. Her mind was not able to accept the arrangement. She loved her father. It did not generally matter what he did to her.

But this was too much for her to handle.

An overwhelming desire to escape took over her. She ran for days, sleeping in trees, and moving at night. By the sixth night, the runaway had reached a small abbey with a stable near the back. Sneaking inside the barn, the eleven-year-old hid in the loft, hoping for a quiet night of sleep. Exhaustion overcame the tiny-framed girl as she settled into the fresh straw.

By morning, whispering voices reached the loft when the stable door opened. Katril, awakened by the sound of the wooden barrier opening, flattened herself as small as her body allowed. The voices drew closer to the ladder leading to her position. One of them climbed the ladder and halted just shy of the last step.

"Will you come out, dear?" the middle-aged woman asked kindly, tucking a gray strand of hair behind her ear. "We have food and drink aplenty here. On this farm, no one will harm you. You have the word of the Mother Abbot of the Cathedral." Seeing the terror and defiance in the girl's eyes, the Mother Abbot continued. "When you decide to come down, we will welcome you to our family and offer you all the protection you need."

Satisfied, the Mother Abbot retreated, shooing the other women away. But not before leaving a small plate of food. The gray-haired Mother knew the girl hiding was broken, emotionally and mentally. Several others had felt the call of the Saints and come to the abbey, but the Mother sensed something different about the tormented soul in the loft.

The events that transpired later that evening proved the Mother Abbot correct.

A storm broke that night with a vengeance. Thunder crashed loud enough to shake the world. Lightning, in shades of blue and yellow, forked and danced over and around the stable. The roof of the stable seemed to sag under the force of the rain. The wind offered no reprieve for the scared little girl. Deciding to hide in one of the stalls, she buried herself under four horse blankets.

Again, the stable door opened with a groan. Only, this time, it was her father. Her screams did not seem to worry him as he locked them inside. She begged and pleaded for his forgiveness. Tears testified of the sorrow the child felt. But only silence came from the approaching male. With each step, she knew he did not care. In Katril's heart, she realized he never loved her. She was just a cook. A maid. A slave. He never showed her any affection or praise. All that he loved was the bottle and the cards.

A vortex of power sank her feet into the ground, and wet soil covered those tiny feet. The strength of a Deity touched every hidden, sealed off part of her heart and mind. The child yearned to be accepted, loved, and respected. All she wanted was a family, and a place to feel safe from the evils of the world. With each horrible memory or forgotten desire brought to light, the divine power amplified. This metamorphosis cocooned the little one in rare energy, raising her off the ground.

Amid the torment of mortal emotions, and the hurricane of celestial energy, Katril heard a calming voice singing a tender lullaby. The song seemed to cut through and focus the power raging inside her. It granted her a haven in the storm that threatened to rip her soul apart. It was time for her to face her fears, but she would not fight this battle alone.

The Mother Abbot, sensitive to such magical awakenings, threw open her window and stared at the wooden structure. Having spent the night in prayer and supplication on behalf of the girl, the middle-aged woman hoped for peace to be bestowed on her latest charge. The display of heavenly strength was nothing the Mother Abbot had witnessed before. She knew the girl was blessed by not one God, but two. The older woman had not seen anyone this powerful in the last thirty years. Others in the sisterhood stood and watched as divine beauty purged the little girl of her terrors.

The stable, forced to contain such awesome power, heaved drunkenly on its side, before righting itself. Before any of the sisters could reach the door leading outside of the farm house, an enormous explosion destroyed the stable. Burnt wood and hay went flying for fifty yards. Such a blast did not harm the stone house, as it was dedicated and warded by their Gods. But every Veritable Mother was shoved back by the concussive blast.

Little more than smoldering rocks and a twenty foot crater were left of the stable.

As the smoke cleared, a new sound emerged. The shrieks of a broken-hearted little girl filled the vicinity with a mournful spirit. The rain was not able to hide her tears while she sat curled in a ball. Her pain and anguish became the storm. And, like all storms, the hurt was beginning to pass.

Strong, gentle hands picked up the sobbing girl and carried her away from the destruction of a broken heart. Contrary to the code of her order, the Mother Abbot refused to heal the child or stem the flow of raw emotions. The gray-haired woman wanted her new charge to remember the torment of a contrite spirit. Such memories had a way of stemming the flow of power until it is became absolutely necessary.

Before reaching the house, Katril had passed out, having no energy left to even respond to any of the Veritable Mothers.

Three days later, Katril awoke in a small bedroom in the abbey. A clay washbowl, housing a pitcher full of cool water, sat atop a dresser near the bed. She noticed her clothes had be removed and replaced with a simple green dress. Confusion, coupled with wariness, fogged her mind. Sitting up, she tried to clear away the mental cobwebs. Flashes of her escape, and hiding in the stable, came rushing back. Before a clear picture could form, the sound of knocking pulled the girl's attention.

The Mother Abbot entered with a cloth-covered tray of hot soup and warm, crisp bread. A tender smile shone on the woman's face as she spoke. "It is good to see you awake, my child. You gave us quite a worry, being asleep for so long."

Fear rippled on Katril's face. She did not want to offend or anger the woman, especially after being shown such kindness. A rich laugh bellowed from the leader of the abbey, calming her mounting fear.

"There is no need to be afraid here, my dear. This is a sanctuary for womankind. You can stay for as long or short as you wish. If you wish to learn letters or a healing art, we can teach you."

"I have no money," the small, timid girl replied, looking down. "I am sorry to be a bother."

The child's almond eyes misted over. A blurry hand swam into view and pulled Katril into an embrace. "My daughter," she heard softly, "you are no bother at all. Here, you are home."

Those feelings of love and trust filled Katril as she inspected the wound of the master trainer. The medic knew his business and had done everything in his power to help. The muscle damage and nerve trauma was so extensive that Striker was never going to be able to fight again. The best the old trainer could hope was just walking with a limp. Striker was about to ask a question but was silenced by the glossy stare in the Veritable Mother's eyes.

Softy muttered words became a lullaby as she recited an incantation. Her illuminated hands hovered above Striker's wounded joint. He had never seen the true healing magic of the Veritable Mothers. Many in the Army called them witches or spell casters. In that room, he felt the awesome power that drove them to fulfill their duties. They were the epitome of maternal instinct. Their sole desire was to help, heal, and nurture others. After a lifetime of war and bloodshed, an old soldier was able to finally see peace. He soon fell asleep, no longer plagued by the memories that had haunted him for these years.

———•———

The next morning, the young recruits awoke sore and stiff. War was a nasty business. These young men were learning it was not all shiny armor and parades. They were allowed a quick breakfast of dried meat and fruit as they were introduced to their new bunkhouse leader. Normally, Striker chose the leader out of the recruits. This offered quite a learning experience, both for the leader and the followers. It looked good on reports when it came time to interview for rank advancements. With so many noble houses represented, however he felt it best to have an outside leader.

A mountainous shadow darkened the bunkhouse as a giant entered and towered over the recruits. His plated boots thumped heavily as he came to a stop in the middle of the room. The lads stopped mid-chew as his deep baritone voice echoed off the rafters.

"I am Pethio. Old man Striker asked me to train you, younglings. You will follow my orders at all times. I care neither for pettiness nor bullying. If you wish to bring honor to your house, pay attention to what is being taught. Nobility is proven by action, not birthright. So, either show it in word and deed or, please, keep it to yourself."

The young men shared disconcerting looks as they silently finished their meal. None of them knew how to take this new addition to their lives. Once they finished, Pethio had them line up into four rows in the arena. The lesser skilled were placed in the front, while the more skilled were placed further back. In Pethio's mind, this allowed those who needed the instruction to learn faster.

"Now that you are all in order, we shall run a lap around the arena. *I* set the pace and you will all stay in your lines. Ready? Begin."

By the end of the five hundred yard lap, none of the boys were able to keep with the Paladin's grueling pace. His long legs and powerful strides were accustomed to long marches, wearing full grip and gear. These lads had a long way to go before being ready for full service, the Paladin thought.

Pethio came to a stop next to the board and shook his head in disappointment. No one was in their respected places, and the lines were a jumbled mess. Sighing, he called everyone to him and lined them up again. Only this time, he had them walk around the arena. His skillful eyes kept a look out for any lollygagging or foolishness. By the time Striker joined Pethio in the middle of the arena, the lads had successfully walked around the arena five times without being called to halt.

As a reward, the Paladin had them run a lap before lining up in front of the board. A mad scramble ensued that ended in chaos, while the fastest of the bunch left the others behind. Striker laughed and Pethio hung his head in exasperation when a handful bypassed the board and went straight for the water barrels.

"Well, my old friend," Striker said with an impish grin, "I never said this would be easy."

Pethio gripped the prayer beads that hung in his war hammer loop. He never understood the chaos of youth. The large man prayed to the Gods for strength with this bunch. The leaders disapprovingly approached the tangled mass of young men fighting over a chance for water. Striker's bugle brought all to heel with a sharp note.

"I leave you ladies alone for half the morning. And what do I get? You lot have lost your minds!"

Striker's crisp tone struck home as they hurried to line up for inspection. Having sweat on their tunics was one thing. But some of the lads were a little free with the cool liquid and were dripping from head to toe. Such lack of discipline got men killed in combat. It ruined well-laid plans. Let the enemy win. The recruits needed to learn that lesson.

"Now that you all have recovered your Gods' given good sense, let's begin!"

His voice commanded no argument from the youth. Striker signaled the other trainers to hand out metal scale mail armor, leather scale gauntlets, and fire-hardened staffs. In all honesty, the trainer hated this part of the training. Not the violence. Such things were common for soldiers. It was the uncertainty. More than a handful of hopefuls got life-altering wounds from those staffs. He just hoped that Katril had the power to heal any damage.

Pethio took over at this point, instructing them on how to wear and move in the armor. Once everyone was situated, the Paladin had them go through basic drills with the staff. Dust clouds whipped up with each passing movement. Grunts trumpeted as the youth imagined they wielded pole arms. Passing from line to line, the giant teacher corrected footing or grips. These were not toys or flights of fancy, but killing strikes. He pointed out the two-handed weapon was constructed to be either a blunt, piercing or blocking weapon, depending on the user. Only the truly gifted ever mastered the two-handed fighting techniques. Pethio hoped to find a few to send to the Paladin Corp after graduation from Battle School.

At the lunch break, Pethio felt confident they had learned enough basics to attempt sparing matches. He, like Striker, prayed for no lasting injuries this time. Striker demanded the youth leave their armor on during lunch. They had to get used to wearing it and moving in it. The meal became a quick affair, since the youth were antsy to begin the next level of qualifications.

With a quick glance to the wooden board, and a horn blast from Striker, the energized twelve-year-olds took off for their places. Trainers and helpers went ring to ring, inspecting armor as Striker explained a couple of new rules. No head shots were allowed, since those had a tendency of killing people. Points were only given to those who disarmed their opponents. Lastly, the winner had to remain in his ring until all the bouts were complete.

Every trainer and helper was present, as this was a very dangerous exercise. Each ring had an officiator to keep the fight from getting out of hand. A blast echoed off the walls as the bouts began. Again, it seemed, the working class took charge. The staff was a common weapon, used by farmers and herders alike, to fight off wolves and other predators.

Deston, paired up with a miller's son, much to his despair, was being thrashed. The boy laughed as the match was called in his favor. He had never won anything before and it felt good to beat a snot-nosed noble. His enjoyment was short lived, as Deston sharply struck the lad in the groin with the staff's end.

Pethio, who saw the entire affair, rushed forward and cuffed Deston with an armored gauntlet. Most people saw Paladins as armored monks, but the sense of justice and protection they harbored for all truly set them apart. They had a sense of right and duty that was born into them and could not be taught.

Medics rushed to tend to the boy as the officiator stripped Deston of the armor and handed him off to the guards. Such actions earned Deston a black mark on his file. He was now forbidden to ever join the ranks in his life time. The Arena was silent as a tomb as the rest of the hopefuls watched the expelled boy sob and struggle against the tight grips of the castle guards, trying to return to his ring .

Pethio ordered all to witness the affair with clear eyes. He wanted the young recruits to know and realize the difference between winning the battle and mercilessly beating an opponent. As his massive frame walked around the rings, he etched in their minds that any and all guild members were to rise above such petty and pathetic actions. If they wanted to wear the sigil of the Fire Brand, they needed to act worthy of it.

The huge Paladin escorted the injured boy to the wooden board as Striker ordered the rest to continue. The large man's words weighed heavy on their young shoulders. Subtly, each one changed their fighting styles to prove their worth. It was not about winning a fight. It became about victory over one's self, and learning restraint. The first set of rounds concluded without another incident. Striker was shocked to see the nobles and working classes were about even.

Pethio called the last of the winners to the center. He handed out tunics and thick, boiled leather helmets, eight blue and eight red. The new game was simple: fight as a group to take out the other team. Katril joined Pethio and Striker while the lads lined up. She always hated this part of the process. More lads were hurt here than in any other part. Pethio inclined his head towards her.

"Lady Katril, I am surprised to see you here. The last time, you swore never to return."

The daggered look she shot the Paladin only added to his amusement. "Well, I am hoping you blockheads stop them before it goes that far!"

As the only non-magic user in their group, Striker always felt the odd man out with those two, but such was his life. His bugle came alive, signaling the start of the exercise.

Karniel got teamed with Finley and six other nobles, on the red team. Although he was not thrilled with the idea, he knew Finley could hold his own. As the exercise commenced, Karniel and Finley realized they had met their match. The blue team was almost completely made up of farmers. Their skill was unmatched by the nobles, who were running scared.

Finley soon found himself double-teamed by a set of twin reapers. These were youth who spent their days harvesting the nation's grain with long sweeping scythes. Their weapons took on a life all their own as he desperately attempted to fight back. He felt the bruises form as each hit connected fully.

The two reapers saw victory before them as they readied for one last assault. Finley, shaking badly, steeled himself for the onslaught. Before the twins could move, a staff sailed through the air and connected with the reaper's chest to Finley's right. The lad dropped ten feet away from the sheer force of the blow. Both Finley and the remaining reaper lad turned to see Karniel bursting forward like a boar. Finley's opponent jumped in the air, hoping to gain an advantage as Karniel wrapped him in a bear hug. Neither of them were prepared for Finley to hit the reaper on the back of the head with such force that his staff broke.

Karniel dropped the unconscious youth as he gave Finley a startled look. Luckily, the boiled leather absorbed most of the blow, leaving only a massive welt on the sandy-haired lad's head.

"Can't be in your debt too much," the Sword Master's son said with a crooked grin.

The two red team members picked up the now abandoned blue team staves and returned to the fray. The fighting continued well into the evening, with both teams exhausted and very bruised. Pethio took pity on the last recruits standing and called a draw, as it was two from the blue team and two from the red. He grinned like a fox in a hen house as he watched the young men sink to the ground. He hoped this would forever remain in their minds. War was not for the pampered or the spoiled. It was dirty, draining, and taxing on the soul, and these lads had not really tasted it yet.

Katril called the medics forward to tend to the injured young men. She walked among them, using a mix of Shaman and Cathedral magic to test their vitals and look for internal bleeding. For all their chest thumping and ego, no one on the military council undervalued her skills as a healer. After checking the last lad, she gave Striker a nod. He silently thanked the Gods that none of the boys had been seriously injured. Having those who did not fight carry their fellow recruits into the bunkhouse, he met up with Katril and Pethio to discuss the exercise.

They walked in silence to Striker's office across from the bunkhouse, the full moon creating a silver shield in the star-riddled sky. The chief recruiting trainer chose to stay close to his charges in case they needed him. The majority of the lads had never been away from their homes and families for any amount of time. He felt it best they knew he would be near, like a father figure. This helped those that needed it, and stopped any foolishness from happening after the lads were sent to bed.

As the three entered the sparsely decorated office, Striker poured them all a small glass of wine. The office/bedroom fit the current resident like a glove. If any item was not functional, it had been removed long ago. On the right side, a long wood-and-canvas cot sat clean up against the wall, with a crisp folded blanket and fluffed pillow. At the foot of the bed was a worn panel locker. This chest housed the most treasured possessions of Striker. A handful of oil lamps suspended in the air from hemp cords. And a small candlestick flickered on the oak desk that had been used since the founding of the Fire Brand Army. All and all, it was orderly and honest.

The silence in the room was deafening. Pethio sat on the stool by the door, while Katril and Striker used the chairs facing the desk on the far wall. With such internal brooding, it was the large Paladin who decided to break the awkwardness of the moment.

"Well, all and all, it could have been worse. No one died, and injuries were at a minimal."

Katril shared a loaded glance with the grizzled trainer at such a comment. Her heart had never understood war or violence. The blood lust that pulsated from those boys sickened her to the core. It went against everything she stood for and wanted to achieve for others.

Striker held her hand in a comforting way. Every year, it was the same for her and her sisters. The spiritual taxation of monitoring the lads during the exercise was bad enough. Having to feel an overwhelming desire to hurt another, to feel what it meant to survive war, was another thing entirely. The enterprise went against everything the female order of the Veritable Mothers stood for and taught in the Abbeys across the country.

"Yes, we are blessed in that," the chief trainer stated, choosing his words carefully. "I have seen it go a lot worse. A few of the lads have real talent. Karniel, Finley, and those two reapers show true promise. The rest, however, will never amount to much more than foot soldiers."

Tears streamed down Katril's face at the cold assessment. Her voice shook with anger and sadness as she snapped and shot up to her feet. "How can you speak this way? How can you be so casual about the boys in your charge? They should be at a faire, or falling in love for the first time. Not learning to take another person's life."

Now the Paladin and trainer shared a look. They had had this discussion before in private, years before, when they had chosen to teach and hold themselves responsible for the future soldiers of the Army.

"My dear lady," the Paladin began with placating tone, "we see them for what they are: scared, nervous boys who want to live long enough to enjoy life. This is why we are tough on them. None of those lads should throw his life away needlessly. If he cannot abide the training, no pride or ego is lost. Yes, we need good strong young men to fill our ranks, just as you need good-hearted, strong young ladies to fill yours. This is not about death, but life. It has always fallen to a few to sacrifice for the many. It is our duty to ensure these boys have the tools to succeed. We do care for them."

The Veritable Mother wiped away her tears and took a calming breath. "Well then," she stated, "shall we get to it?"

The meeting lasted into the wee hours of the morning. They analyzed and assessed each lad, and what he brought by way of skills or strengths. By the time the night watch returned to the barracks, a plan had been solidified and agreed upon.

Life was about to get interesting for the hopefuls. There was only one constant in military life and that was change.

🔥 4 🔥

Striker, silent as the tomb, stood in the bunkhouse before the sun even rose. Each of the recruits was still in bed, albeit to varying degrees. The trainer, looking around the room, chuckled to himself. This was his favorite trick to pull on new recruits. By the Gods, it never got old. Pressing the bugle to his lips, a blood-curdling note released, attacking the senses. The boys jumped nearly out of their skins. Some even reached for the nearest item to use as a weapon. Others crashed to the floor, searching for places to hide.

Not trusting himself fully, Striker closed his eyes. With measured steps, he walked to the furthest wall. It was not proper to have the chief trainer laughing at such a childish trick. The sounds of scrambling youth echoed throughout the room. Cots had to be made hastily. Uniforms were put on in a haphazard fashion. Someone, Gods bless them, was frantically searching for a boot.

The chief trainer reached the back wall of the building and turned to face his charges. Each boy stopped whatever he was doing and snapped to attention. Their commanding officer took a step forward, eyes still closed.

"I am going to go outside," Striker commented. His voice was guarded, void of any emotion. Every ear strained to listen. They did not want to miss a single order. "You lot have five minutes to get my palace in order or, by the Parthenon, you will run until I get tired of watching you." With that declaration, he clipped his heels sharply and exited.

Leaning against the door, Striker's laughter was buried by the sporadic sounds of furniture moving and general chaos. Once composure was regained once more, Striker re-entered the bunkhouse. He spent several minutes inspecting bunks, the state of the latrine, and the general look of the young men. Had this been a real inspection, the lads would have failed. Order was key in the military. Everything had to be just so. The chief trainer took time to show the recruits how to keep a barracks. Sheets had to be wrinkle free. Exercise clothes demanded to be cleaned. For the lads too bruised to stand erect, he offered a balm to soothe the muscles. The military expected perfection and that started now.

They spent the rest of the morning learning how to tend to armor and weapons. Leather had to be wiped, cleaned, and oiled. Blades had to get sharpened and filed to keep their edge. Even their tunics and garments had to be washed and dried to last longer and fight illness. This discipline was what made the Fire Brand army so formidable. Discipline at home met order during war. That was the foundation of success.

After their noon meal, the lads were split into two groups. One went with Pethio for further two-handed weapon instruction. And the other went with Striker. The two planned to meet up for the evening meal. The chief instructor led his group out of the arena, across a cobblestone courtyard, and into a large stable.

"Uh, sir?" one of the reapers began in a very confused voice as all entered the stable. "I thought we were here to learn, not to be punished."

Striker smiled as he opened a window flap. Light poured into the stable as an odd assortment of rope ladders and timber working came into view. "Boys," the trainer exclaimed, his arms opened wide, "Welcome to the grinder!"

The horse stalls and hay loft had been removed to make room for a crazed obstacle course. Striker swung off a rope and gripped a massive cable dangling from the roof. With a strained grunt, he pulled it down as the rest of the window flaps opened, bathing the stable with light. Securing the cable to a giant eye hole stake, he demanded the recruits follow his lead. He zipped, weaved, and danced through the course. Returning to the beginning, he was shocked to see only ten finished with him.

Shaking his head in skepticism, Striker had them run the course again and again. This would not do at all, he thought as he opened a leather folding chair. Beside his seat sat a pile of files with the young men's name and medical exams. He watched each future soldier in turn and updated the records. As they passed him, he issued a check by their names. This way he was able to keep track of their skills and speed.

Once the fastest of them began to show signs of exhaustion, he called a break. He then rolled in a water barrel and, once it was right side up, popped off the wooden top. A handful of young men ran like jackrabbits to the barrel and dunked their heads in it. Striker knew the first to the water were usually the laziest, so he devised a special exercise just for them.

With everyone watered and rested, he opened a tack box and removed several lengths of rope. Teaming up the laziest with the most energetic, Striker paired everyone off, tying them together at the waist. Smiling at his work, he returned to the tack box and removed a small sand glass. After instructing each pair that they had to finish the course before the sand ran out, he pushed the first roped couple forward. As pair after pair stumbled, fell, or snagged their rope, Striker wondered how the other group fared. He hoped Pethio had not lost his cool this time.

Pethio's group had fared a little better, but the Paladin's patience was wearing thin. Since they were a man short, due to Deston's stupidity, the normal exercises had to be altered constantly. The group that ended up with three always fooled around and did not take it seriously. The whispered words that escaped his lips were so unsaintly that his priory brethren were sure to blush had they been present. Snapping at the young men like a chained guard dog, he pulled the extra lad to the center of the arena, having the others form a seated circle.

Using the lad, Pethio went through the forms again, from high guard to Slicing the Forest, and from low guard to Boar Charging Through Water. Over and over, he educated them, using each lad to drive home the point. Bumps and bruises abounded as those too slow or too lazy felt the wrath of the Paladin.

Both groups praised the Gods as the day ended and dinner was served. The two leaders compared notes as the recruits ate and then bathed. Most of the young men could have done better than expected, if they would only pay closer attention. Finley, Karniel, and a handful of others showed the most inkling of promise. And, if they applied themselves, they would have a glorious future in the Fire Brand ranks.

While the trainers were in Striker's office, Katril mercifully left a small vial of ointment on each of the bunks. It was her own blend of oils, dried herbs, and a pinch of magic. She saw the lads as her own children, so, naturally, she wanted to ease their pain. Unfortunately, five of the noble-born youth returned from the baths early and set to hoarding the vials left on the pillows after the healer left.

Karniel, Finley, and the twin straw-haired reapers caught the thieves in the act as they snatched up the last one, which was on Karniel's pillow. Finley tried to reason with his fellow nobles, hoping to come to a peaceful solution. He received a jab to the eye for his efforts. It was a crime in their eyes that such a high born would side with any lower class people. It was that mentality that was the straw that finally broke the tedious control of the reapers. One of the freckled twins ran forward to catch the tumbling boy as rage burned in his eyes.

The estate stewards in the southern and western parts of the country ruled the working class with an iron fist. Harassing and robbing the workers was normal sport for them. Fondling the farm girls, and using them like possessions, was a rite of passage and they relished it. But, in that bunk house, on that day, those nobles learned the true strength of the working class.

The commotion of the brawl was such that Pethio and Striker heard it in the office, through thick stone walls. Not sure what to make of the noise, they rushed over to the bunkhouse and threw open the door.

The sight that greeted the instructors was odd to behold. Three of the five noble house boys lay in a broken heap at the twin's feet, arms and legs broken in odd angles. Karniel had one in a single-handed choke hold against the wall. The offender was slowly losing consciousness. Finley, sporting the beginnings of a black eye, had the last one in a cross arm bar, about to dislocate the shoulder.

The new recruit teachers' worst fear had been realized. Old heart aches and social scars had surfaced with a vengeance. The freckled twins noticed the older men enter the bunkhouse and looked at the fruits of their labors almost proudly.

A loud pop echoed as Finley succeeded in his maneuver. As if to solidify the point, Karniel tossed his victim on the nearest bunk as if he weighed nothing. Defiance stormed in the young men's hearts as Striker stepped forward. He attempted to keep his voice calm while he spoke, but to no avail.

"Do you boys realize what you have done?" he snapped. "Their fathers will demand your heads! Your families will suffer for this." Pointing at the group in front of the twins, Striker continued. "As soon as they come to, they will whine for daddy to avenge them. What in Death's name possessed you boys to do this?"

Karniel stepped forward and reported the stealing of the vials, Finley's attempt at bargaining, and the assault that ensued. Even though the youth took no pride in fighting for money or blood, teaching thieves a lesson was another thing entirely.

Pethio found it hard to fault the young men anything. The Paladin Code was one of god-like justice for all, as they did serve as judges in the less populated areas. His deep voice chastised the boys, but he showed compassion as well. Putting a hand on Striker's shoulder, the warrior priest said his group found no guilt in the boys or their actions. After all, they were not the criminals in that ordeal. Not even the military dared to step foot in the Paladin's jurisdiction, so Striker knew the Corp would protect the lads. Excusing himself, Pethio left the bunkhouse to send a communiqué to his order.

The cleanup, however, was still left to Striker. He sent one of the recruits that had amassed at the back of the bunkhouse to search for Katril. Her magic was sorely needed here. With a tone that conveyed power, he had Karniel, Finley, and the twins reorganize the bunkhouse. They had until Katril showed to finish or not even the Gods could protect them.

The Veritable Mother was in her bedchamber reading when a short boy came bursting in, yelling her name. For a moment, his brain stopped as he realized what she was in, her evening wear. The female healer had been lying on her cot, half covered by a fur blanket, as he entered, but was now covering herself up.

"What do you want, boy?" she demanded, shaking with embarrassment and anger.

He stumbled for words as he averted his eyes. "Fight in the bunkhouse. Bones broken. Striker needs you." He rambled off other incoherent babble, but it was lost between his brain and his tongue. With his message delivered, he was off like a shot, leaving the door wide open.

"The man will be the death of me," Katril muttered as she hurried to get dressed. With her cream-colored gown and green-scaled cloak in place, she rushed to the bunkhouse, armed with a medic kit. By the time she arrived, order had been restored in the bunkhouse. Those hurt in the assault had been moved close to the door, to allow for easier access. The more she assessed, the more upset she became. Luckily, the breaks had been clean, and the dislocation had not damaged any of the nerve endings.

Once she finished with the last patient, her eyes glowed green with power. She seemed to grow, her head almost touching the rafters. Her voice shook dust from the roof. "Tell me what happened," she demanded, her gaze piercing everyone to the soul.

Few had seen the wrath of a Veritable Mother, but the tone of her voice left little to the imagination.

After the four gave their testimony, she returned to her normal size, quite ashamed of her outburst. Opening her kit, she produced extra vials to replace those that had been damaged in the fight. As she passed them out, her gaze turned towards the four boys. She had felt pain, anger, and frustration roll off them in waves as they testified. They knew how bad the situation was, and how powerless they were to stop it. Once the vials were distributed, she gently took those four aside and softly spoke to them. Striker noticed their moods changed as she communicated with them. After hugging each one, and leaving them a blessing from the Goddess, she left the room. But not before giving the white-haired soldier a confident smile.

Looking over his young charges, the old soldier sighed. In twenty years, this had never happened. He knew he would have to choose the words in his report with care, or risk putting the boys' families in even more danger. As the white-haired man turned to leave, he told them all to go to sleep. He heard the softly spoken questions from the youth as he shut the bunkhouse door. He hoped the noble families would not go too far.

$$\text{\reflectbox{}} 5 \text{}$$

With the rising of the sun, the spirit of those residing in the barracks had changed. Breakfast was a silent affair, with Karniel, Finley, and the twins completely ostracized by everyone. For their part, the Nobles chose to ignore the fact that a handful of commoners had beaten their fellows in a fight. Or that a Noble was accused of stealing. Such things were simply not allowed. The rest of the lads refused to associate with Karniel's group at all. This was more out of self-preservation than anything. For they knew the wrath of the Noble houses, and they wanted none of it.

Striker felt like he had been through a laundry ringer as he opened the door to the bunkhouse. Word of last night's fight had spread like wildfire during a dry summer. Rumors filled the local inns as the story grew and drastically changed. Even the staff in the Red Keep were abuzz with the news. Sometime during the night, while the Nobles were sharing wine and favors, the fight had been mentioned to the parents of the beaten boys. Outraged, and reeking of booze, they had marched to Striker's office in the late hours of the night and beat upon his door.

The assault on his office woke him in a foul mood, but he was no match for the ten drunken parents demanding restitution for their children. Pethio, who heard the commotion as he was returning from the bird courier, entered the archway connecting the arena with the courtyard. Striker, seeing his friend arrive, gave him a pleading look for help from the drunken mob of idiots.

"May I be of assistance?" the enormous Paladin asked in a loud voice. With the arch only being seven feet tall, his voice bounced from stone to stone. It created a vibrating blast to those impaired by alcohol.

The sudden entry of a law enforcer put the drunken lords and ladies on edge. The fathers knew being drunk on the training grounds or the Red Keep was an offense worthy of discharge from military service. As such, none of them wanted to face the Lord Commander. Uncertainty festered as they tried to explain their presence on the grounds.

One of the ladies of court took charge of the muttering group and stepped forward. In a sultry, flattering voice, she tried to explain their ordeal.

"Honored Paladin," she began with a bow, "we are here as concerned parents. For we have learned the most distressing news. Our dear children have been accosted and severely beaten by ruthless peasants. We simply ask to see our darling boys and look after their welfare. Surely this is no crime. If anyone needs be punished, it should be those filthy commoners who have no place among our proud and powerful military." A smile crept along her face, as she figured he could not deny a grieving mother.

"My dear lady," the Paladin countered with flat tone, "Your words are one of caring and tenderness towards your young. And yet, their meaning demands punishment for a slight that you have imagined. I was there after the fight and know the cause thereof."

Evil desires filled the drunken lot, as they hoped to find cause for prison or execution for the ones that attacked their boys. Such possibilities were destroyed, however, as Pethio continued.

"Your sons brought dishonor to your houses by not only stealing from their fellow recruits, but they stooped so low as to hide the offense with violence. Such things will not abide in the Red Keep, or in this nation's military." His voice boomed as he concluded. "You can retrieve your sons at the hospital wing and leave the arena grounds. I suggest you do so now."

The sheer size of the Paladin, and the fact that he could probably defeat them all, gave birth to a fear that filled the Nobles and quickened their feet.

Striker breathed a sigh of relief as the parents disappeared from sight. "Thanks, my friend," the soldier commented as he inspected his door.

The hinges were bent, and two of the planks broken from the pounding. He knew the head of the Keep's blacksmiths would not take kindly to this.

Groaning, Striker entered his office and took a draw from his flagon filled with corn whiskey. The arrogance of those aristocrats irritated the old trainer. Such pomp and false pride over some long dead ancestor. All they did was sit in their manors or castles and get drunk while others actually performed the labors that kept them fed, clothed, and protected. He slammed the flagon on the desk with a sigh. With a gentle reminder that the Paladin Corp was taking care of the incident, Striker fell on his cot, hoping sleep, with the aid of very strong alcohol, would overtake him.

As Striker cast his gaze from person to person in the bunkhouse the next morning, silence did not help his foul mood. "Finish eating and be outside in ten minutes," he barked, before he turned sharply and left.

The youth took to eating with renewed energy. None wanted to be on the receiving end of the bad mood that pulsated from their commander.

They scrambled to line up correctly in front of the board. With six no longer in the ranks, the remaining recruits were unsure how to do so. Their confusion was short lived, as Striker had them run laps around the arena. By the fourth lap, soft steps glided along the sand behind the master trainer.

In spite of himself, Striker smiled at the sound. "Are you training to be a Scout, my dear Healer?" he teased, turning to face the sound.

Katril smiled in return, and offered a warm cup of coffee. "I heard about last night," she quipped as he took the cup. "I hope this helps."

The warm brew seemed to melt the stress away with each swallow. With a nod of appreciation, he presented her with a folding chair. She smoothed her dress and sat, regally facing the wooden board, as if expecting something.

Pethio soon entered the dust-choked area, his mind full of the task before him. Every year, this exercise brought out the worst in some of the military hopefuls and the best in others. He prayed to both his patron Gods that nothing bad would happen this go around.

A crew of trainers followed the Paladin, carrying huge iron-hinged crates and over-sized racks of weapons. This new group set to work organizing the equipment in to two teams.

As they continued to run laps, Striker's whip cracked when some of the lads got to close or nosy for their own good.

Once the Paladin signaled all was ready, Striker called the lads to the board to explain the next exercise. Twenty-six chain mail shirts were laid out on a red cloth. Blunted short swords, sheathed and belted, hung next to stringed bows with quivers.

Striker took a calming breath, as this was his least favorite part of the cutting process. Clearing his throat, he began to explain that in battle Men at Arms and Archers made up almost seventy percent of the Army. They were used to protect each other and any Cavalier or Paladins in the ranks. The young men were to take turns being either bowmen or wielding a sword and shield, while the trainers were to attack and try to overpower the Paladin.

The ten trainers smiled at their mentioned assignment while they suited up in their battle armor. This was their favorite exercise for new recruits. This was, in part, because they got thrashed in their year of training. but, for the most part, it was because some were just bullies. They were to act as the bad guys and overpower the recruits. If one of them was able to touch the Paladin, they won.

In the last ten years, the trainers had won eight times. And, looking at the newest recruits, they thought victory would be in their hands again.

The youth got set up in their armor, and were handed a weapon. Half had the bows, and the remainder were bearers of blades. Four-foot rounded shields were added to those with the swords, as Striker showed them how to create a shield wall. The archers, with the protection of the interlocking shields, were tasked to shoot any and all trainers before they reached their group.

Pethio had his warriors lined up in a wedge formation for the expected attack. This maneuver would allow the lads mobility, and give the Paladin added protection against a rapidly advancing force.

The trainers stood about thirty paces away, hitting their wooden swords on their shields. They growled with anticipation as they stared like lions about to feast.

The stench of fear radiated from the youth. It was one thing to fight someone their age, but having to fight a military trainer— well, that was plain foolishness. Many a lad shook from nerves and fright. The few who were not tried to calm the others down a peg.

Karniel glared at the trainers. He knew they relished in the fears of the boys. Yes, this was an exercise, and, yes, there was no promise for fairness on the battle field. But to truly enjoy your opponent's weaknesses, that was bullying at its finest. The green-eyed youth asked to be the boar's tusk in the formation and the Paladin agreed. So there he stood, in front position of the wedge, gripping his shield with both hands. His job was to ground the shield wall, for the others used him as an anchor, and he refused to let his fellows down.

The trainer directly in front of Karniel smirked. He knew how to take out the boar's tusk, for he had done it for years in mock campaigns. Rolling his shoulders, and raising his wooden sword, the rather bulky trainer signaled for his team to prepare. In unison, they tensed like cats about to pounce.

At the sigil board, Katril and Striker studied both groups closely, as they had a bet on the exercise. Smiling with anticipation, the white-haired trainer blew a shrieking note from his bugle.

The hurricane of raw emotions that erupted in the arena was a wonder to behold. Three of the trainers headed straight for Karniel, as the rest spread out like wings on a bird. The fletching of an arrow caressed Karniel's left cheek as it sailed towards the attacking trainer. The once smirking trainer's last second block deflected the arrow, but the maneuver gave the shield wall time to brace for the impact.

Heeding the Paladin's advice, the lads tipped their shield slightly forward, right before the collision. The charging adversaries felt Karniel's strength become amplified as six other youth pushed in unison.

Caught off guard by the well-timed counter, and in a bit of a daze, the trainers were subjected to multiple blows on unprotected arms and legs. Before a strategy could be realized, all three were knocked out from sword blows to the head.

The flanking forces were met with a storm of arrows as their compatriots fell to the ground. The trainers' shields, now covered in arrows, became worthless and were discarded. Using only their weapons and plate armor, they were no match for a wedged arrowhead.

The shield walls separated into two, so as to prevent the trainers from gaining ground. Each one of the lads gained a little more confidence. The plan seemed to be working. A cloud of dust formed, with both groups waxing and waning in their movements.

Finley called for all archers to stand at the ready. Bows creaked and backs strained with the order.

The plate mail attackers, knowing what was to come, surrendered without much fuss or argument. There would be no victory for them this year, but at least they survived with minimal bumps.

An explosion of cheers poured out of the arena. While this was just an exercise, Pethio smiled at the boys while they banged their swords on their shields. Their ability to follow and complete such a meticulous plan warmed the Paladin's heart.

Smoothing out her dress, Katril rose from her seat. "Your flagon is mine," she purred, walking out to tend to the wounded participants.

With a grumble, Striker reorganized and split the group, so they could be attacked by a mixed military unit. The stoic chief trainer had the trainers replace rounded arrow heads and wooden swords for the broken ones from earlier before they left to attend to their wounds. He did not need any more incidents, as most of the lads had never seen combat.

A spirit of victory filled each young recruit as they appeared to bounce on their feet with anticipation. Both teams shouted battle cries while Pethio struggled to rein in his protectors.

One of the young nobles in the wedge formation guarding Pethio sprinted forward. Blood pounded in his ears, full of false courage and battle lust. A handful followed him into the fray. What followed was a complete abandonment of discipline and order. Twenty four bodies crashed in a mad, adrenaline-fueled rage.

Karniel and Finley, unsure of what to do, looked to Striker, but the trainer was blasting his bugle, hoping to calm them down. The effort, however, was futile. The crazed young men quickly became a mob, everyone attacking the other, fully drunk on delusions of grandeur and their own self-worth.

Karniel grabbed Finley and pinned him to the ground as the arena seemed to heave and pitch, waves of energy rolling towards those fighting. They looked towards the Veritable Mother and realized what she was doing. The two lads had no other choice but to hope and pray the magical assault would end quickly.

Katril, having enough of the foolish behavior, became haloed by green light. Her hands, spread wide, came crashing together. Her cupped hands sent a concussive blast straight at the enraged mob. Plumes of dust filled the air as the screams of tumbling youth echoed throughout.

Karniel attempted to stand and dust himself off, but fell on his first two attempts. His equilibrium, momentarily stunned, made it difficult to stay on his feet. A thick fog of dirt hung in the air, stinging his eyes, making it hard to see. A body was heard hitting the ground hard near the far wall of the arena, and then all was silent. Stumbling like a drunken sailor, the powerfully-built young man headed in the direction of Striker, hoping to get some answers and to check on Katril.

The massive twelve-year-old reached the leaders about the same time as Pethio, who seemed unaffected by the blast. They saw Striker cradling the woman's body, silently crying. He knew the amount of power she had used, and how fragile she really was. Such feelings and emotions were taxing enough during a mock battle. But, with such overwhelming chaos, he was surprised the Veritable Mother was still breathing.

The giant Paladin smiled down at his friends. Being a magic user, he was familiar with these types of issues. After speaking comfort to the old soldier, he muttered a prayer of healing and comfort for all present. In an almost reverent manner, he placed his hands on Katril's head and heart. An earthy light illuminated from his hands, restoring her energy and spirit, while putting her into a deep, calming sleep.

With the dust finally settling, Striker had Karniel and Finley carry the now resting woman to her quarters near the hospital wing. A field gurney was quickly fashioned with the weapons rack and red cloth and the boys were off.

Pethio, sensing the anger and disgust churning within his friend, paused before leaving. "It is not their fault," he said in a calming voice. "They have never felt it before."

The older man refused to look at anything but the recruits. His voice, full of pain, quietly muttered three words that shocked the Paladin. Patting his heart-torn friend on the shoulder, Pethio followed the boys with the gurney. A swell of pity bubbled within the male healer. He knew Striker and Katril loved each other, and, after the events of last night, the teacher of hopeful soldiers was not in any mood to forgive.

Casting a final look at the Arena, the giant of a man prayed his friend would not lay a hand on any of his students in his absence.

Even from his high vantage point, in his personal offices next to the Arena, Jaldo, the Army's Lord Commander, was able to hear the gut-wrenching words of his chief recruit trainer. It was no secret that Striker had feelings for Katril. As long as they both performed their duties, Jaldo did not care if their relationship blossomed, for he knew that the Veritable Mothers refused to wed. Not that it was against their creed, but some saw it as an inconvenience, since they tended to move around a lot.

The display of force by Katril, however, did surprise him. It was hard enough to control a man infused with battle lust, but when it was nearly thirty young men, there was no way she could keep her emotions in check. Normally, the past Veritable Mothers yelled or conjured up some rain, but a blast such as that— Well, that was one for the history books. Since war and violence were the opposite of what her order taught, he felt sorry for her and her empathy.

Turning away from the sixth floor balcony, and returning to his desk, the military leader inwardly sighed. Shifting the reports around on his desk, The Lord Commander tried to buy himself more time before speaking to his guests. Their rudeness and arrogance were an insult to his position and rank. But the middle-aged, broad shoulder military man wanted to calm himself before saying anything.

Jaldo often came up here to escape such politicking, and to watch the future of the military. It kept his faith filled and resolution firm. Although his career was ripe with victories and glory, he always hated that he did not have any sons of his own. But since his rise to the highest rank in the Fire Brand Army, he had nearly four hundred thousand sons to care for. In his mind, it was a holy duty and he treated it as such.

He was the one that instituted the families of the hopefuls staying at the Red Keep. Jaldo wanted their parents to know that their sons were cared for, as well as show future applicants the wonders of military service. It was a shrewd move, yet the yield brought more hopefuls each year. It always lightened his heart to see people better themselves.

Unfortunately, the meeting in his office was out of ego and pride, and not for the advancement of others. These Lords had blown right pass every guard, Paladin, and watchman, before coming to a halt in the Lord Commander's ante-chamber. They demanded to see Jaldo and would not leave until they were satisfied.

Banners decorated the full oval ante-chamber, along with a complete set of armor. A desk was added for an aide-de-camp, with two full size benches and several chairs for visitors on either side of the room.

A balding desert tribesman, named Kaveh, stood in front of the Commander's office door, spiked mace in hand, when the lords entered the room. His dark olive eyes passed over the visiting nobles, stopping each in their tracks. It was common knowledge he had thrown a priest out of a window after the visiting clergy had insulted the last Lord Commander. He was not one to be trifled with, for his people took their oaths seriously.

Twirling the mace from hand to hand, the tribesman casually asked them to state their business. Knowing flattery and pomp were of no use, they offered up a sob story of a great injustice to their sons, each adding their own version of events. If they had hoped to gain some type of ally, the land owners were mistaken. For their pleas were met with disinterest. Kaveh had heard from Pethio about the event in the bunkhouse. But the aide-de-camp never figured the aristocrats to be foolish enough to bother the Lord Commander over such a trifle as boys fighting.

Politics meant little to the tribesman. His people did not bother with such honorless ideals and pettiness. He assured the Nobles that the Lord Commander was indeed in his office, but was not to be disturbed. A sharp gesture with his mace killed any remarks that tried to leave the lords' mouths.

Pointing to the benches with his deadly weapon, Kaveh directed the visitors to sit and await his return. Begrudgingly, they sat down, facing the desk. With a curt nod, the tribesman turned on his heels and closed his leader's office door behind him.

Jaldo arched an eyebrow when his aide-de-camp entered armed.

"You have five visitors, Sir," Kaveh reported in a rather monotone voice.

The tribesman's eyes darted to the nearest window before asking if the Lord Commander felt like entertaining guests.

A soft chuckle hummed in Jaldo's throat. He had heard the exchange, and had been surprised they were not sailing out the nearest wall opening already. A simple gesture communicated that the visitors had leave to enter.

With a bow, and still holding his spiked mace, Kaveh opened the office door and showed in the muttering guests.

Entering according to social status, and arrayed in family armor, the first two through the door were the aide-de-camps for the Master at Arms school. They sat, with an air of self-righteousness, in the only chairs in the office, directly in front of the Lord Commander. The other three, who had ties to rather large farming estates, were left to stand or lean against the few pillars in the room. Each one, gripping their sword hilts, was as proud as peacocks. This pathetic display of power irritated Jaldo, since it was customary, even social etiquette, to leave weapons with the Captain of the Watch at the castle gatehouse.

The bearded aide-de-camp, sitting to the right of the desk, straightened his back, shifting to a more dominating position, before he spoke. It was his grasp of politics, and not his military prowess, that earned him the commission he so enjoyed. His words, however, were damned with Jaldo raising a hand.

After relaying that he already knew why they were in his office, and personally assuring them he had the affair well in hand, the Lord Commander rose, signaling that the meeting was indeed over. Much to his chagrin, no one moved.

One of the landowners began to speak, only making matters worse.

"My esteemed Commander," he began, as if to give a grand speech. "We all feel comfort with your assurances, and will relay them to our wives, but that is not completely why we are here. It seems that those pompous Paladins, and the Veritable Mother witches, are also taking an interest as well. What is next? Will the Harvesters also pressure you into not getting justice for the slight upon our houses? We demand to have our honor restored!"

Thanking the Gods that he chose not to carry a dagger, Jaldo stared at the fool rutting around like a boar in the spring. The army leader circled his desk, hands behind his back, so as to not succumb to the temptation of slapping his guests.

"So, there was a slight upon your house?" the Commander asked crisply, still pacing. "Your sons were caught stealing a gift given by the Holy Order of the Veritable Mothers. Such an insult was not taken well by Katril, the one assigned here, nor by the Church or the Shamans she represents. It was my understanding that she healed each wounded boy, even to the point they could walk again. Now if you have no desire for her services, then your boys will return to being cripples."

The finality of his words loomed over the visitors like a wraith ready to exact revenge. None of them wished for a crippled heir. In certain circles, appearances mattered, and a weak heir meant a weak house.

"As for the Paladin," he continued as he returned to his seat. "If you wish to tell Pethio that he is wrong for performing his duties, by all means, try. It is the law of this country that all Paladins have the right to disperse justice and uphold the integrity of *every* citizen. He is currently in the hospital wing, with Katril, if any of you wish to see him."

The off-handed manner of his words wounded the pride of the nobles. They had become accustomed to people cowering to their every whim and want. He was scolding them like they were children struggling to understand a lesson, and they hated it.

With disgust and anger pulsating, they rose and headed for the door, muttering under their breath.

"Aide-de-camps," Jaldo, in an offhand manner as he picked up a report, called from his desk as he returned to his duties.

They turned, somewhat uneasy with the nonchalant manner of his voice.

"You both realize that entering *my* Keep, armed and blatantly disregarding the rules we have here are grounds for discharge from the military, correct?"

The reality of their folly came crashing down atop their arrogant heads and caused their hearts to plummet to their toes.

"Both of you have by nightfall to remove yourselves, your families, and your belongings from the Red Keep or Kaveh will be called to assist you.

Your service to the Fire Brand Army of the Mighty God Kogien has come to an end."

With much deflated egos, they exited and came face to face with the broadly smiling tribesman.

"I do look forward to fulfilling *all* my Lord's commands," Kaveh said, his voice oozing with malicious intent.

The former aides looked to their companions for help, shocked to behold looks of haughty rejection. They had neither status nor power, no money nor political favor to use. They had been reduced to the very thing they despised: commoners

———◆———

The majesty of the banquet hall never failed to impress the Lord Commander. And, after that fiasco with the nobles, he needed something to boost his spirits. It had taken the castle staff almost a week to clean, polish, shine, and dust every inch of the massive room. The undertaking had been an expensive one. But having the converted war room shine like the belle of the ball was worth it. A large maple wood table had been brought in for the occasion, and pewter dinnerware had been placed just so. Lining the walls were small buffets and cabinets. Each one was loaded to capacity with food or drink, with a server ready to dole out the delicious treats.

Smiling and greeting each guest in turn, Jaldo was the perfect host. Lord or Lady, Farmer or Tradesmen, all were seen as equal at his table. The children of the invited families stayed in their rooms, with dinner and a storyteller or puppeteer to entertain them. This way the parents had a much needed night off. And Jaldo was able to observe how everyone would act, especially since children tend to act the way their parents do.

Loving to keep the visitors on their toes, Kaveh had changed up the seating order moments before everyone entered. That year, the guests were seated in the order their sons had joined the recruiting annuls, save for one couple.

The young parents of the Reaper twins that fought the thieving aristocrats were given the tremendous honor of sitting on the right hand of Jaldo. Their confusion was evident when the Aide personally showed them to the chairs. The mother blushed and softly asked if there had been some mistake. After all, farmers were no allowed to even be in the great halls of the castles.

Kaveh assured her there had been no mistake, that the Lord Commander personally wished to meet the parents of the boys that defended the honor of the Red Keep. Unsure of what to do, and not wanting to offend such a powerful man, they sat down, albeit with unease. As a peace offering, Jaldo poured the two farming parents a glass of wine and saluted their boys by name. With the first toast out of the way, stress eased away as the wine and food flowed.

The cheers and merry making from the feast filled the surrounding halls and corridors. Even the Keep's staff seemed to partake in the happy, joyful mood. There were some, however, that did not revel in friendship and mutual respect.

The Rut was aptly named, as it was the rundown section of the Red Keep City. Small dirt lanes and cheaply built homes lined the poorer part of the quarter. Here, any of man's dark desires could be found for a price. Cheap ale and companionship were the easiest to locate. Brothels dotted every other corner. Gangs and other low-lifes controlled the inns and taverns. Though none had gained any true power since the Gang Purge that had happened three years before. Within that lawless quarter, the pomp and ceremony of the military was forgotten. Here, War's true nature became a reality.

In one such seedy tavern, an odd quintet awaited in a shadowy corner. They sat, hood raised, trying to not draw attention to themselves. The inn keeper, Burgess the Portly, kept eyeing the group with suspicion. Their weapons, cleaned and polished, gleamed in the light cast by the roaring fire place. Such finery was odd here, so they stuck out like sore thumbs.

The inn keeper was lazy by nature, and had no desire to call for the Watch. He did not want any unwanted messes in his inn, thank you very much. The Alley Wolves controlled the Inn, and most of the street. They cared little for the nobles or the military. Many such types entered the Rut on a dare, or sought out cheap women. As long as visitors paid, no harm would befall them.

Swinging door hinges screamed as a broad man entered the inn. Scanning the fireplace, and the small table area, he walked heavily to the bar. Chain mail scrapped against plate armor as powerful limbs moved with a fighter's grace. His studded mace banged against the small wood-paneled bar as he sat down with a sigh.

Burgess, seeing the crest on the chest plate, filled a large tankard of ale. He knew this armored man, as did most in the Rut. Few in the Watch ever entered the forsaken section of town, choosing to leave control to the many gangs. This man, however, was not so lazy. Fifty five years of war and violence weighed heavily on his shoulders. His speed and power were unmatched in the army. Even the most murderous men gave him a wide berth.

The Innkeeper set down the tankard with a nod. "Good to see you, Watchman. Got some odd folk here. Don't want no trouble, not me."

Cold, dead eyes met the innkeeper's, and then stole a glance at the small table in the corner. Grunting his reply, the Watchman downed the cheap ale in a single gulp. A sharp metallic ding pierced the air as a Flame Mark sailed towards the rather obese innkeeper.

"My thanks, Master Keeper. Was good like always," the Watchman boomed as he rose from his stool. "Fill five more for my noble friends in the corner. Their sour faces could use a good tankard of ale."

The leader of this rather curdled-faced group turned and issued a defiant glare. "If you bring us that horse piss you call ale, Pig, I will gut you."

The threat became punctuated with a dagger being driven into the warped table. The leather grip groaned as its handle cracked under the increasing strain of the hand squeezing it. Rage, wounded pride, and revulsion radiated off each of the five men.

Like a well-oiled siege machine, they rose and flung off their cheap hoods and cloaks. Decorated chest plates bore the sigils of the Blood Rose, the Blue Vineyard, the Green Salmon, the Black Crab, and the Orange Oak Tree. Every man was a powerful Lord, owning hundreds of acres in land, water rights, and industries. Few were ever able to control as much as they and not be on the White Council. Their purpose was clear: They wanted the Watchman dead.

"Gentleman," the Watchman began in a flat tone, "I am not sure what imagined insult you think I did, but this will not end well for anyone. How about we forget this happened and go our separate ways?"

The leader of the nobles snarled. He had been in Jaldo's office earlier that day and heard the complete foolishness of the Lord Commander. How was he able to allow a peasant to assault a noble? It went against the natural order of class and social castes. They existed to serve their betters, not rise above their allotted place. And they were going to prove that fact.

"Your son almost broke my boy's neck. By the Gods, I will end your line," the Blood Rose noble screamed.

Steel sang as five naked blades escaped their leather confines. The spirit of murder and blood lust overshadowed the torches and the room dropped several degrees. Zawl bared his teeth and growled as the five maniacs charged him, hungry for death. He would protect Karniel from arrogant fools like these, even if it killed him.

$$\textrm{🖑 6 🖑}$$

Karniel knew he was dreaming. Even through his rasped, fearful panting, he knew. Doubling over with his hands on his knees, he desperately attempted to catch his breath. The Rut looked just like he remembered it from all those years ago. The small dark alley he occupied offered little protection. Broken wooden crates and small rotting rain buckets were all that populated the ground. Everything around him was lifeless.

Skills honed from years under the abusive control of a gang yelled at him to keep running. Karniel needed to find a place, any place, to hide. With a dash, the muscular youth was off again. Luck, a deity every street child prayed to, was not with him. Every door and window was locked up and sealed shut. His old haunts were nowhere to be found. Even the North and South gatehouses were barred against him.

To make matters worse, Karniel was not able to find another living soul. Even the bugs and rats that called the poor section home had somehow vanished. With his back against the North gatehouse portcullis, the dreamer slid to a sitting position. Fear ravaged his heart. He was out of time, out of breath, and out of hiding places.

Heavy footsteps crunching the dirt caused the young man to look up. Soulless black-armored boots came into view. The overlapping-plated-steel style of the Paladin armor had become corrupted by the person casually walking towards Karniel. His greaves and gauntlets were a similar design. They taunted the youth's earliest memories. Intricate lines of rich red inlayed the armor in such a way as to give the illusion of veins. The helmet, designed like a distorted bird beak, was blackened like the rest of the armor.

The blood-like pattern came alive as it swirled and boiled. Pulling from the extremities of the plate metal, the red lines snaked their way to the stark white design embossed on the cuirass. Circling around the crest like carrion birds, the blood-like liquid began to gather speed, preparing to strike.

Karniel gasped as he recognized the emblem. There, in the mist of corruption and filth, shone the sigil of the White Raven clan in all its former glory and beauty. Grinning coldly at the shock on the youth's face, the armored man spoke softly but with purpose.

"Join me," he beckoned. "Join me and we can end the pettiness of corruption within the government. There is much to tell you about our past, child. All you have to do is take my hand and your years of suffering will be over."

Karniel was tempted, to be sure. Quick images of memories and long forgotten faces danced just out of view. Focusing on the outstretched gauntlet, movement tugged at Karniel's eye line. In a predatory attack, narrow lines of blood cut into the brilliantly white sigil. Pain filled the sitting young man as the crest seemed to buck in agony and cry out.

Slowly and painfully, the blood filled the Raven crest. Evil jubilation caused the standing man to arch his back in ecstasy. The raw power of death and violence charged within the crazed individual. Karniel yelled in anger and disgust for it to stop. Rising from his seated position, the youth balled up his fists with such power that his knuckles turned white. He knew the man encased in armor was evil with the same surety as his knowing the sun would rise.

Almost all the poisonous blood liquid had filled the once beautiful snow-colored raven. Its death was at hand.

Forgetting his opponent was a full grown man in battle attire, Karniel went on the attack. His formidable years in the narrow alleys and hidden passages of the Rut had taught him that simplicity always won a fight. Using his left hand to knock the open-palmed gauntlet aside, the teen shot forth his right hand in a spear-like manner.

The second his fingers touched the now corrupted Raven, a wave of sickness assaulted the youth. Every abuse the Raven had endured from the liquid was being passed to Karniel. Sheer will power, and a stubborn streak a league wide, kept the youth centered on his mission. Verbal outbursts of pain vomited from both men. Just as Karniel fought to free the Raven, his opponent sought to imprison it all the more.

Time slowed while this battle of wills continued, with each using every ounce of power to gain victory. The struggle became physical as the older man seized Karniel's throat in a last pitched attempt for control. He wanted to dominate everything and no brat was going to stop him.

Hatred burned into the youth like a flame as the grip tightened. The Gods were with the youth though, as the gauntlet was not designed to close completely. Dark spots dazzled in Karniel's vision. His brain and body needed more air.

Snaking his left hand up the armor, the youth opened the bird-faced visor. Light filled the vacancy caused by the opened face plate, temporarily blinding the man. To make matters worse, Karniel was able to smash his thumb into the armored man's left eye socket.

Both gauntlets rushed for the teen's hand, hoping to cast the pain aside. With air energizing him once again, Karniel plunged his entire forearm into the crest, pulling all the toxins into himself. The sickening venom attacked the teen at a cellular level, penetrating bone, marrow, and muscle.

Realization dawned on the sinister man. He felt the power he so coveted being pulled from him. Rage blinded him to all but his goal: domination. Coiling his razor sharp gloved fingers in the youth's arms, and gripping tightly, the malicious male struggled to remove Karniel's arm by violently shaking the youth.

"Oh, little raven," he said punctuating each word with a pointed jolt. "You do not have the strength to defeat me. Fawdake protects and lends me his power. Wake up!"

Power, desire, and the will to fight drained from Karniel with each shake. Feeling an odd sort of peace swell within, he released the urge to continue and slipped into oblivion.

Pethio spotted the large youth he had been sent to collect. The lad had done well in the process thus far, the Paladin thought. It was with a heavy heart that he had to wake the slumbering young man. Shaking Karniel, Pethio did not expect the punch that landed squarely on his chest, nor did he sense the acceptance of death from Karniel.

Casting his right hand over the youth, the celestial hybrid warrior called upon the Saints of his faith. A gentle power flowed from the man as soft brown light filled the room, basking everyone in its radiance. Tranquility eased the harshness of the dream away, and Karniel slowly opened his eyes, blinking rapidly.

"Your father is here," the deep-voiced Paladin spoke. "Follow me."

Confusion danced in the youth's head. "What do you mean my father is here? He is on patrol." Concern and fear, flowing from the dream, entered every word.

With a sigh, Pethio stopped and turned to face his young follower. "If you will trust me a few minutes all will be revealed, my friend."

This comment seemed to stem the flow of questions bubbling up in Karniel. Together, they walked in silence, each wondering what exactly had happened to the watchman.

The Arena hospital wing was normally empty of occupants, but this night was out of the ordinary. A courier had entered the banquet hall and discreetly whispered the series of events to the Fire Brand Lord Commander. The metal wine flute groaned under the crushing pressure of its holder. A pure flame of cold anger burned in the Lord Commander's eyes. So powerful was his energy that the entire room went dead silent.

Rising from his chair, and looking at no one in particular, Jaldo excused himself but insisted the festivities continue in his absence. Nervous chuckles sounded as the hall's occupants toasted their host one last time. It took him less than ten minutes to enter the Arena hospital wing from the southern tower' feasting area.

Stopping in front of the door, he nodded to the watchmen guarding their captain's room. Such an event had never transpired in the entire history of the Red Keep, and Jaldo wanted to know why it had. Choosing to open the door himself, a sober mood struck the military leader.

The Watchman was lying quite still, with linen bandages around his ribs, and a sling attached to his right arm. Dark blood had pooled from the many slices to his chest and abdominal areas. The twinkle that set him apart from his fellows was darkened, forever gone from the world. Striker stood next to the lad sitting on the Watchman's cot, his arm resting on the young man's shoulder in a half hug.

Clearing his throat, Jaldo presented himself to the lad and offered his sincerest condolences. What he was not prepared for was the complete lack of emotion on Karniel's face.

"Your father was a friend of mine," the leader continued. "He saved my life at one of the bandit uprisings near Shaman's Plain."

A lifeless response exited from the lad. "He spoke of you with great respect and remembrance, Sir. Who did this to my father?"

Even with a flat tone to his voice, the others in the room saw how taut his body truly was.

Pethio chose to exit the shadows and step behind the Lord Commander. "Five noble houses joined in ambush," the Paladin reported. "They chose to attack at Zuwl's favorite watering hole. Only one survives, but he will never walk again."

Nodding at the report, Jaldo looked at the young recruit.

"What would you have me do, Son of Zuwl?"

The formal address momentarily pulled Karniel from his rather numb state of mind. Ignoring the impending pressure of the decision, the youth spoke clearly and calmly, measuring each word as if it were a strike in a dual.

"Take their titles, their lands, and their house sigil. Remove their names from the annuls of the Army and any other guild they had business with. No one, either bastard or pure born, sharing their name can or will inherit. Remove their families from the land with a small amount of money. They took everything from me. I intend to return the favor."

The cold, matter of fact tone took those present by surprise. What he wanted was understandable. Zuwl had rescued him from a hellish existence of gladiator-type fighting as a child. Three pairs of eyes weighed the youth and the loss he had to accept.

Taking in a full breath of air, Jaldo considered his options. He knew such an attack held no precedence and yet, how could he punish so many nobles? Placing his hand on the lad's shoulder, he agreed to look into the matter and excused himself. Funeral pyres had to be constructed, and a proper mourning planned.

Pethio, after praying for the lad, also left. He was needed in the Rut to continue gathering evidence and to weed out any living conspirators. Grimly, he nodded to his fellow trainer and left the hospital.

"What will you do now?" the master trainer asked as he uncorked a flagon of beer.

Karniel turned to his teacher. A whirlwind of responses played in his mind, each sounding more ridiculous than the last. In the end, the young man chose to see his home one more time and go to the burial ceremony.

After taking a draw, and passing the flagon to the youth, Striker clasped his student on the shoulder. "You are already better than that lot, so take a day. Mourn your loss. Make peace with your old man and return by the sixth day. We have our own ceremony for those who have passed."

Silently thanking the grizzled man, Karniel returned the flagon.

"Keep it," Striker responded with a smirk. "It belonged to your father. He lost it to me in a game of cards."

Looking at the bottom of the container, Karniel spied two clubs crossed: Zuwl's sigil.

"Head home, lad," the Trainer continued, "Let the Veritable Mothers do their duty."

Six women had entered the room, carrying baskets of linens and oils. Gently, the men were shuffled out of the room. Privacy and respect were needed to honor the dead hero, and the women would see to that.

With his leader's permission, Karniel left the hospital wing and headed for his home. The cool night air swirled as he exited. Thoughts of the meaning of the word "family' conjured images of a dark time in his life and the light Zuwl brought to it.

———◆———

Jaldo lounged in his black walnut chair. The high armrests aided him during long, drawn out debates, of the which this was one. The heads of every school and discipline wanted a say in the punishment affixed to the fools who dared kill Zuwl. Several of the leaders were on their feet, yelling back and forth like idiots.

Varg, Jaldo's second in command, ever hating such useless shouting matches, blew his battle horn. The rumble of voices came to a quick halt. "If you lot are done acting like love sick lads fighting for a dance, maybe we can return to the topic at hand," the rather hot-headed horn bearer barked. His voice allowed for no argument as shifting chairs groaned under the weight of seating men.

Admonishing Varg with a quick smile, Jaldo leaned over the table, fingers forming a tent. "The lad wants retribution for his murdered father. And, judging by the dramatic outbursts, we agree. The question is to what extent?"

Eadala, Lord Justice for the Army, cleared his throat. "Legally, there is no precedence for this action. I understand the lad's anger, as do we all, yet how can we approach the other guilds and explain this action?"

Ever the Politician, the gray-haired Eadala looked at all the options before choosing a single course. Where this ideal was often looked down on by the other leaders, he had kept the Fire Brand Army on point for more than four decades.

"Your wisdom in matters of law and options are unrivaled by even the clerics at the Cathedral, my Lord Justice," Jaldo quipped. "Now we put it to a vote. Do we, the leaders of this Army, choose to alienate the five families and erase their existence from our guild records? If so, do we understand that no one, be it bastard or blood, can inherit or make business with us? If so, let it be known now!"

Jaldo was a bit surprised as every single person present tossed their token into the middle of the table. Never had there been a unanimous vote before, but then again, no one had dared to murder a hero before.

Thanking everyone for their participation, the Lord Commander was the first to toast his dead friend. It was his hope that Karniel would find peace in Zuwl's legacy. As memories were shared of the fallen soldier, Jaldo whispered a question to his Lord Justice, who answered with a curt nod of the head. They had much to do before the funeral. They owed it to their brother-in-arms to take care of his son.

✋ 7 ✋

Karniel sighed heavily. It took him the better part of an hour to reach his father's home in the craftsmen section of the city. His feet, having a mind of their own, followed the path with the young man so deep in thought that he arrived without even noticing.

Memories swam in and out of view as he crossed the threshold of their two story wood-and-slate roof house. An eerie silence covered the room as he looked around his father's house. There were no candles lit or hearth ablaze. There was no sound of books being read or clothes being mended. No laughter at something a guardsman said or weapons training being taught. All that existed was dead, flat silence.

Heavy-hearted, the lad sat on his favorite chair by the fireplace. His emotions threatened to break his spirit. Tears leaked down his face as a single object became crystal clear: a pewter cup, and with it, images of the day they met.

Smack!

Another blow landed on the nine-year-old Karniel, knocking him to the ground. It was fight night in the Rut and Snake had bet all his money on the large, muscular boy. He was a foot taller than the rest of the fighters and easily fifty pounds heavier. It would have been the easiest money of Snake's life.

Most street kids, often called mice, saw fighting as a way to guarantee food or protection, but not Karniel. He hated the blood sport and refused to partake.

Panting from raining blows on the boy, Snake growled in frustration. He ruled the four blocks where Karniel lived with a tyrant's grip. Fear kept his small kingdom in check. The terror of violence or death followed Snake's every step. But, never in the twenty years as ruler, had he seen a child so skilled in the deadly arts and yet refuse its splendor.

Shoving the heavy youth into the back alley, the angry man uncoiled the whip he used as a makeshift belt. Karniel clawed the ground as the forked leather tongue dug into his flesh. The lad's mind yelled for his body to rise and take flight, thereby escaping the pain, but Karniel knew better. If he ran, the punishment would multiply greatly. He just had to bear it until Snake ran out of steam, or passed out from alcohol.

A plump tavern wench exited the building, her hands full of empty ale bottles. She had hoped to get a rest from the gang members' wandering hands. A shocked gasped escaped her mouth upon seeing the raw hide tool sling blood from another cut on Karniel's back. Forgetting the fact her hands were full of glass bottles, the wench froze, dropping her cargo.

The crashing bottles broke Snake out of his abusive actions, but he wanted blood. Turning on the wench, he unleashed the full extent of his drunken rage. A gush of blood preceded the woman's screams, for the whip had torn a chunk of flesh loose from her cheek.

Rage boiled in Karniel as he watched the woman, who had always been nice to the mice, drop to the ground. His young brain failed to understand why Snake was attacking her. Seeing the crate of broken ale bottles, the lad reacted without thought. Grasping one of the bottles by the neck, Karniel charged into the violent chaos.

Snake, smiling drunkenly at his crying victim, hardly registered the impact of the glass bottle. Numbness crept into the gang leader's right side. Confusion replaced rage as Karniel yanked the broken bottle free. The realization of what was transpiring dawned on the man. The bottle had been driven into his spine, nicking the spiral column and spilling his life's blood on the ground.

Offering a pleading gesture to Karniel and the wench, Snake felt the life leave him. In the end, he had no one to mourn him, for such is the end of those who abuse and beat those they are obligated to protect.

Karniel, looking at the wench, took off his torn, rough-knit shirt. Placing it against her bleeding cheek, he smiled sweetly. She smiled in return, silently thanking the lad for his bravery.

Intoxicated shouts filled the air as other gang leaders searched for Snake. After all, he did owe them money.

Fear galvanized the woman into action.

"You have to run," she implored, gripping Karniel's shoulders with force. "For the love of the Saints, don't ever return here or they will kill you!"

Her caring eyes forced Karniel's legs to action. Knowing he was not able to live in the Rut, or seek protection from an opposing gang, the boy ran for all he was worth. He paused for a second at the southern gatehouse before following the main road that encircled the city. He stopped only to catch his breath and to make sure he was not followed. His legs finally gave out in the Smith's quarter, on the opposite end of the Red Keep City.

Despite the warm night air, Karniel felt cold and bone weary. His body shook fiercely as his mind tried to accept what had happened. Snake's blood stained the boy's hands, as if to mock his stolen virtue. Looking for a place to get warm and hide, the lad noticed a forge still glowing.

Ghosting to the back, Karniel used a water barrel, normally used to wipe off etching acid, to clean the blood off his hands, face, and legs. As luck would have it, the lad found a smith's vest his size to wear and he vanished behind the massive leather bellows.

As sleep and fatigue overtook the tall boy, thoughts of the wench's smile, and Snake's last moments, played in his head. Whatever the future held, Karniel issued a prayer that someone would help him.

Morning came early in the Smith's quarter, and so too, was Karniel's discovery. Strong, callused hands jerked the sleeping boy from the protection of the bellows. The Master of the Stag's Crown had no time for runaways or the foolishness they brought.

Yelling at one of his assistants to call for the Watch, the large Master Blacksmith kept a close eye on the trespassing youth. Meanwhile, he demanded an inventory performed for any missing tools, equipment, or material. More than once, street thieves had stolen finished weapons for their turf wars, and the owner of the forge wanted to punish someone for those crimes.

———◆———

Zuwl fought to keep a yawn under control. It had been a long night patrolling the Rut, especially with the death of a gang leader. The Watch Captain could feel another turf war on the horizon.

A newly minted Watchman, freshly discharged from the Army, came running up to Zuwl's patrol, telling him of a disturbance at the Stag's Crown. After the particulars were issued, the Watch Captain chose one other person and signaled for the new arrival to lead the way.

As the Watchmen arrived at the forge, Zuwl took in the scene with a sigh. The rather large Master Smith seemed to be yelling at what looked like a new worker. This was hardly cause for calling the watch, as the lad look properly chastised and sorrowful.

Dismounting with a tired grunt, Zuwl had hoped this would be a simple ordeal and he would be able to head home soon, but he knew better. Smiths were finicky at the best of times, and the Iron Guild guarded its secrets better than the Priests listening to confessions.

"Good morn, Master Craftsman," Zuwl greeted in his calmest voice. "You didn't have to fabricate an excuse to get me to retrieve my weapon. I know it's been a week, but this is a bit much, no?" The Watch Captain placed a hand on the Smith's and Karniel's shoulder, hoping to defuse the tense situation.

Flinching away from the jovial law man, Karniel's eyes never left the ground. His muscles had remained tight since his discovery, awaiting the inevitable beating for disobedience, or a chance to run for freedom.

Understanding dawned on Zuwl's face as the Master Smith explained the lad's transgression. Normally it was a simple matter of shooing the lad along and speaking with his parents, but with not clan sigil, the Smith was duty bound to call the Watch.

Unsure of what to do, the Captain took a closer look at the lad.

Whip marks were fresh on his body, especially across his back and shoulders. Hard muscle moved easily under the young skin, showing a hard life and the ability to fight back. What surprised Zuwl was the boy's self-control. He never uttered a word in his defense, nor attempted to run away. This contradiction puzzled Zuwl something fierce.

Satisfied the Watch had everything in hand, the Master Smith snapped his finger and one of his workers presented a long, thin box. "Here is your weapon, Captain. Try not to break this one, okay?"

With a chuckle, Zuwl accepted the box and stirred the lad towards his chestnut-colored horse.

"What shall we do with you?" the middle-aged Captain asked the boy. "My guess is you have no family or clan and your boss didn't care much for you."

Karniel's only response was a slight head shake. Years on the street had taught him not to answer any of the Watchmen's questions. Such meetings only led to pain, usually at the hand of the Gang boss for getting caught..

Mildly perplexed with the boy, Zuwl told the other two men to escort the lad to their guardhouse. The Watch leader needed time to think and could not help but notice the crowd gathering in the streets. The Captain felt they had an audience of eyes and ears owned by criminal enterprises and Zuwl wanted to give them the full show.

As they left, street runners departed into the side alleys and scurried on rooftops surrounding the shop entrance to report that Karniel had been captured. Realizing nothing could be done, the Gang leaders left the boy to his fate and issued a small bounty for the death of Snake. Not that they actually cared about the man, but the bounty would keep other street mice in line.

Twenty minutes later, the entourage of guards, with the lad in tow, had arrived at the Smith's Quarter guardhouse. Built into the outer wall of the city, the guard station was a simple two room affair. The outer room had a simple table, recently vacated by the morning watch. Wooden plates and cups lay scattered haphazardly, with a pot of soup and a pitcher of milk awaiting care. Normally, the watchmen were not so sloppy, but a death in the city did cause quite a stir, especially if the one killed was an outlaw. The last thing anyone wanted was a gang war spilling into the other sections of the city.

Signaling for the lad to sit, Zuwl served them both food and drink, in the hope to loosen the lad's tongue. Hungry silence filled the room as the street mouse devoured the food without even pausing to breathe. After two more servings, and a satisfied sigh, Karniel opened up to the Watch Captain.

The youth's sudden, albeit guarded, change of heart was simple in nature. He would need protection from the Gangs. Being captured by the Watch brought a punishment of whipping, but Karniel had killed a boss and only one punishment was worthy of that crime. Death. After all, what more could the Watchman do to him?

Zuwl was somewhat off put by the lad's easy manner. He liked the lad from the off. He had had enough sense to not run or fight back, but the Captain was still not sure if his actions were a ruse or the acceptance of a person with no options. The middle-aged man chose to focus his inquiries on the night before, wanting details of both the attack and the tavern wench. Not that Zuwl did not believe the lad had killed someone, even a cornered animal fights back. The implications of the youth's testimony was crucial to keeping the boy alive.

Karniel felt sick to his stomach as he responded with the truth. Bile bit the back of his throat with the thoughts of Snake's blood and the wench's fear. Vomit exploded from him as the realization he had actually killed another human being returned with the force of an explosion on his mind. Tears and shuddering controlled Karniel's body as he fought to somehow right himself.

Zuwl, now knowing the truthfulness of the youth, guided him to a small room and laid out fresh clothes for the boy. The Captain allowed the youth time and privacy to accept such an ordeal and to clean himself. Killing another mortal was hard enough as a trained soldier. But as a child, such a weight could twist and warp the soul into darkness if not tended to correctly.

A seasoned lieutenant walked into the main room with a salute as Zuwl closed the door behind him, protecting the lad.

"Sir, we have completed the investigation in the death of the leader known as Snake. Apparently a bar wench witnessed his demise, claiming his attacker acted in self-defense. She requests protection from rival gangs, who have already issued a bounty on the killer."

Zuwl smiled sadly. He needed the boy's testimony to cleanse the Rut. For years, street gangs terrorized that section. They were like weeds, ever growing and refusing to die. The Watch leader was torn between his duty to his city and the honor of protecting an innocent child. It was true that the criminal element in the Rut needed to be purged from the city. Many a good person had lost their lives in turf wars and the addictive wares sold by the gangs.

Could the rough and rugged soldier sacrifice the life of a street mouse for the security of thousands?

Others might see such a move as best all around, but not Zuwl. He was too honorable a man. He would have to find a place secure enough for the boy, but it had to offer a future and understanding of life on the streets. Another smile graced the rugged, unshaven face of the old military man. Only this one was a peaceful one.

The tall nine-year-old heard the exchange while he was cleaning up. Who was willing to put a bounty on a child, he wondered, as the last flecks of dried blood vanished in the suds and water. His hands still shook from the episode, but his resolve hardened as he thought of the kind-hearted wench. He had to help her, regardless of what they would do to him.

The door, separating the men from Karniel, squeaked with the lad exiting. The nine-year-old straightened and took in a calming breath. He knew there was only one solution to the virus spreading across the Rut. Addressing both of the men before him, the youth spoke with unshaken certainty.

"If I give you the locations of the hideouts and hidden passages in the Rut, will you protect the bar maid and her family?"

Zuwl, seeing the change in personality, and cold determination radiating from the youth, asked a simple question. "Are you a man of your word?"

The Watch Captain had seen his share of battles and the lives lost over leaders offering their men up to the killing fields. He was not willing to sacrifice his men over being too hasty and charging in protected locations like a bull in the spring.

Tender green eyes hardened with an affirmative answer. Even on the streets, one lived or died by their word.

A wolfish grin shadowed across the Watch leader's face. The day had finally arrived.

"Sound a general assembly, Lieutenant," Zuwl said, turning to face the uniformed man. "We will finally be able to rid the Rut of those cancerous gangs, once and for all."

A crisp salute and the clicking of boots preceded a hearty answer. Many of the Watch had lost friends and loved ones to the gangs, and they wanted justice.

With the Watchman leaving, Zuwl turned his gaze to the lad. "Do you promise to be honest with me from this time forward?"

Wisdom and strength infused the one word response. "Yes."

Good, the Captain mused with a mental smirk, the lad shows promise.

Over the next two hours, they questioned each other, as if mentally sword fighting. In the end, a strategy to cut out the gangs was agreed upon. But, more importantly, Karniel had something he never felt before: hope.

The memory swam out of view as the sunlight peeked through the heavy fabric curtains. Karniel wiped the tears from his face and laughed. He wondered if he would meet anyone else worthy of the word family.

8

Varg set back in his chair and finished another glass of water. History lessons were a thirsty business and this one was not close to being over.

"The funeral of Zuwl was an historic event," the Lord Commander commented, remembering the affair with half-closed eyes. "Full honor guard was used, handpicked by the lad, with myself and Jaldo helping to carry the body to the pyre. Zuwl was given the Mark of the Fire Brand, our highest honor to bestow."

Yarmilla, who had been quiet during the tale, excused herself to send a message by carrier bird. She had waited years for the names of those who had hurt her lost beloved, and now she had them. Her heart beat wildly with each step. It was too much to hope that the man she cared for more than life itself was chained like an animal in the Cathedral prison. But she could do one last thing in his honor. Finally, she would avenge her love, no matter what.

With the younger woman's exit, Asiza mused over the story. She had heard a similar one years ago about a man who lost his memories. He had done much good for her guild, even aiding to rid them of some marauders. Scanning the room, she was grateful everyone else was deep in thought or her knowledge of the man would come to light.

A few house staff had refreshed the food and drinks by the time the Harvester leader returned. Regaining her seat, a goblet of wine was emptied to hide her quick breathing. She did not want anyone else to realize her true reason for being there. Sighing irritably, Yarmilla waved the Fire Brand leader on, sensing there was more to the story.

"By the time, I met Karniel again he had surpassed all in his training year," Varg began anew as he regaled them with the White Raven's exploits.

He became a champion of those bullied or mocked, strengthening the weak and defenseless, showing them how to learn, fight, or adapt beyond their own abilities. For these and other traits, he was awarded rank and advanced two years in battle school. Never had they ever seen a young man who was so talented. Some even began to think he was Kogien in disguise, coming to check on the affairs of his army.

Asiza, surprising everyone, asked a simple question. "Did he go on the March of Tears?"

Varg, with a wry smile, answered. "He did and protected not only his unit, but the life of the Desert Lion. Fill up your glasses again. For, *that* is a tale worth telling."

❂ 9 ❂

The City of Tears sat nestled at the southern edge of the Desert of Mirrors, being the northern-most part of the Dazmekian nation. Thick stone walls, thirty feet high and forty feet deep, protected the citizens from the seasonal sandstorms and the odd raider attack. Despite its location, it became a thriving community, with all four creeds having a hall within the upper sections of the city. On this clear, gorgeous day, however, no work would be done. It was a celebration day for all, for the March of Tears had arrived.

Fifty-one booted feet stepped in rhythm down the main road leading to what the locals called the Mouth of the Desert. Streamers and petals filled the air as trumpets and bugles rang out in triumphant accord. Fifty-one light leather uniforms came to a halt at the aged outer gates facing the fiery heat of the desert.

Every one of the soldiers had been allowed to pick one thing that represented their clan before they left. Most of the soldiers proudly showed the sigils of their clans. They prayed to all the Gods that they would survive and bring honor, glory, and prestige to their families. Some chose a banner or ancestral weapon. Others were not allowed such things until they returned worthy of such relics.

This exhibition was a proving ground for the future of the Army. Not only was the environment unforgiving, but, so too, was the refining that it did on every person that entered her sandy lands. There were no social classes or pomp on the march. It would be the group's first taste of true military life. No one in that army unit could foresee the events that would change their lives forever.

Picking up a handful of white dirt, the last of the troop covered his face, neck, and hands. Mentally, he prepared himself for the journey. No fantasies of glory or power clouded his judgment, for he knew what lay ahead. His training might have been rushed, but his years in the Rut made him more than ready. Karniel was not just proving to himself that he belonged. He knew his adopted father's reputation was on the line as well.

Enormous iron hinges groaned as the outer gate opened, allowing wave after wave of scalding heat to pour into the protected city. The fanfare and music ceased as Isaak , the unit's leader and captain, muttered a prayer to Kogien, his patron God. For years, the officer had led the exertion into the wasteland, but this year would be his most trying of them all.

Turning to face his troops with a sigh, the March Leader began the rote speech.

"Younglings," he barked, with authority. "Today marks the completion of your training. From here on, only our beloved Fire God chooses who, if any of you, are worthy to fill the ranks of our Fire Brand Army. Remember your training, guard your flame, and pray that you may be found worthy of the love of your family!"

Hundreds of voices rang out with a cheer. Candles were lit in sacred places as the company of soldiers exited the gate and began their epic transformation. Those on the March were not allowed to share their names with civilians, in case they failed. So the tradition of lighting a candle to the Fire God had begun in every shrine and chapel in the city, asking protection for the unknown soldier .

For hours, the unit of young men marched in the desert, grunting the cadences that helped them keep in time. After a while, the heat and dehydration began to set in, drying skin and chapping lips. An unforgiving sun beat down on them from above, and the insatiable heat waves off the sand cooked them from below. A handful of marchers reached for their water skins in the hope that a few drops of water would sate the thirst that began to claw at them.

Mile after mile, they went on. Over fine grain dunes and rough hot rock. Few plants and animals called that part of the sandy wilderness home, for the environment was harsh and unforgiving.

Isaak studied his unit with a sharp eye as the day progressed. To his dismay, most were about halfway through their small water skins. Shaking his head, their leader almost chastised his soldiers. How could they hope to finish the first leg of the trial if they had no water? Like any other march, he was responsible for his unit's health and wellbeing, but not at the expense of the mission. If there were those that opted for folly and chose to neglect their training, then there was little he could do. All Isaak hoped was that he did not have to bury any of them, this time.

Onward and onward, he pushed them, not allowing them to stop or rest. They had to learn to eat while marching. Any potential stops could kill them, or allow their enemy to escape. Shouting at them to go up and down each crusted dune, the captain saw the realization on their faces that this was no picnic. Yes, these soldiers had gone on long runs at the Red Keep, but her cool winds were long forgotten here. Even the air sliced through the armor and clothing, drying out skin and burning all not use to its rays.

An hour before sunset, Isaak called for a halt. "Alright, ladies, unpack and set camp," he snapped. "You know your duties. Get to it or no one eats."

In unity, they groaned in relief. The sound of packs crashing into the sand, and more than one soldier puking, vibrated across the desert. Knowing their leader was not one for laziness, they quickly got to the task of setting up a temporary rest area. Latrines were dug, tents erected in order, and fires were set. Those on sentry duty set up posts and routes for patrols. With everything sorted, Isaak gave the cooks the go ahead to make dinner. Soon the camp was filled with the smell of meat and soups.

He had the cooks prepare bowls of meat stew and hard bread for the sentries first. This ensured they stayed wake and had energy for their rounds throughout the night. The rest attacked the food like starving wolves. Isaak, surprised by his hunger, even had a second bowl.

Once they had eaten, and Isaak had left to talk with the sentries, the rest of the unit broke up and headed to their tents.

Each canvas tent was large enough to house five full-grown men, equipment, and weapons. To those teenagers, they felt like lavish rooms when compared to the narrow bunks at the Battle School barracks. As this outing was their first taste of freedom in years, many of the lads got into mischief that night.

One young man, Liam, produced a flask of wine and began to pass it around. "Drink up, lads. Compliments of my father's vineyards," he proclaimed with a roguish wink. "The old man will never miss it."

The young men in his company laughed. Being aristocrats, they were used to the easy life and certain prestige. Unfortunately, war awarded no such things.

Each of the drinking young men represented the inner circle of the military order. Their fathers controlled the Heavy Cavaliers, Archers, Men-at-Arms, Scouts, and the Battle School. Never had such an influential group been on the trials before. And, unbeknownst to the young men, their fathers had made wagers on whose son would succeed. They continued to make merry and drink deep into the night, without a care in the world. For why should they be bothered? Their fathers' reputations would protect them.

———•———

The morning came early, and with it, Isaak's command to break down camp and set out again. By midday, they were ten leagues away and deeper into the desert. In this part, nothing existed to break the landscape that began to irritate and hypnotize, just rocks, sand, and a miserable heat.

Careful eyes again monitored those on the desert trial. About half were almost out of water, though something odd struck him. The lone teen from the back of the troop still had three- fourths of his water skin full. Most seasoned scouts could not go this far and not drink more. Eying the lad with suspicion, Isaak called for a halt.

Karniel, feeling his skin begin to burn and become caked in dried sweat, pulled a draw from his water skin but did not swallow. Instead, he held it to ensure his whole mouth, tongue, and throat were hydrated.

A smile ghosted across a middle-aged face as surprise registered within the troop commander. Few knew that particular trick, except the desert tribesmen. Curiosity pricked Isaak and he made a beeline for the youth. Unfortunately so too did the five young men who got drunk the night before.

Liam walked up to the rather muscular Karniel and yanked at his water skin. "Give me your water, little Raven," he snared as Karniel's metallic brand sparkled in the sun. The son of the Heavy Cavalier leader had learned the hard way that alcohol and marching do not mix. His body had used up all its hydration purging the wine, which set him in a foul mood. "There's no way you can beat all five of us," Liam continued, pouring acid into each word. "Besides, your kind doesn't have the stomach to fight back."

The other four lads laughed, feeling quite in control, despite the fact that Karniel was bigger than any two of them put together.

The march leader had a blissfully wicked thought as he walked up to the six soldiers. While bullying was strictly forbidden in the ranks, a duel for goods and plunder was allowed. "What say you, Raven?" Isaak asked while taking the water skin from the young men. "Do you accept his challenge?"

Buzzing excitement blanketed the entire group of teenagers as they broke rank and encircled Isaak and the six young men. Duels were few and far between for the rank and file soldiers, and so all were interested in the outcome. A low rumbling of voices hummed as certain wages for chores and duties were exchanged.

"Sir, I request I receive no repercussions from the duel," the young Raven said, setting down his marching pack. "He is the son of the Heavy Cavalier's commander. I wish neither fight nor feud with his family or kin."

With a wolfish grin that put a dangerous gleam in his bluish-green eyes, Isaak agreed. "I swear on the flame that no harm will befall you and yours as consequence."

With manners that rivaled the etiquette masters from Fiddler's Paradise, Karniel nodded and looked at Liam. "Shall we," he said, with a rather sleepy voice and half closed eyes. Those close to Karniel were disturbed by the almost lazy aura that surrounded the large young man. Either the White Raven did not know who his opponent was or refused to care, and such a cavalier attitude was dangerous to say the least.

Liam motioned for his friends to back away. He was accustomed to having people bow to him, but, secretly, he enjoyed fighting. Not for any good reason, or because of his training. He just enjoyed the sense of uncertainty and the thrill of a battle high. Back in the Red Keep, he would often pick fights with others. It was a good way to hone his skills and assess those training with him. The only reason the aristocrat was not expelled was the fact that the wounds afflicted were never life threatening. In that teenage mind, the angelic blond-haired Noble saw this young social outcast before him as an easy target.

"I will show you the might of the Lion," Liam boasted as he rushed towards his opponent. Traditionally, duels were fought unarmed to show complete and utter dominance of one's opponent. Just before Liam could land a powerful haymaker, his muscular adversary side-stepped to the right and stuck him with a palm strike right in his floating ribs.

The sound of a dry twig snapping trumpeted across the dunes, causing Liam to gasp for air. Sharp pains prevented him from taking a full breath or even standing up straight. He looked up at the young man who had struck him. Neither malice nor anger came from his creamy green eyes. Just a sense of boredom and some slight curiosity.

"Are you ok, Sir Lion? Shall we have another pass," the large youth inquired with a dry tone. Others in the circle chuckled at the joke, as it was always a joy for the common folk to see humility brought to those in power.

Liam felt his face flush as he heard the questions. If the tone had been one of mocking, that could have been morphed into anger for the injured teen, but the insult of indifference was too much to hear. His pride fueled his rage as he stood. This time Liam took his time and tested his opponent. Each young man took turns throwing punches and kicks. Each trying to find the opening to win this physical chess game, but neither became the victor.

"Alright, ladies," Isaak cautioned with a snap, "Either finish this now or I will." It was one thing to entertain his troops, but another to waste daylight on a march.

With his opponent's attention turned to Isaak, Liam struck. The blow landed hard and broke the young man's nose. Blood flowed as the counter attack came into play. The White Raven's fist, closed this time, collided into Liam's neck. The strike would not cause any lasting damage, but it constricted the assaulter's airways just long enough for Liam to be picked up and slammed into the sun-hardened ground.

Liam's tent mates raced towards the young man standing triumphed over their friend. No one should be able to treat a Noble like that, and those ego-driven teens were going to make sure this foolish commoner knew it. Before they reached him, a horn was blown and a voice boomed across the desert like a Deity.

"Enough," the gray-and-brown-haired leader commanded as he had the White Raven lad stepped back. "I hope you lot were not planning to interfere in an official duel. Now I would hate to have to send a bird to the High Command and inform them that their sons are to be disqualified from the trials."

Liam's tent mates helped him to his feet, unsure of what to do. Pride and honor demanded retaliation, but the idea of facing their fathers after being kicked out of the trial kept them in check. That fear did not stop them from staring daggers and scheming of ways to get revenge.

"You, lion cub, will be confined to quarters for the next two nights. And you, raven, will be on night patrol. This is *OVER!*"

The original dueling soldiers had the decency to look ashamed of their actions. For they knew this was not how military men behaved.

Isaak commanded the march to continue, and so Liam took his place at the front of the line.

As they continued, each step caused a sharp pain to spread across Liam's body, courtesy of that fractured rib. Rich brown eyes squinted as that military mind analyzed every movement. And, much to his shock, the son of the Heavy Cavalier leader realized the commoner had been toying with him the whole time. As the sun sank deep into the horizon, so did Liam's cocky attitude.

By the time they stopped for the night, the blond-haired youth was quite depressed. He went through the routine of helping set up camp, but did not say much to anyone. Having been trained by some of the best fighters in the country, the duel should have ended differently. And yet Liam could not shake the feeling there was more to the young man he had fought. His tent mates noticed the brooding, pensive mood and left the tent for a merrier crowd.

As dinner ended, the night patrol began the paramount task of guarding the camp. Three soldiers circled around the temporary haven, with four stationary guards, standard for such a small group. Per usual, Isaak made his rounds to check on the sentries. It was an old habit he had picked up from his first unit leader many years ago. Stopping next to the young man that had fought Liam, the middle-aged man studied the desert sky.

"The stars are beautiful tonight, are they not," Isaak asked, attempting to get the tall and powerfully-built sentry to speak.

"If you say so, Sir. I don't tend to look at them anymore. Too many dreams have fallen by the wayside. Too much loss and death," the young man responded with an amount of experience no one his age should have. There was an almost stoic air about the teen who stood about four inches taller than Isaak.

Unsure of what to say next, Isaak turned and studied the mysterious young man. A subtle scar ran down his jaw line, marring his tan skin. Broad shoulders were slightly hunched, as if they carried a load no one could see. A natural strength was evident, but so too was a deep well of sadness and pain. The military had given this teen a place to channel those caustic emotions, but the group commander was fearful of what would happen if his charge ever truly lost control.

"Every young man here had to pass through four years of basic training, but not you. Is it true you graduated in two," Isaak poised, testing the emotional state of the sentry, but the young man remained silent. "Look," Isaak continued with a touch of irritation. "I have nothing against you or your clan, but I do not know anything about you. The High Command added you at the last minute. No name. Just a clan sigil. Do you have a name, soldier?"

Jade green eyes turned and locked on to those of his commander. A baritone voice answered in a crisp, controlled manner that some would mistake for arrogance. "Sir, I had no name for years. I lived on the streets of the Red Keep until Zuwl, a Captain of the Watch, took me in and adopted me. For some reason, my clan is disgraced and your officers take great pride in reminding me that I am not fit to be here. As for basic training, living on the streets was harder."

This calm declaration shocked Isaak. He, of course, knew of the battle that proved the White Raven clan's downfall. It was a nasty affair and the Old Command wanted a scapegoat. "I am sorry, soldier," the older man replied with sincerity. "I did not know of the abuse you suffered, but you will receive no such treatment here. As for the duel, you could have ended it at any time," Isaak remarked with a wink. "Liam will never forget his first defeat."

As young sentry smiled, the warmth of friendship almost touched his green eyes. "Thank you, Sir. I appreciate that."

Satisfied with the conversation, Isaak slapped the young man's shoulder and began to walk away.

"Sir," the sentry said turning towards his leader. "I was called Karniel, by my father. If you wish, you can put that on the soldiers' registry. I asked the Lord Commander to exclude my name on purpose. False hope is a killer of armies, but false friends kill soldiers. I, for one, do not want to be killed so some blood-thirsty, glory-seeking fool can brag to his grandchildren that he killed the last of my clan."

"Very well, Sentry," Isaak responded. "Return to your duties." The rest of the night passed without incident, but Karniel felt the weight of loneliness ease just a little. Looking up at the celestial diamonds in the night sky, hope began to take root in a heart that had not had any in a long time.

$$\textcircled{?}\ 10\ \textcircled{?}$$

They continued their march into the Desert of Mirrors the following morning. On the way, they stopped by the few small wells they could find to get the much needed liquid refreshment. Isaak took the opportunity to show the young men how to find vegetation suitable for food in the desert. Cool night air did not last long after sunrise and those teenagers were learning to adapt or suffer the pains of hunger and dehydration. Water became a precious commodity, as the fight for survival superseded any alliances or friendships. Their first true test of calm under fire was about to separate the group even more.

Waiting at the first proper oasis was a unit of twenty veteran soldiers. Isaak's men had to fight, sneak, or outsmart the occupying force in order to achieve their goal. The military used these little games to build regiment unity and creative thinking. As well as to show the real effects of physical and mental strain in a hostile environment.

Nearing the natural watering hole, Isaak decided to set up camp two hundred yards to the west. This allowed for space between the two camps, and the ability to hide the number on the march behind a couple of sand dunes. The grizzled campaigner had his troop divide into their tent units, having the tent leaders draw lots to see who would attack first. Each would get a chance to infiltrate, get water, and count the number of horses in the oasis, until they achieved success. The last objective was given to ensure that the soldiers stayed focused on the task at hand.

As the handful of young men gathered in the circle at the middle of the camp, a few were shocked to see Karniel. Though only six people knew it, the White Raven had been chosen to lead his tent the evening after his duel with Liam.

Isaak entered the circle and showed the leaders ten incense sticks fanned out in his hands. Stone-faced and dead of emotion, he walked to each of the young men, letting them pick a stick. As the last lot was chosen, Isaak instructed all to listen. "The one who has the short incense stick come forward."

Much to Liam's dismay, the lot fell on him. He had hoped to watch a few of the other units and see how the soldiers in the oasis reacted to an outside threat. Sighing to himself, the young Noble walked towards Isaak. After a few whispered instructions from his leader, the handsome lad left the circle and surveyed the oasis, wondering what to do.

In the center, there stood a small stone wall that encased the palm trees and reed grass surrounding the well. Most of the desert patrols used it to hydrate and then leave, as the well was owned by a nomadic tribe. The tents of the troops shot off the wall like five spokes on a wheel. Inwardly, Liam applauded the occupying force. It was a textbook defensive structure, simple yet effective.

Seeing no clear way in, Liam called his team to him. "Alright men," he began. "They are using a textbook wheel defense, but have no rotating sentries. Either they are in their tents or they don't see us as much of a threat. Our objective is simple: get water and get the blazes out. As they outnumber us four to one, does anyone have any ideas?"

Efrain, the son of the Chief Ranger, posed a question. "How full does the water skin have to be?" Feeling everyone's eyes on him, he continued. "We can toss one of ours in a tent and grab one of theirs. Since they are all Army issue, who could tell the difference?" Efrain's logic seemed sound, and, without other options, they all agreed.

Opting to wait until the noon sun was at its full strength to begin their approach, the five teens hoped the heat would play in their favor. Each of the young men crept towards a different tent, with the idea that one of them would be successful. They thanked every Deity they knew for a seemingly abandoned camp. Not a single one of the young men realized the mistake they made, or effects they would pay for later because of it.

Efrain reached his tent first and, gambling a peek inside, slowly moved the tent flap aside. There was no one in the tent, only gear and equipment. Easing himself inside the rawhide structure, the wiry-built youth searched for any and all water skins. He found them covered under horse blankets, next to the saddles. Replacing the one on the bottom of the pile with his empty one, Efrain looked out the tent flap. Not sentries appeared, but the lightly-tanned teen could see two of other tents and prayed that his mates found the same luck he had. Removing himself from the tent like a wraith, he took off towards his camp with care. The sound of shouts and running feet added speed to his flight, the fear of getting caught causing small feet to take off like a shot.

His fellow soldiers met him with cheers as the ebony-haired youth fought to catch his breath. But the sound of Isaak's voice broke his reprieve.

"Well done, son," the unit commander said with a laugh. "You did not have to outrun your team though."

Efrain smiled a sheepish grin and raised the water skin in triumph. Applause thundered and all congratulated him on a masterful heist.

"Well, it looks like success, gentlemen," Isaak continued, arching an eyebrow. "Shall we taste the water?"

Efrain, Liam, and the rest of their team gathered and each took a swig from the rather large water container. Sharing a laugh at the ease of the exercise, they all took another gulp from the water skin to solidify their victory. Now no one would dare question their prowess in battle and the skill that all Nobles innately possess.

The feeling of sweet triumph was halted somewhat by Isaak's next question. "So, how many horses were there?"

Looking at each other quite confused, they turned to him and answered. "We saw no horses, Sir."

Isaak smiled and asked for the water skin. "So," he began, studying the markings on the corners of the leather vessel. "You found their water skins unattended?"

Efrain nodded to the affirmative. He and his tent mates rocked with nervous energy. A worm of doubt began to eat away the joyous spirit.

Still smiling, Isaak continued. "Were they under something or out in the open?" Efrain replied that they were hidden under horse blankets. Any hopes of a lasting celebration were crushed with one final question. "Did you lads check the water for poison?"

With faces burning as bright as the sun beating down on them, Liam and company felt true terror for the first time in their lives. All Nobles lived in fear of poisoning. Many had seen the horrifying effects first hand. A healthy respect and fear had been taught since infancy to those five lads and now they were in a wilderness, leagues away from any chemist or healer.

Karniel, realizing what had happened, snatched the water skin and smelled the outside of the lip. "It smells slightly of almonds and jasmine. If I didn't know better, I swear they poisoned the water in preparation for our attack. Not enough to kill, mind you, but you five are in for a very bad night."

Wide spread shock erupted like wild fire. Calls for the medic and pleas to Isaak were heard above the panic. The unit commander allowed the panic to reach its apex before calling his men to order, with a stern voice. He aided the medic, who doubled as the chief cook, as he checked out each of Liam's teammates.

Once they were all checked, and the medic issued his diagnosis, the medic corralled the victims to their tent. Isaak gathered everyone around . "Men, do not ever think war is easy. This exercise shows us that any opponent will lie, cheat, and steal their way to victory. All of you would do well to remember that."

Pointing at the well, he continued, "Those men guarding the well know every trick in the book. Hell, they are old enough to have written it. Please take this seriously. If this was an actual offensive, Liam and his team would be dead. I do not want to bury you boys."

Each young man pondered Isaak's words. For some, this march was only a game, a way to ease themselves into the Army. For others, it was a way to gain family honor by simply finishing the tasks. After all, the Fire Brand would not put their lives at risk on purpose, would they? Most of them, though, did not realize it was a way to show the realism of war. War was not pretty. It was not fought with rules and comfort, nor was it won with ease. These young men began to realize that war was a dirty, messy business. They had not even scratched the surface of its filth.

Isaak left his charges to discover their own thoughts and retired to his tent. It was smaller than the others, but big enough for a cot and a folding writing tablet. He lit the oil lamp that hung from the tent pole and eased himself onto his cot. He was about to loosen his bootlaces when Karniel parted the tent flap.

"Sir, may I come in?" the youth asked before entering.

Isaak sighed and waved him in. "What is on your mind, Raven?"

Karniel cocked his head to the side and grinned. "You knew the water was poisoned. Just like you knew there would be no horses at the well."

Isaak stood to his fullest, which made him almost eye to eye with his tallest soldier. "Are you accusing a senior officer of endangering his men? Careers have been ruined over even the gossip of such things."

Karniel shook his head but did not back away. "No, Sir," he replied. "I was only pointing out the facts. You knew someone would try to gain water other than using the well. I'm willing to bet it's done at least once every march to that well. How much nightshade did they add to the water?"

Isaak threw back his head and laughed, causing the oil lamp to sway in its container. "My boy, there are precious few who know that poison, and what it can do. Pray tell me, how did you know it was nightshade?"

Now it was Karniel's turn to smile like a wolf overlooking a flock of prey. "As I told you, much of my youth was spent on the streets of the Red Keep. In certain alleys and byways, there are shops that promise street kids hot meals and a warm bed. We learned to avoid them because the food was laced with poison and those kids disappeared. Besides, nightshade dissolves completely in water, but you need something to mask the taste. Jasmine usually works best."

"Well, now," Isaak proclaimed as he sat back down on his cot. "You are full of surprises. I ask that you teach your team what you can to prepare them for reality. Most of those boys out there have not the foggiest clue what they are in for."

Karniel remembered the looks of shock and disbelief as his peers realized the water was poisoned. They had no idea about the hardship of fighting and surviving in a hostile environment. "Sir, I will do what I can to aid them," Karniel responded. Turning back to the tent flap, he paused and turned to his unit commander. "How old were you at your first battle, Sir?"

Isaak looked in the direction of the young man, remembering that moment in his past. His eyes seemed to lose focus as he answered. "I was a week out of the Master at Arms training school, newly appointed to a regiment in the Salt Marshes, when we were attacked at night by raiders."

The commander's bluish-green eyes glossed over as the scene of that night came rushing back to him. "I can still smell the smoke of burning tents and hear the screams of my fellow soldiers as they were run though by spear and sword. I swore an oath that if the Gods protected me, I would make sure the young men of our army would not be so unprepared for battle."

Karniel left the Commander to his thoughts and the memories of death and destruction that haunt all who make such sacrifices.

———•———

The dawning of the next morning brought its own difficulties while the nightshade did its work. Liam and his teammates were retching so bad that few in the camp had any desire to eat, much less take another run at the stone water well. Morale was quite low for the troop as Isaak made his rounds. They needed water, not only for the next leg of the march, but for the afflicted soldiers. The only way out that Isaak could see was to parley with the Captain in charge of the oasis. He did not particularly like this option, because they had no advantage for trade.

So Isaak called all the tent leaders together to see what they had to barter. Most of them only had their standard kits, with precious few commodities. The niceties of life were not afforded to the new soldiers. They had to earn those privileges through rank or valor in battle.

One of the tent mates in Karniel's team, a young man by the name of Tomas, asked if anyone had any alcohol. Isaak gave the young man a bewildered look, but the charming clansman from the southern region smirked as he stood. He walked into Liam's tent and exited as nonchalantly, but with a flagon of wine in his hand. "Rich folks can't go without their wine, Commander. I am sure those poor soldier boys protecting the water would love a little taste of home, Sir," he said quite puckishly.

"Alright, Tomas, if your tent leader is endorsing your plan, this is your campaign. Show us how you forest clansmen do your business," Isaak replied with a dare.

Much prejudice was held against the forest people to the south of the

Ghromheim Mountains. They were labeled tricksters and thieves. Bandits and rouges. They loved nothing more than fooling those to the North into deals they would only regret later. Tomas was this to the extreme. He earned quite the reputation as a card shark in basic training. It got so bad the Battle School Master had banned the young man from playing cards and dice.

Tomas' smile never reached his canary yellow eyes. "How far can I go, Sir? I know you fancy Northern folks are a pampered lot. Don't want to be hurting no feelings, but you know how sensitive you Northerners are."

After counseling with the tent leaders, Isaak responded to the fiery red head rogue. "Soldier, those are enemies of the State," the unit commander said in his most commanding voice. "We need supplies, food and water. Any and all attempts to gain the advantage has been approved by this council. Son, if there is any truth to the rumors of your people, now is the time to prove it."

"Very well, Sir," Tomas replied. "I will pick my team and we will get you the supplies needed." With an approving nod from his leader, the lithe young man made fast work of rounding up all the highborn soldiers and getting as much wine or spirits as he could. Luckily, five of the country's most premier winemakers had sons in the troop. As expected, they could not leave home without the sweet nectar. In total, Tomas gathered six flagons and fifteen flasks of alcohol. This treasure trove would be enough to tempt even the most disciplined of soldiers into abandoning all reason.

As for his troops, Tomas went with a small elite team. Studied military tactics and bravado would do him no good in this game. He needed street savvy, quick thinking individuals who did not mind bending the rules to make good their mission. Thankfully, not all the unit came from the pampered halls of the nobility. There were two horse thieves, a street hustler, and three street mice to boot.

"Right," Tomas began. "I only need enough time to whet their whistle and then we got it. Karniel, can you whip up a batch of that same mess they used on Liam's team? After all, Liam was nice enough to donate his father's best vintage to the cause. It would seem a shame if we did not return the favor."

The lads snickered at the quip. Most of the noble born recruits saw themselves as a cut above the common recruits, and, as such, treated those from working families with disdain.

"It is doubtful they will fall for the same trick," Karniel responded. "But I might have something that will do the trick." Rummaging through his kit, he found his prey at the bottom. Smiling, Karniel pulled a leather pouch from his bag. "This," he explained, "is used by medics to make patients fall asleep. It is odorless, tasteless, and mixes best with dark liquor. Trust me, boys. It will work."

Just like Liam had done, Tomas waited until the sun was at its strongest. He needed the heat to force the soldiers at the well to remain in the shade of their tents and for their bodies to crave liquid . As bold as brass, he sauntered to the western edge of their camp. "Hello to Fire Brand Soldiers," he yelled with gusto," I've come to trade fair spirits from the South for water and supplies."

A grizzled, gray-haired Master-at-Arms named Harold answered his call. "Who are you and what do you have to trade?"

Tomas perked up with a grin. "My name is Tomas, Good Sir. Can I approach the camp? It makes no sense for us to be yelling across the desert like heat-stricken fools, does it now?"

The Master-at-Arms groaned but waved Tomas to approach. "Do not do anything foolish, Boy. I am not above smacking you back to your village".

Stopping just shy of arm's length from the stocky leader, Tomas bowed. "Tis an honor to be granted leave to enter your camp, Good Sir. I only wish to barter wine and spirits for water and spare food. We have copious amounts of the best vintages. Lion's Roar, Ranger's Trek, and Harvester's Ale, to name a few. Would your men like a flask or a flagon?"

The last he made sure to speak loud enough for the entire troop to hear. He knew it was military policy to keep the more junior soldiers to the back at times of trade or parley. He needed their homesickness and irritability to kick in. It would make the fiasco easier to sell.

Karniel and the other lads could hear Tomas calling to the Master-at-Arms as they emerged from the camouflaged hole they had dug earlier. They headed to the east side of the well, using burlap cloth to protect from the scorching sand below and sun above. They belly-crawled towards their target, stopping shy of the tent line. There, they began to slowly move the sand away to create a dip just big enough to hide their bodies. This way they could move at a moment's notice and still remain hidden from view. They had traded in all their normal armor for looser, more sandy-colored clothes to blend in with the surroundings.

By the time his team was set, Tomas had everyone's attention. He learned they had been stationed at the well a good week ahead of the Trial and that all the remaining wells were likewise occupied. Smiling at this information, he decided it was time to begin the game, as his father called it. Sitting on a pile of rope next to the Master-at-Arm's tent, he cleared his throat. "Sir, can I have your name? All this pomp and ceremony is a thirsty business, and besides you have me at a disadvantage."

The confidence and boldness of Tomas made the hazel-eyed Harold uneasy. How could this young man be alone and have the authority to speak for his troop, he wondered. Signaling for a patrol, the forty-year-old man chose to delay the parley. "My name is Harold of the Red Keep,

Master-at-Arms with the Heavy Cavalier unit out of the City of Tears. You can address me as Sir or Master-at-Arms, *boy*."

Inwardly laughing at the arrogance of Harold, Tomas appeared properly chastised. "A thousand pardons, Sir. I meant no disrespect. All I wish is to trade and then be on my way. Tis easier than fighting and less painful too, don't you think? We get water and you and yours get prime alcohol that would normally cost a month's wage per glass. Everyone wins."

Harold eyed each of his men. He knew they would want the liquor. Most could not even afford it by the glass, and now they could have quantities of it for the mere cost of a few skins of water. He dared not say no to the young man, or they would never let him hear the end of it. Thankfully, the single patrolman he had sent to check the parameter returned and signaled the all clear. Harold returned his gaze to Tomas with a wicked thought. "Alright, we will trade, but you must sample the liquor before we do, little man."

The lad from the south grinned from ear to ear. "Oh Sir Harold, nothing would please me more. I just can't promise how much would be left for the rest of you." With a grunt, Tomas uncorked the first flagon of wine and took a long draw. With each gulp, he could feel the disdain and envy growing in Harold's troop. He knew he had them, even if they did not know it. With a satisfying sigh, he studied each of the men as he lowered the flagon. "Well, boys," he exclaimed, "who would like to trade with me first?"

In a mad scramble of shouting and shoving, military order became lost at the well. Harold glared at Tomas, who, for the time being at least, let chaos reign. A shrilling whistle pierced the madness.

"If you lot do not act like proper soldiers, then no one will get to trade," Harold growled. "Line up with whatever you wish to barter. Make it snappy!" He knew he had lost control of his men. What shamed him more, though, was the fact he had not seen it coming.

Once Karniel and the others heard Harold's men lining up, they crept from their holes. Their orders were simple: Find any and all food or medicine and get out. Karniel and Tomas were hoping to play up the accepted practice of letting young desert raiders "steal" commodities. The Red Army Commander saw it as the cost of using the desert every year, and thus accepted it. Using the burlap as giant bags, they plundered the two eastern tents. Karniel instructed them not to take anything that could be personal to the soldiers, as the desert tribes would not cause such an offense. One of the horse thieves decided to act as a lookout to ensure they could slip away at a moment's notice.

The moment all those provisions were secured in the burlap, and the sacks were tied off, the lookout gave the signal to exit. Each member had a sack over their shoulder as they proceeded to head north of the well for about a hundred and fifty yards. Once reaching that distance, they made the long trip to the western side of Isaak's camp, so as not to arouse attention from the bartering.

By the time all the trading had concluded, Tomas had twenty water skins full to bursting, four extra boot knives, and a yew bow with a full quiver. So happy was he that carrying such a load was not a burden. He even began to whistle a merry tune. The roguish youth was joined about half way by the lads who had liberated Harold's camp of provisions. Each helped ease the load and walked triumphantly towards their awaiting comrades.

Later that evening, Isaak praised the young men for their ingenuity and cunning plan. Everyone shared in the celebrating, happy to see fresh provisions, medicines, and water. Each young man took turns telling their version of the day's events. And, as the night progressed, the stories became more and more embellished. This would be a night they would always remember. There were no social castes or political circles, just young men who were truly enjoying the bond that such a brotherhood created.

The next morning, as was customary, Harold and his soldiers came to Isaak's camp. Most of Harold's troop were hung over and could not remember most of the previous evening. Each of the leaders was given a chance to meet and council. Their troops were given the chance to mingle and share experiences from past campaigns. This allowed the more experienced to share wisdom, and aid the newer generation on their march.

Harold, however, showed no respect as he entered Isaak's tent. His ego and pride were still recovering from the chaos that had ensued the day before. "Your *boys* poisoned my men," he roared at Isaak, "and I demand retribution!"

Isaak was lying on his cot as the infuriated Master-at-Arms entered. As he finished reading a communiqué, he chuckled at the accusation. Although he knew Tomas' plan, none of them could have calculated how deflated Harold would feel over the whole ordeal. They did not know that the pompous leader had risen early to perform an inspection and found all of his men sound asleep in their bunks. No one had bothered to patrol or even post a sentry. As if to add insult to Harold's wounded pride , the medicine-laced liquor had knocked them all out right after their dinner.

"Sir, my men performed their duties with the utmost precision. Their objective was clear and their execution clean," Isaak responded with long suffering. "I have already dispatched a report detailing the event, and received permission to continue on our way."

Isaak handed Harold the small-scripted paper. "As you can see, we are to break camp and resume our march." Getting up from his bunk, Isaak began to put on his traveling armor. "If you wish to lodge a complaint, then please feel free. Otherwise, my men and I have a long march from the Oasis of Dreams to the Fire Temple ruins, and we really do need to be on our way."

Harold's fist ground the paper to bits.

Glaring at the March Captain, Harold went ballistic. Charging forward, he struck Isaak across the face with his gauntleted left hand. The backhand strike caught the victim completely off guard and gave Harold the few seconds he needed to launch Isaak out of the tent.

The camp's inhabitants turned towards the tent at the sound of Isaak's partially-armored body hitting the sand with a thud. Karniel, Liam, and Tomas ran to their unconscious leader's aid and called their teams to arms. In under a minute, Harold and his men were surrounded by armed young men in a diamond formation. Each spear tip was held ready to be bloodied in the defense of their leader.

Liam knelt on the right side of Isaak and began to check his vitals as Karniel and Tomas took up positions at his head and feet. Liam started at the feet and began to work his way up, the same way he had been taught in Battle School. He gave a silent prayer of thanks, as none of the bones seemed to be broken and his captain was breathing normally.

Tomas looked at Harold, like a predator searching for his next meal. They both seemed to be eyeing each other, as if to weight the odds on who would move first. "Is this because of yesterday," Tomas inquired, pointing at Isaak. "Our job was to outsmart you, which we did. If you can't stomach that, *old man*, I'll beat your worthless carcass right here and now." As if to seal the threat, Tomas lobbed a wad of spit that landed square in Harold's right eye.

Harold laughed madly as he wiped the spit away. "You wish to duel me, boy," he said with condescension. "You Southern inbreeds are not worth my effort. However, I will enjoy instructing you on respecting your betters."

The older soldiers sidled, glances darting between the two groups. They had no desire to fight with the young men. In fact, they had earned their respect, but a fight between unit leaders was an entirely different thing. One wrong move and more than military careers would end.

Harold's men backed away and took a knee, creating a circle inside the diamond as Liam and Karniel carried Isaak's body to another tent. They were met by their unit's medic, who took over administering aid. Liam grabbed the medic's spear and took his space in the diamond. Karniel, however, ran to help Tomas prepare for the duel.

Tomas, much to Karniel's surprised, opted for a light leather set of armor. Although not the smallest in the unit, Tomas' arms and legs were half the size of Karniel's. "Use your speed, Tomas", Karniel pleaded. "He has years of experience on you."

The Southern lad stared into Karniel's eyes as he grabbed his shoulders. "Brother, I intend to kick his pompous ass, even if I have to cheat. Now if you don't mind, I have a name on my dance card."

Before the lithe youth took a step forward, a familiar voice halted him.

"I appreciate your zeal, lad, but allow me to defend my own honor."

Isaak stopped just shy of the two young men, putting the last of his armor in place. Karniel smiled and shook his head at his leader's stubbornness.

"Sir, would it be prudent for you to proceed?" Tomas inquired. Secretly, he wanted to beat Harold to a bloody pulp, but respected Isaak too much to steal his retribution.

Isaak saw the concern in Tomas' remark, and it surprised him. "Well, lad, being prudent has never been my strong suit, but if it makes you feel better, you can be my second." Tomas agreed with a flamboyant bow. With that settled, Isaak turned his attention to the pacing Harold, who sneered at the show of concern by the young men for their leader.

Fully arrayed in his chest plate, armored gauntlets, and boots, Harold was an imposing figure. His stocky frame spoke to a power that had been sharpened over years in battle. In his mind, strength and might reigned supreme. Sentiment was a fairy tale for religion. It was past time these new soldiers learned this doctrine.

Smiling in a sinister manner, Harold had to admit he would have preferred to crush Tomas. But completely destroying Isaak was not a bad consolation prize. "Which would you prefer, youngling," Harold demanded of his opponent as he threw a sword and an axe at Isaak's feet.

Without taking his eyes off Harold, Isaak retrieved the sword. To the shock of all, he used a mighty double overhead strike to break the axe handle. Driving the sword into the sand, he began to circle his opponent and speak to everyone present.

"You came into my camp under the guise of peace and brotherhood. Your soldiers broke bread with my *men*, praised them for their ingenuity, and even saw them as equals. But your *pathetic* ego and pride could not stomach that a handful of cadets bested you. This is not our way. We protect and defend. We inspire and encourage. We are not bullies!"

Roaring the last words, he flew like an arrow towards his opponent. Harold sank into a defensive position, but was ill prepared for two heavy boots that came crashing into his chest. The chest plate took most of the damage, but not enough to prevent Harold from getting knocked to the ground. In a daze, he shook his head, as if trying to recalibrate his brain. His blurry eyes came into focus in time to see Isaak's right gauntlet smash into his face, knocking him further into the sand.

Sitting on Harold's chest, Isaak rained down blow after blow as his anger channeled into pure righteous indignation. He had been taught since infancy that those who donned the armor of a soldier dedicated themselves to a higher calling. They were to be the shield that protected, and the sword that defended. But, more and more, high ranking officers forgot that purpose and became drunk on their own power. Isaak's last blow was followed by a sickening crunch as Harold's jaw finally gave way.

With a grunt, Isaak stood, panting from exertion. All eyes followed him as he walked back to his tent, staggering under the stress of the fight and his own demons. Even though everyone felt his actions were justified, he felt ashamed for losing control. The blood dripping from his hands seemed to mock the man that had spent a lifetime honoring the military code and his own ethics.

The rest of the afternoon passed without incident. Karniel, Tomas, and the rest of their troop watched Harold's men take down their tents and head back to the City of Tears. Harold, too bruised and broken from the duel, had to be carried off on a kit. As he was carted past the younger troops, Harold gazed at Isaak's tent with his undamaged eye. Rage began to grow as he went past, and an oath, silently spoken, was struck.

By the time dinner had been eaten, and patrols set, the very depressed March Leader had yet to emerge from his tent. A dark cloud hovered over that area of the camp and no one wanted to be on the receiving end of it

Karniel, Tomas, and Liam volunteered to stand sentry that night. All three were worried about their leader; however, Liam seemed to be the most conflicted. As the other two tried to devise ways to overcome the next obstacle on the march, the young aristocrat's mind kept returning to the events of the day before.

While Tomas, Karniel, and the rest of their lot were busy pilfering supplies and water, Isaak had come into Liam's tent and checked on the poisoned young men. He even shared water and food from his own supply. This was to be expected from any leader of the Army, but Isaak took the time to sit and listen to each lad under his charge. He asked them of their hopes, dreams, and aspirations, and took the time to commend them for said desires. No answer was silly or seen foolish to Isaak, as he treated them with a sort of reverence.

This feeling kept running through Liam's mind, until it finally boiled over.

"Right, I'll be back quick as a wink," Liam said as he left his companions with confused looks. He came to a sliding halt at Isaak's tent, unsure of what to do next. The flap lay draped closed and undisturbed. Gathering his wits about him, Liam parted the flap and entered. A single candle flickered as the air moved in the tent, but the March Commander stayed sitting crossed-legged on his cot. Liam had no desire to interrupt what appeared to be some type of meditation or praying, but the tent owner's eyes had opened.

"What can I help you with, Liam," Isaak asked in a rather calm voice.

"Well, Sir," the young man began. "All us lads are worried about you.

You had no supper and hadn't left your tent since the fight. We aren't sure what to expect in the morning."

Bluish-green eyes shot from Liam to the tent flap and back to Liam. "All us lads, huh? Do not take this the wrong way, son, but you're a terrible liar." The leader chuckled at his own joke. "Why are you really here?"

Liam sighed and stared at his boots. He felt like a moron barging into his leader's tent.

"I just want to thank you, Sir. I know it's expected of leaders to check on their troops. My trainers would do such things, but you showed genuine concern for us. It wasn't an obligatory thing, Sir. My tent mates and I appreciate that."

As he finished, Liam stood with pride, for he had never felt such things before. The respect of a commanding officer, the friendship of brothers, and being judged on his merits alone were no longer only ideals, but a reality.

Isaak groaned as he uncurled his legs. "I am honored by your concern. It is my duty and privilege to do right by all of you. Not because it is expected, but because, after losing my own wife and son, I have the chance to make you into the men I would be proud to call my sons."

He continued as he rose off his cot. "I stayed inside this whole time to rest my body and calm my soul. You will taste battle and nothing you do can prepare you for the blood lust that ensues. I pray you lads do not get lost in that addicting tidal wave and never come back. Be better men than me. Fight when you have to, but know the difference between winning the fight and destroying your opponent."

As Liam mused over his words, Isaak stretched his sore muscles. He then walked over and opened the flap for his visitor. "Now, if you please, report to the others that I intend to break camp and leave before dawn. Off you go." Liam saluted with gusto and left to convey the message. Isaak smiled and blew out the candle. It was past time to continue on their journey.

❦ 11 ❦

The candelabras flicked as Varg removed his gauntlets and set them on the table. A light breakfast had been brought up earlier and the water and wine restocked. For this tale was longer than he remembered and Varg wished to make himself comfortable. He had not spoken at this length since the Red Keep trial. He did not care for that ordeal either.

"As you can see, my friends, Karniel did not start out a bad man, nor do I believe he is one now. He showed respect for his commander, his unit, and his men. I dare to say, he lived by those codes his entire life."

All but the Priest nodded in agreement. "If that were true," Mathis retorted, "how is it that he left the Army and had his brand removed? Is it still tradition to receive a brand at the end of Battle school, and a name at the end of the Trials, or has that changed?"

Varg stood with abruptness, knocking over his chair in the process. The Priest's response shook him to his core. No one outside of the military was privy to these rituals. Taking a calming breath, he responded. "How is it you know so much about our traditions? We allow your Paladins and healers certain liberties, but they are not present during such affairs. No one is!"

The struggle to keep his wits about him was coming to an end and his fist slammed into the table. If Mathis knew more than he let on, then Karniel was going to be condemned for sure.

This time Mathis felt ill at ease. Though each guild helped and aided the others, certain things were kept secret. One could even say sacred, and if any outsiders knew, well it would not bode well.

"My dear Lord Commander," the dark-skinned, hazel-eyed Priest began, hands up as if surrendering. "I feel no honor in knowing your traditions, nor am I trying to insult or one up you. I need to know as much information as I can get. I will not have another bloody revolution on our hands. We all know what happened at the Battle of Shaman Plain. The trial of that commoner leader led to a full revolt for ten years and almost destroyed our country. It took nearly one thousand years to repair the damages. Please help me understand this young man so an honest judgment can be passed."

Everyone understood the pleas of Mathis, and such a plea cooled some of that hot rage boiling within the Lord Commander.

All their guilds had lost someone or something dear to them during those years. Halls had been burned; homes had been destroyed. The land still bore scars of that dreadful time. The entire country almost tore itself apart. Were it not for the momentous efforts of the first Council of Four, there would have been no country at all.

Varg sighed as the weight of his calling and role came back to him. Glancing at Asiza, he chose his reply with great care.

"I understand your fears and concerns. Your knowledge of us notwithstanding, I am shocked at your desire for the history of this young man. If my information is correct, he is being held by your Questioners as they try to get to the 'truth'."

Yarmilla, who had been beyond quiet during Varg's discourse, burst forth with a barrage of questions.

"What do you mean Questioners? I thought they were disbanded for torturing innocent people? Have you forgotten what you promised us? How could you let this happen?"

Her anger shocked all in attendance. Even though she was not one to shy away from doing what was needed, the tears that streamed down her face spoke to a personal connection. Asiza arose and consoled the Harvester with a caring embrace as she cried into the Shaman's torso.

"I suggest," the Shaman stated in a flat voice, "you begin to answer some of *our* questions, Mathias. The sooner, the better."

Mathias wondered at the state of Yarmilla. What had happened in her life to despise the Questioners so? Alas, that question would have to wait as he felt distrust radiating from all in the room.

"If you would like the truth, so be it. I just pray you use your skill to ascertain the reality and honesty of the situation. What Yarmilla said is true. They were disbanded. After the ten years of bloodshed and horror, they had become a force that enjoyed pain and evil. They captured all who opposed them, regardless of affiliations or guild caste. At first, the Order acknowledged their existence. And, in some twisted capacity, accepted them. However, as they accrued money and power, the Order sought to end them entirely. Much time and effort was extended on this front. Despite this, two escaped.

"The one presiding over the heretic's interview was the younger of the two. The older one was apparently killed by your White Raven, along with some other men, when they detained him. In truth, these events were not disclosed to me until yesterday. I dispatched carrier birds to each of you the moment I was told."

The very room seemed to darken as Mathias completed his narrative. The reality of the situation became fully realized by all. If a twisted, evil man had Karniel, how long was he able to last?

Asiza, still embracing Yarmilla, nodded. "You speak the truth, Sir. It seems events are in motion that we are not privy to, nor can we control."

Filling a goblet full of wine, and handing it to the relieved Priest, Varg began to speak. "There is more to his story with us, and it will have much bearing on his future after he left us. Get the lass comfortable," the gruff soldier ordered with sadness in his voice. "She needs to hear this."

🔥12🔥

With the first leg of their march completed, the youthful troops were in high spirits. Tomas, Karniel, and their rag tag group of teenage knaves were seen as celebrities, with even the blue bloods showing them respect. Isaak was proud of his men, for he no longer saw them as just potential soldiers. They marched without complaining, aided others with their duties, and truly became a unit. He thanked the Gods for them. By the time they had marched the fifty leagues from the well towards the ruins, they all looked forward to a rest.

No one knew who had built the Temple, but all agreed it was once a majestic wonder.

The outer wall had since been demolished, yet its foundation had somehow survived. The inner wall had been rebuilt in the last thirty years for training and military games between the Fire Brand Army and the Desert tribes. Each foundation stone of the inner wall was five feet across and nine feet long. Twenty of these mammoth stones ran north to south on either side, with ten running east to west. These four walls stood twenty feet high, with ramparts included for extra protection. The courtyard had enough room for a latrine, water well, a small exercise yard, a store house, and tent area.

The young men shouted for joy as the Temple came into view. Most wanted to make a break for it, but Isaak's commands kept them in a true military line. Having gone that far, many of the youth were full of energy and vigor for the next challenge. Once the troop entered the arched gate to the south of the once holy building, their leader set to work ensuring sentries were stationed on rotation, armor was repaired, supplies were accounted for, so that his men were ready at a moment's notice. The middle-aged commander had no desire to come up short in the game that would test the group's mettle. It was considerately cooler in the shade of the massive walls, so the lads had no problem working until dusk.

—————◆—————

Unbeknownst to Isaak and his troop, their movements had not gone unseen. A pair of seedy individuals had followed them in secret, along a parallel set of dunes. Common sense dictated that they were from the desert tribes, for their long flowing, sandy-colored garb was similar. That, however, was far from true. The plans of the villainous duo were far more nefarious, and the commander of their particular group was only biding his time to strike. Upon seeing the troop arrive at the Temple, the two darted for their large reptilian mounts hiding a few yards behind a sandy mound and galloped off to report to their leader.

Popping the leather reins, the spies pushed their lizards to the peak of their speed. Even though the gait of these eight-foot long creatures was awkward at best, once gallop-stride was achieved, nothing could catch them. Having circumvented the Temple by almost half a mile, the watchers headed due north for five miles. After about an hour astride their mounts, a haphazard array of tents appeared in their view. The military prided itself on making order from chaos. In comparison, the lot in that camp seemed to roll in chaos like a pig in mud.

Entering the camp, the riders were halted by a mountain of a man covered in black and red snake tattoos. The self-proclaimed gate keeper of the camp, few dared to ask his name, but most called him Warden. This violence-loving behemoth ran the day to day affairs of the camp, as well as kept the others in line. His vast, corded muscular arms grappled both the bits with a jerk and held them in a death grip.

"You boys are late," he commented as he smiled dangerously, the lizards struggling in vain to free themselves. "Gareth has been expecting you. You best to be hurrying."

Sharing a quick glance, the men dressed as desert clansmen casually dismounted, trying to show the mentally warped shot caller that he held no sway over them. Despite the nonchalant walk towards their commander's tent at the center of the camp, two sets of feet moved with increasing speed as Gareth departed his tent and walked purposefully towards them. His six-foot frame and broad shoulders were impressive enough, but his deadly personality and wit were what created his legend.

Like most men his age, he had served as a reservist in the Army, at least until his time ended abruptly in scandal. He was as ruthless as he was charismatic, and failure was never allowed, even if it meant going to very cruel extremes. His blackened leather armor matched his mood as he silenced the words trying to escape the watchers' throats.

"I expected you two days ago," he said in deceptive quietness. "What kept you?" Gareth never yelled or screamed at his men. A word spoken sternly yet softly inspired more fear than roaring like a lion.

Both of them vomited a quick narrative of the troops' march and the fight that had ensued between Harold and Isaak. Gareth rubbed his two-week-old beard. Harold, the Bandit knew, was a hot-headed fool, but a decent campaigner. So if these young men had managed to best him, then this would not bode well for his plans. Gareth hoped to kidnap the sons of the Military Council and ransom them. Or, better yet, recruit them to his cause.

"See to it that Senka finds her way to speak to me. I have a special task for her," the blue-eyed, dark-haired leader commanded as he turned back to his tent.

Being so dismissed, the two men broke into cold sweats at that command. Feeling like a hare tracked by a hawk, these two had hoped to gain favor with their boss, not be filled with trepidation. They feared to displease their leader, yet this order made them wonder about their choice to join the outlaws.

They had no desire to find the Lady of Shadows, or interrupt whatever she was doing. Her tent was not hard to find, as most of Gareth's band gave her a wide birth. Not that the tent was uninviting or menacing, but the sounds that radiated from it gave most of the group night terrors. Resigned to the task, both men wondered what punishment Gareth had in store for them once they returned to duty.

Weaving a long path through the camp, they nipped a bit of food from the cooks and stopped to get an update from their sergeant. After thirty minutes of avoiding the exiled, rough linen tent, the two men approached the canopied entrance. A young feminine voice became slightly audible from the darkness within.

"What do you fine young men seek here?" she asked in a sickly sweet voice. "Enter, enter. There is no need to be afraid." The hypnotic tones in her smoky voice caused the men to enter without hesitation or thought, despite the unnatural chill in the air.

As their eyes adjusted to the dim interior, a petite young lady came into view. She was lying quite provocatively across a straw-filled mattress, her ebony silk robes loosed around her. "Don't be shy," the honeyed words continued. "Come in and rest."

The taller of the two had enough mental strength to relay Gareth's message to their hostess.

"Why thank you," she replied as she rose. "Now it's time for your reward."

The screams that exploded from her tent proved to the camp once again what happened to those who failed the bandit leader.

Once night fell on the desert, and the stars shone in all their majesty, Senka crept like a ghost to meet with her confederate. Surrendering herself to the Void, the dark mage passed into Shadow and Darkness.

Using a form of element morphing, the attractive young lady was invisible to all, save the most powerful of Shamans. Passing a handful of camp fires, the Lady of Shadow overturned stools and flicked cups out of hands with small wisps of magic. She knew it was childish, even petty, but watching the horror fester in these scum made her feel right at home. Circling Gareth's three pole tent, she felt the irritation and anger buzzing in the horse skin structure like an active beehive. She wondered what had her ally so worked up this time.

Gareth leaned over a folding leather-and-wood rod table, studying an enlarged map of the ancient temple. It was quite vexing, as the structure had but one entrance and enough stores to last a fortnight. To further complicate the problem, he knew the desert tribes were converging to march on the Fire Brand outfit within the week. There was precious little time to waste if he was to realize his plan. Muttering a curse, he reached for his cup of wine, only to find it was not there. Gareth turned sharply to the right and let fly a small dagger as his arm fully extended.

A blackened dust cloud surrounded the knife mid-flight as Senka sat on a chair, calmly drinking. "Your reflexes are getting better, Gareth," she teased as she threw her right leg over the arm of the chair. "Soon you may be able to sense me before I enter your tent, though that would take all the fun out of our little game."

Gareth did not allow himself to get drawn in by her tease. He knew the runes she had cut into her black leather armor only shone red after she had taken a life. Normally, he did not care how many lives were absorbed by her perverse magic, but tonight he needed her to focus.

"I have a request of you, my sweet. I need to know if the young men we hunt are truly in the Temple, and if so, which tent is theirs. As I am sure you are aware, those noble types do not mingle with us common rabble."

His words struck their mark as black fire danced along Senka's long, thin fingers. "Oh don't worry about that," she answered as she began to juggle the flames, bouncing them from finger to finger. "I will find your little treasures. Just promise me I will get to play with them before their time with us is through."

Gareth gave her a sinister smirk. "My lovely Shadow, you will get all the play time you want."

Twenty minutes of shadow jumping later, Senka crawled to the top of the ring of dunes surrounding the Temple from the north side of the building and glared. Silver light reflecting from the full moon, with torch and wood-burning urns, hindered her ability to dark jump. As she searched for another way in, her thoughts turned to her younger days in the Shaman's guild and her own trial.

Ever an eager learner, she earned a student position after besting all in her village in a contest of magical aptitude. Her parents dotted on her, claiming she had the gift and would return lost honor to their bloodline. Being a fast learned had gained her some rivals in the beginning, but she persevered and soon won over her starkest opponents. Together, they swore to be the best arcane users the Shaman guild had ever seen.

Senka and her confidants discovered shadow jumping quite by accident. They first used the forbidden skill to pass from shadow to shadow and sneak past the Library Guardian. This allowed them to obtain more and more knowledge. By surrendering themselves to the Void, they simply disappeared from view and detection. This use of the jump slowly began to corrupt her group and tempt them to darker and more apostate skills.

The more skills they learned, the more the lust of power took hold. The taint that had, in the beginning, been so faint, now ran rancid in their very souls. Oaths and sacraments soon followed, all hidden from view and performed deep in the very mountain they once swore to protect. A final ingredient was needed for them to complete the spirit-charring ordeal, but the Defenders of the Goddess Thoprac stepped in at the last minute, due to one of Senka's ranks turning spy.

All thirteen had been shackled and brought before the Guardians, the ruling council of the Shamans, and the Oracle, the living mouthpiece of the Earth Goddess. Such a gathering had not happened for a thousand years, not since the Heretic last poisoned the land.

Senka, out of all her confederates, refused to renounce her devotion. But it was her shadow magic attack on the Oracle that got her promptly cast out of the Guild, as well as her citizenship to enter any and all cities, under pain of death. Her name was blotted out of the records, with only her image as a testimony to all the corrosive nature that was the Shadow arts.

She wandered for a year, from hamlet to hamlet, avoiding any and all contact with people. Meanwhile, her hatred of the Shamans, and all the guilds, festered in her like a cancer. Her family, the same people that taught her to accrue power and skills, renounced her and acted like they had no daughter. Even her village marked out her name from their histories.

As her exile lengthened, her powers dwindled. Death and constant blood sacrifices fueled her powers. Without those, her body began to decay. She lived in constant pain as she became weaker and more frail. Drifting from graveyard to graveyard, her body could sustain itself enough to stay alive, but not repair the damages. A shade of her former beauty and youth, she aged some twenty years in a matter of weeks. It was not until she happened on Gareth robbing a caravan on the Green Highway that her pain lessened.

Gareth and his band had been watching the tax routes for weeks, hoping for them to become lax with security, as they tended to do midway through their tax runs. All he needed was a moonless night and their victory would be assured. Fate smiled on them both as a bank of cloud cover passed over and darkened the night sky.

Smarter than the average hedge robber, the bandit leader had his men attack four miles from the inn. It was where the soldiers would add more men and fresh horses for the remainder of the journey. Spears and pole arms bit deeply into the legs and torsos of the taxation guardians as the bandits burst forth from the hedgerows on either side of the dirt road. Although the bloodthirsty thieves lost five men in the process, all the soldiers guarding the gold had perished quickly and without a cry for help raised.

This murderous act fueled Senka as never before. With a blood-curdling scream, her body floated some six feet off the ground as those departed souls rejuvenated her body and her powers. A swirling cocoon of dark magic enshrouded Senka while her screams continued to echo up and down the dirt road.

Gareth and the remainder of his men ran towards the scream, thinking to silence a witness. But, instead, they were forced onto their knees by the sheer concentration of dark magic in the air. Then, all at once, a massive explosion hurled the bandits back several yards.

Senka, still floating, zeroed in on Gareth and bid him rise. Casting a reassuring look to his men, he got to his feet with a touch of swagger and bowed. His pomp and gesture meant little to Senka, for she saw right into his blackened heart.

"Your hatred of the Army pales in comparison to mine for my former guild," she stated. "But I have need of one such as you. If you help me destroy the Shamans, I pledge my powers to help you destroy the military."

Gareth looked at his men, the stench of their fear assaulting his nostrils. "My Lady Shadow," he flattered with a grand, open-armed gesture, "these pathetic fools I offer to you as a gift to seal our partnership."

While the traitorous leader walked towards the female mage, tentacles of black energy snaked towards the betrayed bandits. As the newly minted partners embraced, those arcane appendages of Senka's will coiled themselves around the men. Paralyzed by fear, the magic crushed their bones and absorbed the souls of the wicked.

Thus began a twisted and quite violent partnership. They fed the darkness within each other, while taking note of all broken parts. Some would blindly call it love, and, in a way it was, but their agreement was conditional, even doomed to failure.

The call of the night watch on the Temple wall pulled Senka from her memories. Mentally berating herself for not paying attention, she realized the Moon had shifted. The western side of the temple now cast a huge shadow on the exterior ground. Smiling manically, the dark mage took off in a mad sprint and dove head first into the shadow before anyone could notice her.

Moving from shadow to shadow like a fish in murky water, she was able to see distorted images of the young troops and the layout of the camp. Gareth had been able to give her a description of each of the lads. His plan could be achieved with any of them, but his main prize was Liam. The ruthless boss of those desert outlaws wanted Commander Piloni to experience the indescribable sensation of being at someone else's mercy.

Ghosting from tent to tent, Senka finally found Liam's bunk at the far north end of the courtyard and slid in under the hide wall. Enough shadows were cast by the fire, and the lads moving about the interior, that the shadow mage was able to stay partially hidden in the Void, but still feed her hungry blade should the need arise. All the young men before her were well fed and strong. Looking for a lad that matched the description she was given for Liam, Senka realized her prey was not present.

Listening to the typical whinnying of spoiled Noble offspring, the intruder was able to surmise some important information about her prey. He had volunteered to stand watch during the night, much to the shock of his tent mates. His attitude had changed a little every day since fighting with Karniel, and his fellow nobles were not happy with it.

Efrain, now the de facto leader, commented to the others that Liam needed to stop taking a shine to those commoners and remember his pure blood lineage. Most of the other boys agreed with him. None of them liked being one-upped by commoners, but Efrain despised being bested by Tomas and Karniel. In his mind, no commoner should ever be on the same battlefield as a Noble. It was an uncivilized notion.

Senka's lip curled as a soft growl escaped her lips. She had seen enough to know Liam was here and that she would relish breaking these condescending brats. The thought of their agonizing screams at her hands was enough to keep her blood lust at bay for the time being.

Passing fully into the shadow, Senka decided to search for Liam. His odd desire to spend time with commoners did not set well with her. Could a Noble truly see another as an equal, or was it a ploy to have others do his bidding? She searched for about fifteen minutes, looking in every tent, corner, or room. She found him instructing a weary watchman on how best to stay awake during the night.

"I find it best to move constantly and focus on different things on my patrol," the handsome young man declared in a firm but gentle tone. "Try to gauge the distance between you and an object. That way if we need to call for a volley of arrows, or a ballista strike, you already know the hardest part." The tired young man smiled in amusement at Liam and thanked him for his advice. "Right," Liam continued, "off ya get. I will cover the rest of your watch. We have less than two hours til sunrise, and you need some sleep."

The young soldier gave a crisp salute and retreated to his tent as Senka returned to the Void. Something about Liam bothered her and she did not like it one bit. Here was a Noble being polite to, even helping, a commoner for no reason. It rubbed her the wrong way, for she could find no ill will in his heart.

The gems in the night sky twinkled a little brighter. The dark Shaman cast an over-the-shoulder glance at the young man walking the North wall patrol. She had to report all this to Gareth, and he, most likely, would not take it well.

Riotous laughter and yelling echoed throughout the bandit camp. None of them worried about being heard or seen by the soldiers at the Temple or by the nomadic desert tribes. The temple was too far away and the closest tribe had been taken care of two days before they had settled to wait for the Fire Brand hopefuls. Nopale liquor had been served with supper, leaving many of Gareth's men too intoxicated to touch their toes.

Some cloud wisps were dissipating right over the bandit leader's tent when the Lady of Shadow returned and gave her report.

"Well he appears to be nothing like his father," Gareth stated as he paced back and forth in his tent. "This social wedge that has been driven between the five of them, do you think we can use that? Could you influence those young men so their distaste for Liam grows to hatred?" The former soldier knew there was nothing worse for a unit than friends becoming enemies over ideology.

Senka sat crossed-legged on the folding table, pondering over what she had seen and heard. Liam was different and his kindness was eating away at her resolve like a slow-etching acid. "It is possible to influence them in such a way," she answered, finally looking up at her partner. "How badly do you want this to go? I could conjure a dream for their leader to send out a patrol. Or would you prefer I get them to kill Liam? Either way, you win." The suggestion was real, but her heart was not in it.

Gareth turned and gave Senka a smoldering smile. "My lovely dark goddess, you have given me a truly wicked idea. Conjure a dream so that Liam and the other noble brats stand watch together, but have that pathetic Efrain be in charge. With any luck, we will be able to capture them all." He clasped her hand in his and kissed her delicate fingers. "We make such a lovely team, you and I."

She nodded, unsure how to take his sudden show of affection as she slid off the table. "I will begin preparations after I rest for a bit. Isaak will have interesting dreams this night." With that, she left the tent, walking within the camp instead of through the Void. The cool night air brushed at the strands of hair that had come loose from the bone sticks she had inserted to hold the locks. Void magic would not help calm the storm of conflicting feelings raging within her.

Passing by where the cooking fires were ablaze, she took a plate of roasted meat and flat bread. An expression of gratitude slipped out from her mouth before she realized it, causing the balding and abused cook to freeze in shock. No one appreciated his efforts, and to hear it from the Lady of Shadow, the cook did not know how to react.

Realizing what had happened, Senka played it off with all the grace of a drunken duck, and returned to her tent, not emerging until the next night.

🔥 13 🔥

At the Temple, morning exercises came before the red sun blazed in full glory over the horizon. Soon the whole courtyard was filled with the sound of clashing wooden swords. Although his men had been trained and tested with edged weapons, Isaak figured it best to use the leftover wooden weapons they found in the storehouse. This way their swords did not lose their sharpness nor get warped. Everyone, with the exception of the day watch, was either striking wooden palls or using a partner in dueling exercises. As he walked among his men, Isaak noticed a rather disturbing occurrence.

Tomas, Karniel, and Liam were lined up against Efrain and two of his tent mates. It was odd enough to see a Noble team up with commoners, but, odder still, the combined team moved with trained grace. As this was to be a practice run, the combatants were only supposed to go at half strength. However, Efrain and his friends were attacking at full power, even attempting to completely overpower their opponents. Tomas and others were strictly defending, refusing to sink to their attackers' barbaric mentality.

The March Commander smiled as he realized this action only infuriated the young nobles even more. He decided to allow this fiasco to continue, purely to see how quickly the enraged Nobles would lose. In Isaak's mind, it was time to put all this caste stupidity to bed. They were all equal under the Fire Brand Banner. If the young men did not learn that in the Desert, then future campaigns would end in utter failure, with countless unnecessary deaths.

Tomas' grin had not left his face ever since Efrain all but demanded to spar with the southern clansman native. Behind those twinkling eyes, the roguish teen could guess why the young Noble wanted to fight him. Ego and pride had always been the aristocrat's downfall and Tomas was happy to teach Efrain the error of his ways.

With each block of Tomas' hexagon shield, Efrain became even more sporadic, losing his cool and forgetting his training. Abandoning his shield all together, the Noble used strong double-handed blows to tray and knock Tomas off balance, but to no avail.

Every enraged strike was met with a deflecting guard. Side jab and block. Back hand strike and block. This dance continued for fifteen minutes, with Efrain becoming more and more unhinged. He screamed several curses towards his opponent's mother and sisters.

The other lads ceased their practicing to watch this odd exchange. Tomas, true to his nature, kept laughing each time he halted a strike, knowing full well it would drive Efrain over the edge. This, and the fact Tomas had tossed his wooden sword aside minutes into the fight, drove Efrain into a maddening rage.

Efrain's eyes shot venomous hatred at Tomas as he tried to find a weakness. Realizing brute strength was not enough, he opted for more underhanded approaches. Kicking a foot full of sand at Tomas, he charged, hoping to employee the same tactic that Isaak had with Harold. Only the plan backfired horribly. As Efrain's feet connected with the shield, Tomas used his right foot to flip the bottom of the shield up into the air. This caused Efrain's feet to slide up the face of the shield and his head and back to slam into the dirt with a loud crash.

Isaak yelled for room as he surged forward with the medic. They did their best not to move the young Noble's head and neck as they performed the initial examination of the unconscious aristocrat. As the medic felt around the shoulders, neck, and head, Isaak had everyone but Tomas return to their duties. As the crowd dispersed, Tomas felt torn as concern and justification battled in him. He never felt any true ill will towards the Noble. But his constant remarks of commoners being weaker than their betters were enough to make even one of the exalted Saints swear.

Tomas' conscience became eased somewhat as the medic proclaimed nothing was broken and Efrain was only knocked out. He also suggested giving Efrain something for pain, as he would awaken with a vile headache.

Isaak sighed in relief as the medic reported everything. Losing a soldier was to be expected, but to lose one to such a bone-headed stunt, well, there would have been hell to pay for sure. Especially since his father was a powerful man, and those in power had no claim to the truth; they just wanted someone to blame.

Efrain moaned as Tomas and the medic carried him to his tent and placed him on his cot. The medic left instructions with his tent mates that he was not to be disturbed until he woke of his own volition. After Efrain was properly bedded down, Isaak pulled Tomas aside.

"I want to know exactly how a training exercise turned into a full-fledged brawl," he demanded with a growl.

Tomas dropped his gaze. "Sir, ever since we got the water skins, and Liam began to spend more time with us, Efrain and his "blue bloods" have been giving us a hard time. Snide comments about our lineages, how we weren't worthy to clean his boots, and bull like that. I never wanted to hurt him. I just wanted him to shut up. Most of us joined to be part of a group, outside of class or caste. To be seen as who we can become, not what we were born. You have been the first commander to truly live by those principles.

"If his daddy gets his knickers in a twist because his boy got thrashed by a commoner, oh well. Efrain should have stopped, but he didn't. I threw my swords to show that I meant no harm to him, but he just would not stop. His ego will get someone killed. Gods forbid it's one of my mates, because then I *will* kill him."

Tomas finished his testimony in tears as Isaak studied the southern young man. For a long time, he had been the one to duck responsibilities and duties. But now he had finally found acceptance, and, for the first time in his life, a true family outside of his clan at the port city.

"Lad, listen to me," Isaak advised as he placed his hands on Tomas' shoulders, "you have a good thing going here. Nobles will always see guys like us and think we are below them. It's a fact of life, but trust me when I say to let your victories do the talking. You and the lads did well with Harold. I'm proud of the man you are becoming, but don't let some idiot ruin your life. We still have two more stops before this is over. Show them they can't afford to discount us."

Tomas looked up at his commander and smiled. "Thank you, Sir. My Pa would have liked you a lot. I will get back to my duties now."

Isaak shook his head and chuckled as Tomas walked away. He thought how fine of an officer Tomas would make one day, as long as no more crackpot moves were made.

—————◆—————

The lowering of the sun brought the activity of the troop to a dull roar. Food had to be prepared and most were relaxing after a long day of drills and sparring. As always, the sentries were fed first and then sent to their respective posts along the walls of the Temple. By the time the moon became a sickle in the sky, the camp was at peace.

Efrain had not wakened by dinner time so he was left alone while his tent mates had their turn to eat and mingle among the troop. His dreams became dark and twisted as he feverishly tossed and turned in his sleep.

He saw himself atop a hexagon shield being carried before the Red Tribunal. Trumpets were blaring and confetti littered the air as he was brought to the front steps of the Keep. A giant staff struck the ground and all became silent. The Lord Commander and his two generals, along with the military inner circle, awaited Efrain at the top of the steps of the massive stone fortress.

He gulped nervously, but felted triumphant as he was lowered. He knew this day of victory would come. And, now, in front of all the citizens of the Red Keep, it had. He stared straight ahead as he ascended towards the leaders Efrain had hero-worshiped for years. It was those men that ensured all that entered the main doors of the castle knew the articles that governed the Army.

Each step had been inscribed with a tenet of the five units. The first four were white for the Battle School. The next four were a pale yellow for the Men at Arms. The following four were an orange-yellow for the Scouts. The next four were a rich, vibrant orange for the Archers. And the last four were a rich, blood red to represent the might of the Heavy Cavaliers.

The words on the steps seemed blurred as the dreamer passed each one, causing a worm of fear to wiggle within the teen's soul.

Finally cresting the last step, Efrain was shocked to see all eight men, in their ceremonial armor, bowing to him. A small part of his mind felt this was wrong, but an overwhelming sense of confidence swelled in him. He turned, with his arms opened to accept praise of the crowd, only to find the corpses of his fans piled high in the courtyard.

He swiftly turned back, but found the eight leaders of the army also dead, mere shades of their former selves. Efrain, in a panic, ran for his father's body, only to have it dissolve into smoke. The dreaming lad screamed while he ran into the Red Keep. The tapestries and banners were moth eaten as he darted further inward. The full sets of armor that lined the halls had become riddled with rust and lost their shine. The entirety of the Red Keep seemed to rot and die as he ran from room to room, looking for a place to hide.

In his frantic state, he ended up in the Judgment Hall. It's raised, red marble seating shone brightly as he entered. The emblem of the Army covered the floor in a giant mosaic. The hexagon shield, with an axe and spear crossing behind it, had always given Efrain a sense of pride. The sound of applause pulled his eye line from the floor and towards a lone figure in black leather armor.

The armor-wearer stood, leaning over the wall, right in front of the larger tribunal seats. "You have allowed your army to die," he began. "Commoners and street urchins run unchecked among the ranks of this once powerful enterprise. You and the other nobles have become fat and lazy, unwilling to purge the unworthy from the Red Keep. They caused the decay you saw. They are a cancer. A threat to the very fabric of this great country."

The armor-clad stranger leaped over the wall and strolled over to Efrain. "Do you wish to prevent this great catastrophe? Do you wish to restore honor to your name, unit, and country?" Seeing the lad nod with energy, the man continued in a prophetic tone.

"Help me prevent the corruption of this place and I swear, before all the Gods, that you will be seen for the hero that you are. Help me stop this apocalypse."

Efrain felt the tears run down his cheeks as he thought of his family, especially his father. If he could save his father and the others on the Inner Circle, then honor dictated he should. The Red Keep had been his home for years. Every good soldier should defend such a holy place.

Efrain wiped away his tears and steeled his heart. "What can I do to prevent this downfall," he asked the stranger in black.

The stranger smiled at the request. "Just listen to me."

———◆———

During the night, the medic periodically checked on Efrain. He had been running a slight fever earlier, and had been tossing and turning quite a bit. Luckily, the fever broke halfway through the night, as did the thrashing about. A thankful medic left Efrain to sleep about the third watch, and the injured lad managed to rest the rest of the night uninterrupted.

As morning came, Efrain awoke a little sore, but full of purpose. Burdened with the knowledge of a horrible future, he could still see the ruin of the Red Keep every time he closed his eyes. As he got prepared for the day, the promise made in the fever vision, and the instructions that had been received, played again and again in his mind. The young Noble knew the time would come, and it would come soon, to show the entire troop that none shall taint the might of the Red Keep.

Exiting the tent, the wiry-built sixteen-year-old scanned the temple grounds. Only one in every four soldiers was of Noble blood, and this gave birth to a well of hate that began to overflow deep in his tender soul. Why did this happen? How was it that the ruling council did not see the threat these commoners posed? Several more strange and frightening thoughts clouded Efrain's mentality as he passed up all the well-wishers shouting for joy at his speedy recovery. Appearing to be in a daze, the mentally-strained young man struggled to put one foot in front of the other as he exited the Temple courtyard. Leaning against the outer wall, the black-haired soldier's breathing became rapid and shallow.

His mind battled the dark influences that attacked his very soul. Could he dwell among so many that the dream deemed as unworthy? Could the mission be accomplished? Should he warn his father of the impending doom?

Suddenly, a calming influence seemed to caress Efrain's mind and soul, dulling it to the questions racing through a very troubled soul. The quiet influence gathered his thoughts and brought all the chaos into focus.

With this newfound peace, the youth returned to his duties, full of purpose and vigor. There was a mission to complete and the youth would not dare to fail.

———◆———

Senka, drenched from head to toe in her own sweat, strained as she uncurled her legs. The power it took to not only send the dreams, but to maintain a tranquil connection with the young man, was quite taxing on her small-framed body. Having straightened out her legs, the mage laid on her back, with her arms and legs extended to their fullest. She needed to work out the stiffness fast if she was to report to Gareth in a timely fashion.

Starting with the extremities, she rotated each joint and filled it with shadow magic. She had learned this technique as a shaman apprentice. It was meant to be a meditation ritual, and a way to stay connected to the Earth. In the Shadow arts, its main purpose was to heal the body after long exposure to the more powerful spells. As each of her joints became invigorated, she began to sense the pull of her connection to Efrain get stronger with each passing second. She felt his body react to rigorous sparring as each blow landed. Laughing at his inability to defend himself, she completed the arcane ritual. Now fully infused and healed, she headed to leave, but discovered Gareth entering her tent.

"Did our little experiment work?" he asked with a hopeful grin as he stood to his full height. His military cut brown hair rubbed the ceiling of the tent as the male walked a turn around the interior.

Senka was shocked at his brazen act of not only entering her tent, but his actions of questioning her. Swelling with power, she replied rather curtly. "Your plan worked, but not how you expected. You did not tell me someone in that camp was of Shaman decent. He shielded the leader from my attacks, but another was not so lucky."

Gareth seated himself on her cot and looked at her like a parent expecting their child to lie. "Who," he countered, "is the puppet?"

Cold anger fueled Senka as she responded. "One of your precious Nobles took hold of the dream and now believes all commoners are destroying his beloved army from the inside like a virus. He has been instructed to await your command."

Gareth stood and straightened his shirt. "Well, that is not what I wanted, but it will have to do." As he walked past her, he paused to look her way. "If you ever deviate from my plans again, little shadow, I will kill you myself." His eyes held none of the friendship she had come to expect over the years. Allowing the threat to hang in the air for a moment, he departed and left Senka incensed with fury.

—————◆—————

The day continued without incident at the Temple. Training completed and lunch had been served when Efrain asked to speak with Isaak in private. Never one to refuse his soldiers' need for help, the leader left his plate of stew and hard bread to follow the young man. Efrain guided Isaak towards the rear of the temple, claiming to want to discuss the incident from the day before. As they reached the small building that housed the dry food and training weapons, Efrain drew his wooden sword and struck the back of Isaak's head with a powerful blow, knocking him unconscious.

As he bound the feet and hands of the march commander, Efrain snarled at and reveled in the ease of his deception. Opening the storehouse door, Isaak was pitched in like a sack of grain. Upon completing his task, Efrain rose and spat at the feet of his victim. In the young Noble's eyes, Isaak had no place in the new military, or in the country for that matter. As he left the bound troop leader, the magically-controlled puppet felt very pleased with himself.

As Efrain returned to the rest of the troop eating lunch, five miles to the north, Senka exploded from the cool shade of her abode and dashed to Gareth's tent, knocking down anyone in her way. This was not how the plan was suppose to happen, but puppets don't always like their strings to be pulled. Having arrived at the bandit leader's tent, she demanded to see Gareth. Shockingly, the bodyguards did not let her enter. The camp knew she had displeased their commander, so the fear they once had for her was gone.

Knowing any appeal to those men would fall on deaf ears, the already irritated woman conjured up tentacles of shadow magic. A purple hue encompassed the petite frame as the guards were coiled up and flung into the air as a child would throw their toys in anger. Each man flew some twenty feet in opposite directions before landing on tents nearby. Fury pulsated from the purple fire outlining Senka as she entered the dimly lit tent. Gareth had the decency to look shocked as he and his dark-robed companion felt the pure majesty of the Lady of the Shadows.

"Your plan had better come to completion today," she said as her smoky voice filled the tent with the dark, cold rage. "The young man you had me soul string is attempting a coup. He wants what you promise him and he wants it *now*!"

With a growl, Gareth darted out, shoving Senka aside. Too many plans and deaths had been cashed in to see the middle-aged man's revenge be lost to the stupidity of a teenager. Tightening his sword belt, Gareth called his men to arms, screaming for his lieutenants to line up their raiding parties for battle. He wanted the sons of the Nobles spared. As for the rest of those poor, useless souls in the Temple, they were of no consequence.

Killing a few dozen weak teenagers playing soldier would put a smile on the attacking army's face and Gareth knew it. They were cowards at heart, with no real skill and too lazy to earn an honest living. Just the right kind of disposable fodder any self-respecting bandit needed.

When he reentered the tent, the roguish commander's face failed to mask his bewilderment as the giant of a man was knelt in front of Senka. Clothed in robes seen in the Mystic Isles, the guest had somehow teleported in the tent some ten minutes earlier, claiming the ability to empower Gareth's whole military force with skills beyond their comprehension. Before a single word could be uttered, the black-haired former soldier was dazed as a flick of Senka's wrist sent him careening out of the tent and dangerously close to a cooking fire.

Warden, who was calling for his mount, saw what transpired and ran to his leader's aid. Gareth was already on his feet by the time the juggernaut arrived. Signaling for Warden to bring an extra lizard for him, he dusted himself off with a laugh. A dangerous gleam sparkled. Gareth was sure to gain his prize before the sunset.

Jumping in the saddle, with the thrill of battle coursing in his veins, Gareth directed the mount towards the edge of camp. The majority of his army was lined up and waiting his express command. Unleashing his short sword, the bandit leader signaled his forces to march towards the Temple and victory.

14

Just before preparation of dinner, a cry of alarm alerted the camp as the north side sentry spotted a dust trail heading their direction. The whole Temple became a beehive of activity as armor and weapons were located and put in place. Tent units became organized into fighting teams, each one ready for battle. Those on the wall looked on with awe and fear while Gareth's troops arrived, only a hundred feet shy of the wall.

The leader of the attacking force smiled at the young men, seeing himself some twenty years earlier. Dropping the raw hide reins, the chief raider stood in his saddle, much to the dislike of the reptilian mount. Cupping gloved hands around a thin-lipped mouth, Gareth began to address those within the wall.

"Hello to those in the Temple. My men and I seek the sons of the Inner Circle. We know they are in there, and if they will give themselves up, the rest of you can either stay here or be about your march. You have until sunset to make a decision. Remember, the loss of five is much better than a slaughter of fifty five"

Panic ensued in the heart of every young man as Gareth completed his speech. They had been trained to handle battle scenarios, but only in training, not in real life. Most of Isaak's soldiers had never been in a fight to the death, and more than a couple were losing control of themselves. What happened next truly wounded the morale of those within the wall to its core.

Efrain, full of dark energy and self-righteous bravado, called his fellow Nobles to him. Each one had also grown up in the Red Keep and trusted him more than anyone else.

"Men," he barked with authority, "this is the day, and this is the hour. Those commoners will toss us out to save themselves. They care nothing for the blood our families have spilled for generations in their defense. They envy us and our upbringing. For they are weak and deserve neither our help nor our pity. Watch, they will abandon us to be tortured and die at the hands of bandits."

HIs words shocked the young aristocrats. More than one face showed conflicting emotions, as they did not know who to believe. Liam ran over to the small group, yelling for them to take up defensive positions. He eyed Efrain with suspicion. None of the teenage nobility had moved.

Karniel, realizing something had to be done, yelled at Tomas to prepare his bow and gray goose quiver and stand at the ready. Be it blind luck or a blessing from the Gods, Tomas was a dead shot with a bow at four hundred yards, picking off moving targets with ease. This, and the fact that most of the Archer Corp was Southern, had contributed to him getting accepted by the Archers even before he had officially finished training. Karniel hoped Tomas could either pick off the leaders or wound enough of their mounts to cause despair in the ranks.

Tomas had two of the units on the North wall with him, facing the bandits, along with an additional unit on both the northwest and northeast corners. This allowed for a more secure front, if the bandits chose to scale the wall. One of the remaining units acted as a reserve, stationing themselves along the stairs leading up the wall. Karniel called for the remaining two to head to the Southern gate, on the off chance an attack came at their rear. The young nobles, however, heeded Efrain's words and stood in the middle of the courtyard, refusing to help.

Worry wormed through Karniel's heart. Isaak was nowhere to be seen. Shouting at the last reservist on the stairs, Karniel sent him to hunt for their leader. Watching the soldier leave, a whistle from Tomas pulled Karniel from his dark mood as the archer waved the White Raven teen over. Once he arrived at the middle of the Northern wall, Tomas voiced concerns about their armor and weapons.

The spears allowed them reach during a siege, or if the bandits were to use ropes. Their short swords allowed them to move with ease in close quarter combat. The marching armor was a whole other beast. It was designed out of boiled leather to be lightweight and durable, but it was not designed for actual war. Reluctantly, Karniel nodded in agreement while they both studied the outlaws.

Each member of this ruthless band was armed to the teeth with a combination of weapons. Small axes and dirks were tucked into belt loops. Long swords and war hammers were swung across backs or tossed from hand to hand. Every man had identical metal scale armor, with braided leather gauntlets and greaves for added protection. Few chose to use helmets, seeing the youth as no true threat. Some took to taunting their opponents, even going so far as riding up to the wall and swearing at Isaak's troop.

Amid this brutish verbal abuse, Karniel and Tomas walked calmly up and down the wall, offering a smile and words of encouragement. The two tent leaders wanted the young soldiers to remain calm. To remember their training. And, most importantly, to have faith in themselves and their units. True leaders do not give in to fear. They boosted the morale and confidence of their fighting men, and Karniel and Tomas were such men.

As the sun sank further into the horizon, a faint rumbling could be heard in the Temple and without. It seemed concentrated in the middle of the ruined stone structure, but being so subtle, no one was quite able to pinpoint it. Bewildered looks were shared by all present as the noise continued.

The lizard mounts became more agitated as the vibrations and sound rose, digging their claws into the dirt and whipping their tails. This rumbling distorted their ability to both see and hear. The giant reptiles used sound to see in even the darkest of locations. Now everything was a distorted blur while the vibrations attacked the very center of their brains.

The bandits struggled to rein in their mounts, as what was merely an annoyance became excruciatingly painful for the four-legged creatures. Gareth and Warren had to abandon their saddles. Their beasts reared up and bellowed, thrashing about like beings possessed. Gareth, rolling forward and rising into a combat stance, was not sure if his beast would attack or run. Stealing a glance to the left and right, he took in the pitiful scene. Over half his men were either trampled or fighting bucking mounts. Despair and ego battled within his soul. Never had he lost a fight, and he could not afford to do so to untested teenagers.

A wide geyser of sand and rock broke the bandit leader's resolve as it exploded between the attacking force and the northern wall of the Temple. Debris created a cloud of dust that blinded the attacking force, adding insult to injury. The bandits had been preparing for an easy fight against unprepared youth. The sudden display of a mage was quite disheartening to the bullies.

Warden, without leave from his captain, issued a call for retreat. He had seen Shaman magic before, and he wanted none of it ever again. He'd lost comrades to a small outfit of Shaman women at a shrine, near the Salt Marshes. The flailed, burning corpses of his fallen men still haunted the behemoth, and that fear got the better of him.

Glaring at the Temple with a snarl, Gareth turned and followed his retreating band. The sound of cheering youth echoed in his ear like a bug he wanted to kill. Each step hardened his resolve for revenge, and he swore a murderous oath to all the Gods he had forsaken long ago.

Wonder and amazement filled the defending teens' eyes. The seemingly powerful band of bandits somehow dissolved into a heap of disarray and chaos. Shouts and prayers of thanksgiving erupted into the air as they watched the outlaws retreat further into the wasteland.

Tapping Tomas on the shoulder, and signaling for him to follow, Karniel ran towards Liam and the other aristocrats. The bulky young man hoped to head off what was likely to follow: anger for the betrayal. They had just avoided one blood bath, he did not want another.

Before they reached the young aristocrats, hoping to stave off the coming attack, a miracle happened.

Isaak, with a blood-spotted bandage and a few lengths of leather, emerged from his tent. He had stripped to show his chest and bare feet, calling all to halt with the authority of the War God. Sweat and fatigue rolled off the older soldier's body from his injury. He knew what was soon to occur. And, in the hope of stopping any potential violent reprisals, he ordered everyone to stand their ground.

Years of military training stopped the youth in their tracks, with some still on the wall and others entering the courtyard. The Temple became electrified with a typhoon of anger, fear, and shame. The barefoot man pulled power and rejuvenation from the Earth while crossing from his tent to where the mutinous teenagers stood defiant.

Coming to a stop just shy of arm's length, Isaak considered Efrain and his insubordinate actions. Movement caught the leader's eye line, Efrain's hand suddenly reaching for his weapon. Time slowed with the teen clearing his blade of its sheath and aiming for his target's throat. A sad smile danced across the leader's face. He half expected an underhanded move, just not one so full of rage.

With a snap of his wrist, one of the leather strips coiled around the centerpoint of Efrain's sword, just below the sharpened point. Lunging his right leg forward, and dropping his center of gravity, the middle-aged man yanked the remainder of the strip with both hands, his torso twisting to the left. Powerful corded muscle and righteous fury sent the sword and the attacker sailing into the air. Efrain was momentarily stunned, his face and body brutally crashing into the dirt. This gave the unit commander all the time required to bind the rebellious youth's hands and feet with the remaining lengths of leather. Efrain, regaining control of his faculties, began to flop around like a fish, cursing his leader and swearing vengeance upon all who did not aid him.

The brash action of the tied up youth shocked everyone. Refusing to aid in a battle was bad enough to lose a commission in the military; but attempting to kill a commanding officer was punishable by death.

An army of cold, emotionless eyes turned on the youth that had sided with Efrain. Shame radiated off them like heat from a blazing fire. They knew their actions would be remembered by all who stood ready to fight.

Isaak ordered them be put under guard in their tents as the last light of the setting sun sank into the horizon. They were to be treated like prisoners of war, and expected to act as such. Pointing to Liam, Karniel, and Tomas, he signaled them to meet in the sparring yard. The march leader wanted as much information as was available before casting a verdict that would change the future of several people.

Soft words and whispered conversations popped up like weeds, with everyone dispersing for their regular duties. Extra watchmen were needed on the walls and a new guard roster was made to keep the prisoners under control.

Tomas, running from the wall, was the last to join the discussion. His quiver rattled as he used his shoulders and back to unstring the bow. Smiling like a drunken idiot, he punched Isaak on the shoulder and said, "It's good to see you made it, Sir. But why were you in your tent bare foot?"

The inquiry struck a chord with the other two teens. They were also wondering why it appeared that their leader had been hiding during the attack.

The laissez faire attitude of the Southern left much to be desired, but Isaak was not surprised by the question. If he was in their place, he would have asked it as well. Their march commander provided an account of his assault, with what he was able to remember.

What they did not know was that it was Isaak who had caused the rather abrupt explosion of earth. His sweet wife had, many years earlier, discovered he had some small skill in the Shaman arts, and had attempted to teach him. Since he never wanted to hone those skills, any action or usage with the elemental arts usually came in moments of anger or distress.

All three were shocked at the account, but none more than Liam. While anger and disgust were shared among the lads, an overwhelming pool of sadness weighed on the future leader of the Heavy Cavaliers. He had been friends, even childhood playmates with Efrain. They, and others in their tent, had trained together, fought together, even hunted together. His brain was not able to understand this odd chain of events. Clearing his throat, and wiping away the tears streaming down his face, the young nobleman began his petition.

"Sir, few know better than I the gravity of Efrain's transgression. By our traditions and laws, you should have him tried and executed for crimes against the Military Code of Conduct. Nothing less than death is fit for the crimes at hand. I do not excuse, nor will I attempt to beg for leniency. But understanding the reason behind someone's actions is just as important as how they did something.

"During the standoff, he kept spouting nonsense about commoners plaguing the Army and how all Nobles will be offered up as a sacrifice in some great rebellion. As I am sure you know, many of the older houses feel this way. But to say that nearly eighty percent of the Military will rise in a coup is absurd. *This* is not the boy I grew up with. His words and actions seem strange, almost alien to me. Is there a way to help him?"

Liam's pleading looks passed from person to person, hoping for someone to aid him. His audience shared a knowing glance. They could testify how rare honesty and integrity were in anyone. That, coupled with the supplication for a friend, caused them all to pause. Subconsciously, Isaak rubbed his chin while the other lads became very interested in the dirt at their feet. After expressing thanks for his testimony, Isaak assured him that every consideration would be offered to the young nobles. A sad smile cracked across Liam's face.

With that, the bloodied leader dismissed the teens to their duties and retired to his tent. He had a lot to think about before the morning.

———◆———

Diamond specks of light populated the dark blue sky as the first stragglers of Gareth's military force arrived at camp. They were dust-covered and purely defeated.

Only a handful of the weaker bandits had been allowed to stay and prepare for the incoming troops and their prey. Campfires blazed, and food was cooked, while they awaited their leader's glorious return. They stayed busy, doing anything to put some distance between themselves and the infuriated female pacing in Gareth's tent. As well as the oddly cloaked man within.

With the majority of the force entering the camp begging for water, Senka tore out of Gareth's tent like a hurricane. Although she felt Efrain's defeat and subsequent capture, what truly had her ire up was the presence of a Shaman in the Temple. She wanted, no, lusted, to have that Shaman's head hanging from a pike outside her tent. Although she had sensed one with the gift earlier, the one that caused the ground to shake and erupt had to be a fully trained mage, with years of experience and power. Few contained that much skill in the arts, or so she thought.

A dark physical presence, fueled from years of wanting revenge, possessed the female pacing to and fro in front of the bandit leader's tent. Clinching her hands in rage, small bursts of energy spouted off her like a leaky hull. If she did not find a target soon, the whole camp would feel the deadly force of her magic. The only calm in her tumultuous storm was the stranger, who opted to stay with her.

The mysterious, yet powerfully built figure spoke a few words while they awaited the former soldier. Instead of prolonged conversation, he chose to meditate and cast a looking spell over the Temple and its inhabitants. He knew the truth of what had transpired but did not share with Senka. Leading the Lady of Shadow away from the returning bandits, they stood and watched the embodiment of defeat. Much to the Stranger's amusement, he saw the once proud bandit king reduced to a sun-burned husk, complete with a sword belt dragged behind him.

The five mile trek was nothing to the Desert Folk that ruled the sands and dunes. But, for Gareth and his lot, thirst and heat exhaustion had long set in their miserable hooks. The setting sun offered some peace as the desert cooled, but, to the defeated group, it did little to calm the hatred in their leader's heart.

Watching this ragtag group fight over water and cool clothes, the dark-robed man emitted a distasteful smile. He needed the strongest among them, and if they decided to attack each other like dogs on a bone, so be it.

Gareth pushed past the last of his men with force, with the sight of his tent giving him a surge of energy. Entering his abode, he stripped off his leather cuirass and pauldron. The cuirass, having dug into his burnt skin, was sent spinning through the air in a fit of rage. He had been defeated. The sting was made infinitely worse with the realization that students, *students,* were the cause. The full force of his downfall came crashing down into his soul, his fists colliding with the folding table, smashing it beyond repair. His broken table was flung out of the tent flap and hit an approaching guard, a savage yell bellowing from the tent.

A wild fury seethed within the hunched man as Senka and the Stranger entered the once immaculate enclosed pavilion.

"This was supposed to be easy," Gareth wailed, still hunched like a crazed animal. "Your little puppet was ordered to weaken their resolve, not strengthen it. And another thing," the bandit king continued, regaining his focus to a razor's edge. He wanted their heads. He wanted to win, but, of greater import, he wanted someone else to blame. "How in the blazes did they cause our mounts to lose their bloody minds?"

The Stranger smiled a wicked grin as Senka barked her responses. They became so consumed in their argument, they did not notice how the enigmatic man had poured himself a drink and now sat at leisure on Gareth's cot.

They are as petty as children, the reclining man thought as the verbal altercation was reaching its climax. Both participants had brandished weapons, and were about to attack, when a queer sound broke through the blood pumping in their ears and the volcanic anger in their hearts.

Leaning into a large down feather pillow, with his feet elevated on an extra set of Gareth's armor, the Stranger continued to clap at the theatrics display of childishness. "Now, before you two kill each other, how about we take a breath?" Two sets of icy glares fixated on him as he admonished them like children. "Please do not get me wrong," he said with his hands out front. "I have no desire to halt your little tantrum. It is, after all, quite amusing.

"However," he paused to take a sip, "if you two debutantes truly wish to obtain your goals, allow me the honor of helping you."

Any comments or snide remarks were squelched while the bickering duo were forcefully smashed to their hands and knees. An ungodly voice penetrated not just the tent, but into their very minds, as the still reclining man began to laugh maniacally.

"You both lack the power to fulfill your goals," his voice began, while raking through every hidden part of the soul. "You are weak, unruly, and short-sighted. I will allow you *this one chance* to feel true power and all the glory it holds. You see, I collect individuals with certain gifts and abilities.

"You," he venomously spat, shots of pain rippling through the bandit, "were nothing more than a reservist, hoping for a better life. Deserting your unit over some imagined slight, an entire unit died for you. Now you want to torture your former unit leader's son. Such childish whining is pathetic. You're just playing at being a king, like a child plays at being a man.

"You, sweet pouty child," Senka vomited as the force caressed her very spirit, "were excommunicated, cut off from the Shamans you long held in such high esteem. Your *sin*, if it can be called that, was desiring every bit of magic you could acquire. You prance and dance like a tavern wench in heat, weaving weak spells and dark charms. How could you ever be called the Lady of Shadow? Are you the Queen of the Dead? If you both are done wallowing in the mire of humanity, join me and become true forsaken!"

The voice and force dissipated like the morning dew as the kneeling couple shared a hungry look. The now standing Stranger smirked while they swore allegiance to him. Good, he thought, this makes a complete set.

❧ 15 ❧

An eagle's cry rang out as the second group of torches was lit by the night watch in the Temple. A rich, velvety sky offered the perfect cover for the bird of prey being used as a courier. The large-feathered flyer circled the walled camp several times before spotting the gloved hand of Isaak. The unit commander stepped out of his tent as soon as she screeched her arrival.

Normally, few of the marching soldiers would not care about a communiqué from the City of Tears. But the last twelve hours had not been normal. Much to the chagrin of the cooks, plates were dumped, or all out abandoned, as those eating took off like jackrabbits towards the messenger bird. Isaak, seeing the incoming horde of teenagers hastily approaching, decided to reenter his tent for his own safety, and the bird's. A wall of bodies quickly formed around the tent, anxiously awaiting any news.

Inside, the eagle preened in disinterest atop Isaak's cot. She cared not for military business, just the chance to rest her wings. The hanging oil lamp swayed, casting waves of light across the small table. Isaak, sitting on the three-legged folding stool, was shocked to see what lay in store for his unit. The eagle's message was odd indeed, but, on the off chance the unit leader's report had not reached the city, the enclosed orders had to be followed. As feelings of sadness and anger welled up again, he penned his response to the military council. Surely they were not able to overlook a bandit attack, as well as a coup in the ranks.

Giving his response a once over, and being satisfied with it, somewhat weathered hands rolled and sealed the paper. Like most of his profession, Isaak was not a man of letters. Any education on that front had been given during his stint in Battle School. The military saw the need to educate even the newest recruit to read and write. Long experience had taught them that poorly written intel was more damaging to a military force than no intel at all.

Elevating his very tired body out of the seat, Isaak woke the sleeping bird and enclosed the message in the tube tied to her foot. She angrily tried to dig in her talons but realized the half-hearted attack was not able to penetrate the armored-leather gauntlet. With a laugh, the leader opened the canvas flap to release the eagle and almost head-butted Tomas.

The youth's shock, and the jockeying for position throughout the ring of young men, was the last straw for the temperamental bird. Talons flashed and feathers flew as she tried to take off and escape the claustrophobic environment. Isaak, having no choice in the matter, pushed her off into the air. A cursed screech escaped the eagle as she circled the tents and left in a huff.

The flood of anxious eyes that had watched the eagle leave were now fixed on the middle-aged man holding a piece of parchment. Fear and excitement was shared by all, while a voice on the wall yelled, wanting to know what was happening.

True to form, and realizing he was about to have a riot on his hands, Isaak called his men to attention. Part of him laughed at the bated breaths and energy in the air. The lads seemed like children before a holiday.

"Men, stand to," he began, easing himself through the throng. "We have received intel that a massive group of desert tribesmen are heading this way. They are expected to arrive in two days' time. This attacking force will have one very simple objective: to take this Temple. Ours is harder still. We must defend her at all costs."

A ripple of laughter tore through the lads. The majority of them saw the tribesmen as nothing more than desert vagabonds. Free-loaders who the military allowed to stay in the wasteland no one wanted. Most had never seen a desert tribesman or the awesome power they possessed.

Isaak knew better than most the strength of the Blessed Ones. He explained the history of the exercise and how, for the last fifty years, the Fire Brand banner had been captured forty-seven times. This new information, along with the fact they were fifteen soldiers down, quickly choked off the laughter. The realization of the coming assault was beginning to take hold of each young man.

This was no unit of fellow soldiers or weak-hearted bandits. These were Masters of the Desert coming to defend their honor and home.

Smiling at the inexperience of youth, Isaak signaled all to follow him to the storehouse. By the time they reached the commander's former prison, a sober mood covered the Temple like a blanket . Opening the door, their leader pulled out a large wooden chest. He had Liam and Tomas pass out its contents. Meanwhile, he pulled on a large iron ring attached to the floorboards, and submerged into the depths beneath it.

One of the best things about the desert was its weather consistency. An underground cellar, such as the one below the Temple storehouse, was able to house large quantities of food, armor, and weapons without damaging the goods. The stone sub level had been built by the original engineers of the religious structure. It was eighty paces long by seventy paces wide. This made preparing for a siege not only possible but ideal.

After ensuring the steel and leather were free of rust and tears, Isaak surfaced to explain the coming exercise. Blunted weapons and steel armor were to be used in the young men's first real taste of siege warfare. Seeing the excitement buzzing on his troops' faces, the grizzled warrior could not help but smile. Swirling colors of blue and green took on a new shine as Isaak recalled his trial. Unfortunately, this was no time to reflect. There was work to be done.

Pressing the metal mouthpiece of a horn to his lips, a cold shrill ripped across the courtyard. The march leader needed the energetic, raw group focused and on point. Opening a cloth map of the Temple, the lean yet muscular man welcomed any ideas on how to defend their home base. A verbal avalanche of ideas rang out, causing the middle-aged man to smile. He knew how long and boring siege warfare was. Having these young men participate in the planning was the only way to keep them from flying off the handle later.

After two hours of piecing together ideas, and finally reaching a viable strategy, the lads were sent to their bunks. Dreams of victory and glory filled the Temple as the soldiers finally fell asleep.

Efrain, however, had no such delusions as he shifted his weight yet again, hoping to find some area on his body that was not sore or stiff.

The restraints had been loosen and retied several times since his capture. This would ensure no loss of limb from slowed circulation, or permanent nerve damage. A plate of bread and a sliced apple sat untouched next to him. Out of pride or ego, he refused to eat anything. As he flexed and strained against the leather straps, the nobleman was able to hear the commotion with the eagle and the subsequent planning. Knowing they had received their plans for this leg of the march, sadness stung his watery blue eyes and tinder heart. The desire to defend Dazmek and her citizens was real and deeply engrained in the prisoner. Such a betrayal the young man had never felt, nor could he fathom the lack of understanding from his peers.

Did they not see the truth? He continued to wallow in his fog of depression, with rage and self-doubt taking turns in this emotional dance. Never had Efrain felt so alone. Hundreds of miles from everything that gave comfort and stability, the isolation of the desert was taking its toll on the spiritually ragged sixteen-year-old.

The state of woe was forcibly exiled by a powerful focusing of the wiry lad's mind. Every physical sense became heightened as power surged through lean, youthful muscles. The soreness and pain were forgotten and healed as Efrain's body somehow strengthened itself. Rejuvenated muscled bulged against the leather strips, a desire for freedom almost overtaking him. Fiber by fiber, the restraints tore, getting Efrain closer and closer to success.

A soft call for patience tickled his mind as Efrain had nearly broken the raw hide strips in half. Confusion took center stage in the nobleman's young mind, for he wanted nothing more than to be free and be among his friends and fellows. A harsher demand for obedience tore through the connection with such force fear was the only emotion left in the mortal puppet. Pulling his knees to his chest, the teen sobbed pitifully as arcane lashes assaulted his resolve. How would he able to save his family, friends, and country from the coming devastation if he was tied up like a common criminal?

———◆———

In the privacy of his canvas abode, the Stranger glared at Senka and Gareth. For the second time, the puny teen had almost broken through the Dark Mage's pathetic attempts at soul weaving. Rich green orbs raged with deadly fury with each passing second. Soft as a Spring breeze, but corrosive as acid, the Stranger ordered a full disclosure of the kidnapping plan and what magic had been employed.

This time, there was no vomiting of information or petty blaming. Simple, informative answers were given, nothing more.

Behind lidded eyes, the true ruler of the bandit camp paced with leisure. The plan was simple and effective, if not crude and short-sighted. With his broad back turned to the latest in his collection, the powerful master of martial and arcane arts decided on a different approach.

"Our plan will not be felt across the land on its current course," the robed man explained. It was time for these pawns to understand what was at stake. "Gareth, round up your most trusted fighters and make for the coast. My ship awaits you. Leave your tents. Travel with light rations and water. The rest of the rabble will serve as a distraction for those seeking retribution for your bloodthirsty escapades."

The Stranger paused for a moment, as if to fit the last piece of the puzzle into place.

"The Captain will be vexed when you arrive. Say the title of Volshebec and the crew will set sail for a predetermined destination. There, your true training will begin."

Shock registered on Gareth's tan face as his blue eyes widened. Never had he abandoned a mission, much less one so close to fruition. Despite the fact that the man standing before had at least a hundred pounds of hardened muscle, and the grace of a killer, the thirty-five-year-old voiced his dislike of the plan. It was cowardice. Plain and simple.

A predatory grin slid across Volshebec's face. His massive frame turned to look into the eyes of the man that dared accuse him of being afraid.

"You doubt me, *Soldier?* What has your childish pursuit given you, boy? Once Senka arrived with her corrupted magic, you willingly sacrificed all those bandits for power and greed. I am merely requesting you do the same again."

The truthfulness of the statement stung Gareth deeply. Gold and land had never truly held a special place for him. The former field worker wanted power and the freedom that comes with it.

"My goal is at hand, *Mage.* What can you offer me *now,* besides a whisper of a promise?"

Knowing the smaller man before him would never be on equal footing with him, Volshebec nodded with a wicked sense of respect. It took guts to stand before one such as himself. The bandit had no advantages or skills that could best the male mage, and yet he dared to question. That type of inner strength could be tempered with the right amount of fear, so long as it was kept in check.

Tapping Gareth on the forehead, the powerfully-built arcane user smirked with glee. Golden light, full of radiance, poured out from the touched area and coated the bandit leader. A rapid series of breaths rattled from Gareth. His blue eyes rolled back until only the whites showed. The golden-hued energy coated every inch of the man, sinking under cloth and armor.

A growl, bestial and ancient, rumbled deep within the thirty-five-year-old. Something older than the land had taken hold of Gareth's soul and anchored itself deep within. Knowledge of tactics, fighting styles, war, and politics settled into his mind as his nerves and muscles flickered and twitched. The experience of an army's worth of soldiers was now ready to be utilized.

The sheer weight of the gift caused joints to buckle, and Gareth crumbled like a house of cards in a thunder storm.

Eyes green as the summer grass took in the bandit. Few could have survived such a transformation. Volshebec was glad he had not wasted the magic on a weakling.

"Once you gather yourself, my General, follow my instructions and such a life as you never imagined will be yours."

Staggering like a newborn foal, the empowered bandit departed the tent and began to choose an elite number for his assignment.

Jealousy was not an emotion Senka was accustomed to, and, as such, the female mage wondered what game this Volshebec was playing. Watching her partner in crime stumble into the night, she could not help but wonder what was in store for her. The lithe-built, brown-haired woman had never felt such concentrated power before. She would have died trying to perform such a feat. The name Volshebec felt familiar to the woman, like a rumor whispered in shadow. But, before Senka could make the connection, her attention was pulled elsewhere.

The male mage had begun to unfold a plan that was dastardly and cunning, with a final move that most game masters would never see coming. It would require patience, timing, and no small amount of power.

With each step explained, Senka's yellow eyes widened with excitement and lust. The road to her vengeance was going to be paved in blood and broken souls, and she was to begin right away.

———◆———

The next morning, the Temple became a chaotic mess of activity for the coming siege. Armor had to be shined and oiled. Leather ties needed to be trimmed or replaced. The swords, arrows, and spears had to be inspected for dullness, and even the slightest speck of rust. Isaak's unit took to their duties like ducks to water. An excitement bubbled up across the Temple in anticipation. Even those who had followed Efrain performed the more menial tasks of filling sand bags and water skins with a thankful heart. With those tasks well in hand, others prepared a mountain of torches and oil cloths. Isaak knew light was their greatest ally in the coming battle. If there was no place to hide, sneak attacks were nigh impossible.

Food and medical supplies had to also be stocked and inventoried. Cooks handed lunch off to the crews, as the meal had to be eaten on the move. By sunset, a cry was heard from the west wall. Isaak and the tent leaders ran up the stairs to see the outline of a lone rider in the midst of the setting sun.

The shadowy figure rode back and forth twice on the closest dune, as if to issue a challenge. With his horse rearing up on its hind legs, the rider blew a bone war horn. The Fire Brand leader swore. He knew what was about to transpire, and his troop was ill prepared. The rider's horn somehow conjured a massive number of desert people that seemed to materialize out of thin air.

The teenagers on the wall fell silent as a tomb while the giant horde marched towards the Temple. Any ideas or thoughts of the glory of battle turned to dust as their mouths dried up. In a menacing fashion, more horns echoed through the desert, calling what appeared to be an innumerable force to encircle the Temple completely. A deep booming voice cried out with authority as the mass ceased marching about fifty yards from the wall.

Tomas, unbeknownst to the others, had drawn and notched an arrow, ready to let it fly at the slightest whisper of trouble. Never had the teen seen such a force. A sense of dread filled the Southern clansman as he readied himself. If it had not been for Karniel grabbing the notched arrow, and breaking off the tip, Tomas would have dropped the approaching rider with an armor piercing arrow buried deep in his chest.

A white flag, bright and clean, unfurled in the hot desert wind as the rider approached within speaking range. His sixteen-year-old voice carried a serious, no nonsense tone. Thick with accent, he began his address.

"Fire Brand Commander, I have been chosen to convey the regrets of the Blessed Ones and the honorable Desert Lion. Our beloved game will have to wait until a matter of supreme importance is amended. Found not fifteen miles to the west, a small cluster of our people is dead, murdered in their homes. Honor demands we right this iniquity and grant them freedom to enter Paradise. You have been chosen to speak with the Desert Lion. Make ready for his arrival."

Having concluded his message, the teen spurred his horse and returned to his place in the swarm of warriors that surrounded the ruins.

Isaak, in true military hospitality, ordered a small pavilion erected in the center of the courtyard. Cooks ran to get fresh, cool water, some dried fruit, and cups for the visiting leader. Respect and honor was everything to the Blessed Ones and the Fire Brand Commander intended to keep the peace. Giving the pavilion a once over, he ordered the ranks stand at attention in the courtyard and on the wall. All would face the archway as the Desert Lion entered. None of the young men on the march truly understood the honor bestowed on them, for this great leader rarely spoke to anyone outside of his people.

Isaak felt a little out of sorts, having to meet such a leader in plain marching armor. Cleaning himself and his armor as best he could, the Army leader ordered the south gates be opened for the soon to arrive guests. In no way could they afford to offend the gathering of battle hardened fighters, hell-bent on a swift and bloody justice.

Hooves thundered across the hardened sand and a small detachment of riders entered the temple. Ten strong, cream-colored horses came to a halt a few feet from the pavilion. Each rider bore a blue robe with an embroiled fang on his chest. They were the Lion's Fangs, the personal protectors of the Desert Lion. The riders dismounted in two rows of five, drawing their swords in a salute, while a lean, pure black horse proudly cantered into the awaiting courtyard. It was adorned with tassels along the reins, with thin silver letters embossed along the leather saddle.

His rider was another story entirely. Light blue linen robes created an air of wisdom and power yet kindness and good nature. Snow white hair was held in place by a keffiyeh with a beaded band. Soft leather boots sounded as the Desert leader dismounted and saluted all within the walls with a jovial smile and a wave. Moving with strength and purpose, the longest living leader of the Blessed Ones headed for Isaak and the pavilion. The sound of steel sliding home sounded every time he passed his personal guards.

The smile widened on Isaak's face with each step of his guest. It had been many years since their last meeting and that had been quite interesting. Honor and ceremony was just as important to the Fire Brand Army as it was to the Blessed Ones. The hosting leader opened his hands wide with the final step of the visiting leader. Clasping each other's forearms, they each promised peace while the talks began.

The Desert Lion groaned slightly as he eased into the folding chair. "Oh Fire Brand," the older man spoke, "I will miss our games this year." He plucked a date and began to chew.

Isaak smirked and responded with a puzzling look. "We stand ready to meet you and yours on the field of honorable battle, my Lord Ashur."

A gasp trumpeted from the ten honor guards at such a breach in etiquette. No one was allowed to address the Desert Lion in such an informal way, especially not some lowly captain of untested boys.

Ashur's risen hand silenced any potential outbursts. "'Tis true it would have been a remembered fight. Why, I can remember a young, brash soldier who outsmarted not only my people, but his as well. If memory serves, that was the last time your battle flag was seen."

Raising a cup in honor, Isaak took a sip, as if to acknowledge some hidden truth.

"Alas, the Gods of Sky and Sand demand we avenge our fallen loved ones with extreme prejudice," the white-haired leader continued with an air of sadness. "Men die in battle, this is honorable. But to slaughter women and children in their sleep is a blight against the very Gods that give life." A pure fire blazed in Ashur's creamy yellow eyes, while he described in detail the burnt tents and mutilated bodies found by his scouts.

The sheer description was such that two of Isaak's young men broke ranks and retched against the wall. Even in the halls of the Battle School, there was a code taught to protect all women, children, and non-combatants. War was violent, but soldiers were to hold themselves to a higher code of conduct.

The Fire Brand unit commander offered his condolences and support in the enterprise of hunting down the filthy vermin. Soldiering was one thing, as both parties tend to understand the obligation of violence. But murder, well, there was no forgiveness for that crime.

With gratitude, the Desert Lion declined the offer. According to their traditions, they alone were responsible for bringing the offenders to justice. Isaak's unit understood the desire for vengeance and restitution. If the Desert People had accepted their leader's offer, each lad would have gladly helped.

A polite smile radiated from Ashur as he surveyed the refreshments. "It is so rare to find someone accustomed with our ways, Fire Brand. How, pray tell, did you know the way to welcome us?"

Isaak took a turn to smile, albeit slightly puckish. "Oh, about fifteen years ago, I was captured in a siege battle here. One of your people, a very honorable Leopard, tended to my broken wrist. As you say, my Lord Ashur, it was truly a remembered fight. I seem to recall, in the heat of battle, your company somehow misplacing our battle flag as well," the march leader teased in the way old soldiers do at times.

Both surprise and realization danced across the white-haired man's face. His jaw dropped in shock, as if he was seeing his host for the first time. "So you were the one that earned the title Elam, the Vanishing One. I have spent years pondering how you were able to not only retrieve your flag, but you gained ours and my very independent niece," Ashur said pointedly.

That siege had been the only spot on his rather successful tenure as the Desert Lion. The legend of the Elam had gained much notoriety throughout the tribes. Never had there been a more thrilling tale of an ordinary man that performed extraordinary feats. Such grand stories were used by the Desert tribes to educate and inspire the younger generation to become better than the last.

Feeling not only the looks of his own troops, but of the honor guard as well, Isaak blushed a little at the praise. Being a true soldier, he never saw the need for expecting attention or praise for doing one's job. It was to be expected, and so he performed to the upmost.

Ashur's admiration of Isaak grew while watching his reactions. A healthy dose of true humility was imperative for a leader, and the man sitting across from him had the making of a great one. It was the Blessed Ones' tradition that leaders were not to seek praise or fame of the world, but to serve the people and protect all in righteousness. This was the main reason why most of the desert people did not venture into the lands to the south. Politicking and dishonorable deals were against their way of life.

Regret echoed in the Desert leader's voice. "I wish we could have met under different circumstance. Alas, the time for pleasantries is over. On behalf of my people, I ask that you and your sons stay within the Temple and not interfere. If we chase any of the bandits here, then by all means, protect yourselves. We aim to kill them, down to the last man. Offer none of your countrymen asylum."

The coldness of those last words washed over Isaak as they both rose and clasped each other's arms. Ashur's honor guards were already saddled and ready before their leader reached his horse. With one foot in a stirrup, Ashur swung his right leg over his mount with the ease of a man twenty years his junior. "If the Gods permit," he offered in passing, "mayhap we can continue our game."

With a salute, Ashur produced a small coiled silver horn. Three notes announced not only the Lion's departure, but the mobilization of the desert army. The Fire Brand soldiers shouted their own battle cries, to lend power and strength to the departing allies. Liam, Tomas, and Karniel arrived at their leader's side atop the wall in time to see the heavy archway door seal close the southern gate. Ten young men were called to place a heavy cross beam into braces on the back of the door, locking it in place.

Isaak, his troops knew, would offer no quarter to those who killed innocent people, especially bandits.

Unable to keep his inquiries to himself any longer, Tomas, quite impishly, rested his arm across Isaak's shoulders. "So tell me," he playfully began, "you stole our banner, their banner, and their leader's niece? How in the blazes are you still alive?"

His playful tone died with the look Isaak gave him. Dropping his arm and backing away, Tomas offered his apologies. Karniel, cuffing Tomas on the back of the head, looked at Liam with an exasperated gaze.

Knowing the jest was not meant to insult, Isaak answered, but his soul seemed a thousand miles away. "If you must know, she became my wife, and yes, I still have both battle standards. Would you three please see to the pavilion, and have the others return to their allotted duties?"

With that, Isaak followed the progression of the tribal army, taking in every detail. Part of him wanted to follow them into battle. There was a purity to the Blessed Ones' way of life, and it gave the Fire Brand leader the most precious of all life's gifts.

So lost was Isaak in his internal struggle that he did not hear the three young soldiers salute and leave.

The three youth had everyone disperse and return to duty. The cooks returned the uneaten fruit to storage and used the water for the soup they were preparing. Karniel, berating Tomas for his foolishness, untied the ropes of the pavilion and gathered the hammered stakes. Any retort from Tomas was muffled as the cloth tent slammed into his face. Sensing the bickering would not stop, Liam pulled them both aside and rehearsed to them the story Isaak had told him earlier.

Each took turns seeing their leader in a new light and realization that the life of a soldier was froth with heartache, pain, and loss. Such were the costs that befall those willing to sacrifice their lives for the protection of a nation.

16

The Desert Lion swore loudly against the insufferable wind. His horse, experienced in battle and weather, refused to move one more step. Dark clouds converged on the horizon as soon as they departed the Temple. The churning storm seemed to devour every star and light in the sky. The closer they got to the bandit camp, the more dangerous the weather became. Yellow and green lightning flickered like a viper's tongue across the sky. Claps of thunder deafened all in the area, making verbal communication all but impossible.

Feeling his mount's muscles lock in place, the Desert Lion looked up and down the battle line. Frustration caused his teeth to grind as his whole party came to a halt. Many had dismounted, attempting to coax or lead their mounts. Offering a petition to the Gods above, Ashur saw the clouds swirling like a whirlpool. With each pass, the wind became increasingly more powerful, kicking up a swell of sand. So forceful were the passes that grains of sand began cutting through fabric and flesh. Heavy scarves and rawhide bucklers offered little protection from the unnatural brutality of the storm.

Seeing there was nothing for it, Ashur called for a massive retreat. He dared one final look towards the bandits' camp. Fear seized his heart as Volshebec appeared to materialize from nothing, standing at the eye of the storm.

Blackened steel armor absorbed any celestial light as lightning escaped his outstretched, gauntleted fingers. Bright as blood, the sigil on the chest plate warned all of the impending doom. A heavy spiked mace hung loose at his side, thirsty for death. Looking dead in the desert leader's eyes, the powerful mage smiled. He knew the old legends and what had been prophesied.

Terror rippled through the air as Ashur's mount came alive and sprinted away. For the first time in his life, dread commanded the Desert Lion. The

Forsaken had returned, he thought as he caught up to his people, just as the stories had foretold.

The unnatural storm raged all night long and nipped at the heels of the retreating horses. The sand stung their flanks like a whip. The speed of the retreating force did not seem to affect the dogged clouds. By the time they finally reach the great stone Temple, no torches were ablaze, nor was there a watchman to be seen. The defeated force decided to take shelter on the opposite side of the powerfully-built stone structure, hoping to cut some of the strength behind the sand and wind. Quickly forming a black mass of thick horse blankets, the Desert Tribesmen covered not only themselves, but their animals as well. Prayers were uttered as reins were tightly grasped.

At the hour the morning sun would normally shine brightly, the dark swirling clouds began to ease and disintegrate. The landscape surrounding the Temple had changed drastically overnight. On the north side of the Temple, a wall of sand and dirt had created something of a natural incline. It stood eighteen feet tall at its highest peak, and stretched the entire length of the wall. The pile had become so compacted that a full grown man was able to walk up and down the embankment and be fully supported.

Thirty-six horses had died during the storm from sand suffocation. Each one was a cherished partner to a very powerful tribesman. Wailing was heard throughout the area as their riders bid farewell to their beloved horses. A spirit of mourning passed over the tribes as thick pelt and canvass tents were erected in the Temple's shadow. Never had any of them seen or even heard of such a storm as they had the night before. Some of the Elders wondered at its meaning, and if the Gods had turned on them.

Once the community of tents was erected, Ashur called together all the heads of the tribes and the societies. Privately, he wondered if anyone else had seen the armor-clad being, or if his fears had played a cruel joke on him. His ponderous mood became infectious upon all who entered the leader's tent. One by one, the leaders from the Elders, Hawks, Leopards, Serpents, and Scorpions entered the spacious dwelling. By the time the last war leader arrived, few words had actually been spoken.

Cups of coffee, wine, and water had been offered to all attending. Normally, Ashur's wife would have had that honor, as her voice was always welcome in council. The Lioness had other matters to attend to, as her station was one of comfort in times of need. This time, however, the Desert Lion, himself, personally poured the cups and welcomed his guests.

Eirini, a thin but tall-framed man, leader of the Water Seekers, ducked under the tent flap and dusted off his thick riding robe. A moist cloth was offered for his face and hands, as was customary for a family member. He graciously accepted, battling to control the shock of being tended to by his nation's leader. Such violations of protocol were unheard of among the Blessed Ones. Discreetly eyeing the other guests, the Water Seeker could see their shock as well. Clearing his voice, the younger man spoke to his elder leader, in a matter of familiarity.

"Peace unto you and yours this day, Ashur," he said with a slight incline of his head. "I hope you have brought us here to explain what happened."

Normally the Water Seekers brokered peace and harmony, but the calm accusation caused the leaders of the Leopards, Hawks, and Serpent societies to jump to their feet. They began yelling and blaming each other for the previous night's failure. A shadow of a grin passed over the ambitious accuser's face. He had never liked his uncle, the famous Ashur, or his well-earned reputation. Old offenses and perceived mockeries crept to the forefront of the minds gathered as the young Water Seeker positioned himself in the desert leader's seat at the head of the low laying table. With chaos growing with each yell or angry gesture, they looked to the very man who had caused the argument for justification.

The Water Seeker leader's smug basking in the lime light was short lived, however, as a trumpet sounded so loud everyone present had to cover their ears. A look of disgust radiated on Ashur's face. So fierce was his scowl that the once angered leaders sat down like punished children. Everyone knew who had the real power over the people and none of those present were stupid enough to anger their caring leader.

Hands still shaking with fury, Ashur took a calming breath and a drink of water, allowing the cool liquid to relax not only his throat but his soul. He needed them to focus and act with one mind, not like angry children stomping about. If the enemy had returned, it would spell ruin for everyone, not just them, but the nation to the south as well.

Pacing to vent off some of his irritation, the Desert Lion expressed his gratefulness for them coming. He verbalized his regret and sympathies to those who had suffered loss. Now that he had their attention, the crucial part of the meeting could be addressed. The tent seemed to grow colder as he relayed his experience in the storm and the being he saw at its center. Alarm captured the leaders, and many downed a glass of wine to calm their fears. All knew of the ancient evil, and what form it would take, but they had hoped to never see it personified in their lifetime.

Eirini sighed and swirled his drink before speaking. "My dear fellow leaders, surely you do not believe in that old ghost story. There is no proof of such a being, and if there were, why would he return now? Yes, the storm was unnatural, but it could have been the Gods enacting revenge on our behalf. For all we know, the bandits were completely destroyed and our minor losses were just that, minor."

The logic of his words seemed to, in part at least, calm the company. The older leaders knew better than to believe the charming words of ambition. Over half looked to Ashur to continue his report. They not only believed in their society's traditions, but had an understanding that came with experience.

"If the storm was truly the work of the Gods," Ashur rebutted, "why did it follow us like a slave driver? How is it that only certain leaders were stricken with loses while others were untouched? In my nearly thirty years as leader, I have never seen such a powerful event. Scoff what you will, child, but do not make a mockery of our beliefs." Decades of loss and experience energized his words. He had faith that the Gods of Sky and Sand would protect them, so long as they showed proper respect.

Eirini's demeanor was that of a pouty child during the rest of the meeting. No one even looked in his direction or asked for his opinion.

The Hawks offered to ride out and contact the remaining clans throughout the desert, and the three port cities along the coast. The Leopards offered to send a patrol to scout out the bandit camp, to make sure the murderers were indeed dead. The scouting patrol, however, was rejected, since it was still not sure if the Forsaken were close by. They were given the honor of aiding the Lion's Fangs with protecting Ashur and the rest of the tribal leadership. The Scorpions and the Serpents had already set up a defensive perimeter around the camp, so their task was to maintain it.

Satisfied that everyone had a plan, and duties to keep them active, Ashur thanked them once again and ushered them out. The Water Seeker chose to stay behind, still sitting in Ashur's seat. Seeing this out of the corner of his eye while gathering up the cups and pitchers, the Desert Lion felt amused at the small act of defiance. He knew the Water Seekers were seen as weak or even useless to the other societies. In truth, he used to see them that way, too, but with the coming calamity, he sensed they would come into their own.

Putting the dishes on a small table, Ashur turned and eased his body onto a pile of pillows at the foot of the table facing Eirini. The younger leader, crossing his arms and closing his eyes, still refused to acknowledge the older man's presence.

A rich laugh burst forth from Ashur. "My boy," he began in an eased tone, "I get that you wish to lead. There is nothing wrong with that desire, if it is reined in and used to help your fellows. What happened to that fiery boy who was destined to lead our people into the future?"

Watery blue eyes opened and seemed to calculate a response. "They see me as less than they are," the Water Seeker said in a flat tone. "They will never see me as an equal. In my youth, I fought harder, ran faster, and did more than any of them. Now that I am the youngest Water Seeker to ever hold the title of Peacekeeper, they look down at me."

Ashur, rising from his reclined position, stepped up to and knelt before the young man. Enclosing his hand in Eirini's, the Desert Lion swore to his fellow leader that their people needed him now more than ever. They were hurt, ashamed, and beaten. Many leaders had forgotten the ability of asking for help. And, as tempers were sure to fly, they would look to the young man for guidance in such a troubled time.

His words seemed to reach the Water Seeker, as he felt ashamed for his actions and apologized. They embraced as family and Eirini departed to tend to his duties. The older man was soon left alone with his thoughts, worried about what to do next.

———————◆·———————

Isaak came to as he felt someone shake him. His legs felt stiff and sore from sitting on the wooden steps of the sub level all night. Reaching to retrieve his fallen prayer beads, the Fire Brand leader felt his back pop and crackle. A chuckle pulled the older man's attention to his left. A steaming cup of coffee met his gaze, and he accepted the warm liquid with appreciation.

The Fire Brand leader had pulled his sentries long before Ashur's people had reached the Temple. He did not need Shaman training to know the incoming storm was magical in nature. Feeling the unholy power in the air, Isaak realized the canvas tents would not hold up to the abuse that was coming their way.

Ordering everyone into the stone cellar, as the winds picked up and the sky darkened, Isaak knew it was their only hope for protection. With the food and water stored there, they could last a couple days if need be. After counting all his troops, and sealing the hatch behind him, the march commander eased himself down and took up a sentry position on the steps. Silently pleading to the Gods for the well-being of his charges, callused fingers worked a string of prayer beads as prayers were recited to appease the forces of eternity.

Tomas had volunteered to wake their dozing leader. He respected the man for his willingness to stand guard over them during the storm. With the exception of his da, Tomas had never seen such a protective leader before. The youth's admiration for his captain grew during the night as whispered conversations were shared about Isaak and his past. Even the imprisoned nobles had something good to add about their leader.

According to the barrack gossip, Isaak had been an exceptional youth. He was made unit leader while still in the recruiting process, and led his Battle School year in both personal merits and mock battles. Once his year's march was complete, the four training schools each offered him a place among their ranks. His legend grew with each day, until that fateful attack in the Salt Marshes. Galvanized by both pain and hatred, he rallied the remainder of his unit and killed every bandit that dared cross his path.

The Fire Brand Inner Circle, so impressed with the young man, offered him a commission as Regional Captain over the Marshes. They even traveled the two hundred and eighty miles to personally award him their highest honor: the Diamond Dragon for bravery and selfless sacrifice in the face of insurmountable odds. Much pomp and celebration came afterwards, but Isaak chose to move closer to the desert, to be nearer to his wife's people.

Such tales lasted into the wee hours of the morning, each one more fantastical than the last. Soon after, the whistling wind and rocking lamplight created an almost wave-rocking atmosphere. Sleep overtook the lads as Isaak kept watch with his pray beads slowly circling in his hand.

With the coming of dawn, and the end of the storm, food had to be prepared and someone had to peak out and see the damage it had caused. Without so much as a by-your-leave, Tomas scurried up the ladder right past Isaak, excited, like a child at their first faire. Planting his feet, and bending his knees, the Southern jokester grunted with exertion, as the wooden door was heavier than before. The hatch finally gave way and sunshine and sand poured into the cellar.

The scene that filled Tomas eyes brought him to silence. The wind, spinning off the thick interior stone walls, had knocked over the small ramshackle storehouse. The tents were in a twisted mess in the Northeast corner, almost completely buried in sand. The wooden practice men were caked with dirt, while the latrine somehow survived with a mere three feet of dirt piled in front of its door.

Those who had finished eating followed Tomas out of their underground vault, pausing after a few paces because of the damage. A ring formed around the cellar, the lads unsure of what to do first. Isaak, nursing another fresh cup of coffee, organized the tent leaders into work shifts. Each tent had to retrieve, clean, and pitch their tent, clean off one of the practice men, and shovel the dirt over the side of the west wall.

Moans and groans sounded, but the lads got to it once they felt Isaak's icy stare. The Fire Brand leader walked along the wall, making a full circuit, to ensure no one slacked off. The cooks had chosen to stay in the cellar with Efrain. The fourteen other young nobles were given the delightful task of cleaning the latrine. It took three hours of hard cleaning to restore the Temple to her former glory.

Isaak had ordered the archway doors opened. He had seen the enormous Desert Tribe camp during his walks around the Temple. Unsure why they were still there, Isaak thought it wise to send an envoy to Ashur. That way he would be able to petition an audience and find out what had happened. Mulling over those in his command, a smile creased his face. He needed someone observant, yet respectful, smart, yet not easily shocked. He knew just the young man for the job.

———◦———

Karniel felt like an idiot, dressed like a military officer. His field promotion to Fire Brand Envoy was so quick he had no time to refuse. Isaak had him carry the army banner and a shield, as a sign of peace, but they were so awkward the lad spent most of his time balancing them. He met a young man named Eirini at the edge of the camp and was ordered to follow his long strides. Karniel was sure the robed tribesman wanted Karniel to trip and fall, as each twist and turn became increasing harder to maneuver. During one tight corner between a tent and a pile of horse muck, the military envoy swore he saw a smirk flash across the face of his guide.

After what seemed like forever, they arrived at a massive tent, guarded by four sets of heavily-armored warriors. Karniel swallowed hard, his nerves abandoning his reason. Each guard stood ready to attack, appearing to collectively weigh the soul of the youth. Sweat poured down his back as each second passed. Blood pumped in his ears. The sound was so loud he could not hear the Water Seeker talking to him.

"Fire Brand!" The crisp command bounced around the enclosure, catching everyone's attention. Eirini relished in belittling the guest, his heart continuing to harden over what had happened with his sister.

Karniel almost dropped the banner as he quickly tried to regain composure. Things were not looking well for the young envoy and, with each passing moment, he felt even more foolish.

"I said we are here. Were you listening or gawking?" The Water Seeker's tone was caked with condescension and disgust. Karniel's very presence seemed to insult the tall, wiry man.

Heat waves steamed off the Fire Brand soldier's face. He had not heard a word and now was deep in the Tribesmen's camp. Even the horses seemed to be eyeing him with a disapproving glare. "Right," Karniel said, displaying a false sense of readiness. "If this is the Desert Lion's tent, then I thank you for your honorable guidance. I await the Desert Lion's grace."

Eirini was not prepared to be addressed in such a formal way. Those words were reserved for clan or society leaders, and he was never treated as such. Feeling somewhat shameful that he had tried to make the lad look like a fool, the tribesman parted the tent flaps and signaled Karniel to enter. A look of shocked amusement filled Eirini's face as he followed the envoy inside and let go of the flap.

Those near the surrounding tents were shocked to see the politeness of Karniel. An elderly man, tending to Ashur's horse, commented that it was wasted on the arrogant guide. Very few of them liked Eirini. He seemed content on causing problems and then fixing them. This backhanded way of obtaining power soured the value placed on the peace brokers. That was why most did not see the Water Seeker as equal to any leader. But here a Fire Brand had offered the smug young man such honor. Maybe they should do so as well.

Karniel's eyes needed a moment to adjust to the dim interior of the tent. The sound of liquid being poured caused the lad to lick his lips in spite of himself. The armor was burdensome and offered little chance for his body to stay cool. He felt shocked as Ashur came into view and embraced him in a hug and kissed both his cheeks. The southern young man's stiffened back and locked joints were not sure if they were going to attack or run. His discomfort tapered a little when Eirini broke into a fit of laughing.

"I told you he would freeze like a hunted deer," the younger desert tribesmen said as he doubled over. He slapped his leg and spilled some of his cup's contents on the lush blue robes of his office.

Anger threatened to boil up in Karniel and get the better of him. He had at least sixty pounds of muscle and years of hard training on the laughing man. Knuckles cracked with force as his strong hands balled up ready to smash the man's face.

"That is all, Eirini. You can go." The request came from behind the infuriated youth. Ashur had walked passed Karniel to open the canvass flap as the amused man bowed and exited. Ashur, releasing the flap, allowed the tent to return to a dimly lit arena. Bowing his head, the Desert Lion handed Karniel a cup of cold water and signaled for him to sit at the right side of the head of the short table.

"I must apologize for the rudeness of my nephew," Ashur commented, sitting on two horse hair pillows. "Ever since his sister left us, his attitude has been poor indeed."

Not trusting himself to speak, the youth only nodded in reply. His anger was still present, but was abating as the Desert Lion spoke. There was something in the older man's manner that reminded Karniel of Zuwl, and, just like that, anger was replaced with sadness.

Touching the gold braid on the Fire Brand uniform, Ashur laughed in a teasing way. "Such finery is not worn by us. It has no purpose in battle and could be pulled or snagged on a weapon." His comment was not meant to be rude but to gauge the type of man across from him.

The teen's eyes looked at the braid with little interest. It was true it had no function, and, since he had not earned it, it felt foolish to have on a uniform. "To be honest, Sir, I just got the promotion and am still getting accustomed to all it involves."

The honesty of Karniel struck a chord with Ashur. Having met with several high-ranking army personal most of his long life, the white-haired, yellow-eyed man found the lack of ego a refreshing change of pace. Only one or two of the southern army officers had the intelligence to honor the Desert people's customs and traditions. Smiling, Ashur found himself warming to the youth.

"I would be honored if you call me Ashur, as it is my birth name. How are you called, Sir Envoy?"

The teasing question caused the last of Karniel's anger to vanish. "My name is Karniel of the Red Keep. To be more accurate, its poor alleyways. As for the 'Sir' I have not earned that title, so Karniel will be fine."

"Well, you seem to be moving up in the world, Karniel," Ashur responded in kind. "You should be proud of all you have accomplished. Now, drink up. Negotiating is a thirsty business."

For the next hour, the midday sun tried to claw its way into the tent and ruin the peace talks, but to no avail. They shared all the information on what had happened the night before. Karniel did grow quiet during the description of the Forsaken. He had seen armor like that before in a dream, but not since his adopted father's death. A sense of foreboding slithered its way into the rest of the conversation as a peace was brokered between the two armies.

Before they rose from the floor, Karniel had one final inquiry. "Why did you give me a hug and kiss me on the cheeks?"

A playful twinkle sparkled in Ashur's eyes. "It was a twofold gamble. On the one hand, it is the traditional greeting of peace between families, and since you represent my niece's husband, it is expected. On the other, I needed to see how you would react to both the greeting and my rude nephew. Your army has a history of attacking without reason, and I needed to know if you were one of those foolish men who see an insult where none exist."

As they walked to the exit of the tent, the logic appealed to Karniel's sense of fair play. If he was in Ashur's place, he would have done the same thing. Before departing, Karniel told the desert leader Isaak wanted to meet with him, that day if at all possible. A puzzled look appeared on Ashur's face at the request. With a shrug, all the youth was able to say was that it involved a personal matter. As soon as Ashur agreed, Karniel saluted and headed back towards the Temple, carrying the banner and shield.

As the departing youth vanished in the throng of people, the Desert Lion wondered about his future meeting with Isaak. Alas, such things had to wait, for two very angry looking Leopards were heading his direction fully armed. With a sigh, and an eye roll to the heavens, he parted the tent flap for his new guests and prepared himself for a verbal barrage.

🔥17🔥

Karniel mentally praised the Gods as he was allowed to remove the bulky, thick uniform. Even though the wind had been heated by the sun, turning it hot, it felt nice and cool against his soaked shirt. A crowd of his fellow soldiers encircled him the moment he entered the Temple. Everyone lobbed questions so quickly the youth felt like he was being interrogated. No sooner had he answered one, two more entered the fray. Yelling at the top of his lungs, Karniel shouted for them all to stop.

"Don't you lads have something better to do," Isaak asked, walking up to the mob. "If everyone has completed their duties, then I am sure an inspection of grip and gear is in order."

The lads scattered like rats abandoning a ship at the sound of the veiled threat. Armor had not been tended to, as they had been busy restoring the Temple and rebuilding the storeroom. A failed inspection meant running around the Temple, or digging and filling holes for hours, and no one wanted that.

Seeing they were alone, Isaak picked up the uniform coat and dusted it off. In his hurry to be free of its confinements, Karniel had dropped it, not even thinking that it was borrowed. A sheepish grin appeared on the lad's face, not sure what his commanding officer was about to do.

"I never saw the reason for such a thick uniform," the older man said as he inspected the coat, ignoring the fact it was dirty. "They are hot, bulky, and make a person look like one of those iron soldiers sold during festivals. I am glad you were able to fit. Your shoulders are much broader than mine. I don't know who left it in the cellar, but they must have been a giant of a man."

Breath escaped Karniel's lungs that he was not aware he was holding. Thanking his leader for the use of the uniform, he began his detailed report on the guard movements, the number of tents he had seen, and the overall attitude of the camp. Even Ashur's odd greeting was mentioned, but only in passing.

Isaak, looking past Karniel towards the small town of tents, and smiled at the cleverness of Ashur's gambit. The Desert Tribes were renowned for their shrewd business dealings and cunning strategies. The mention of Eirini's attitude and treatment of the youth bothered the unit commander a lot. He knew his wife's brother was angry over her choosing a southerner, but he had hoped those feelings would have lessened with time.

With Karniel reaching the end of his report, Isaak permitted him to get cleaned up and return to his normal duties. As the lad headed for his tent, Isaak singled out each of the other tent leaders in the courtyard and called them to him. Ordering them all to stay within the thick stone walls, their commanding officer explained he was going to secure peace with the visiting tribes. One of tent leaders asked if they could at least have a look out on the wall, but Isaak gave a negative answer. Such actions showed a lack of faith in a truce and that was not needed here.

After he got assurance from each of them, he left a heavy threat in the air. No one was allowed to speak or visit with Efrain until he returned. The emotionless pools in his eyes chilled them into compliance. With that well in hand, he headed to council with Ashur.

Sharp memories of his wife began to bubble to the surface the moment the massive gates closed loudly behind Isaak. As he passed the thick pelt tents, he felt the pain and love he had experienced all those years ago. Without thinking, he allowed his fingers to graze the rough animal hair on the passing tent. That action conjured up the most vivid of images of the day he met his wife.

Screams vomited from the Fire Brand youth as a group of tribesmen held him down to set his broken wrist. Two bones had been severely damaged by the Scorpion's spear, but, praise be, they were able to heal the youth and stabilize the injury. A female medic coaxed him into drinking a tonic for the pain. Quickly, the effects took hold of Isaak and he was carried to a tent deep in the Blessed Ones' camp.

He was still able to hear the cries to arms of his fellow soldiers, even in the middle of the opponent camp. His soul ached to rejoin the fray. Never had he felt more alive. Never was his purpose clearer. The lad's body had other desires than fighting. A strong, sweet temptation for sleep clouded his mind and lulled him into a false sense of peace.

The battle lasted well into the evening. Both sides were drained of both soldiers and energy by the time the moon rose to control the dark cobalt heavens. The Fire Brand Army thanked the war god for the full moon that illuminated even the darkest of corners. This stroke of good fortune allowed them to save the torches for a darker night, while being able to see exactly what was happening in the attacking force's camp.

Medics within the Temple tended to both fighter and prisoner alike. Traditions and rules of engagement allowed for the healers to not be harmed, as it was not their place to fight. Balms, ointments, and tonics were handed out as fast as they were found, the wounded now reaching forty-three in total. Luckily, only one of theirs had been captured.

The Blessed Ones' attacking force faired better than their opponent. Only eight were truly injured, but four of their number were held prisoner. Battle plans were concocted over meals in the main tent as leaders had their societies repair armor and replace broken weapons. A soft snore produced an eye roll from Eirini, that year's leader. They had to move the captured soldier into the main tent after four botched attempts had been tried to rescue him.

Rolling up a cloth map of the Temple, Eirini remarked snidely about the true nature of the southern women. Everyone but the Leopards laughed at the crude joke. Winning the prideful leader's favor was a quick way for the tribal youth to move through the ranks since the desert people allowed their youth to command every aspect of the attack. Most of the Desert Lion's personal guard were a few yards away in case something went array.

As the voices left the tent to resume the offensive, Isaak opened his eyes. He had been awake for most of the meeting and learned a great deal about their mentality. Inch by inch, he eased from an inclined position to a sitting one. The pain in his wrist was dull, but he lacked full range of motion. Softly, his feet touched the carpeted floor. He put his full weight on them and stood, only to be met with a shock.

A slender dagger came to an abrupt stop, just short of his feet. The blade was no more than five inches long and maybe an inch thick. It had been designed for one single deadly purpose: silencing sentries.

Bending to grip the bone handle, the Fire Brand lad laughed. "Had I jumped, you would have another wound to clean," he said, handing the blade back.

A lithe-framed girl came into view. Her cinnamon-colored hair had been pulled back by a thin leather cord. Her eyes, guarded in shadow, had watched the young man and knew he was not asleep. Even though a mere three paces separated them, she did not move. She had heard stories of Fire Brand soldiers mistreating females. Her gloved hand pointed at the paper-covered table and demanded he set it down there.

His left hand went up slowly, palm up, signaling he meant no harm. The knife-wielding hand placed the dagger on the table and slid it out of range.

"I will not hurt you, nor could I if I tried," he said, signaling to his hurt wrist and acknowledging the liquid medicine in his system.

The serenity in his voice confused her. Being a good judge of character, the lithe desert girl was at odds with herself. Was she able to trust him? Was he as bad as the others in years past? Several more such questions riddled her brain as she tried to get a bead on the young man before her.

Any discussion was a moot point as Isaak had tied his hands and feet with a length of rope next to his makeshift bed. Bewilderment and wonder filled her as she questioned her prisoner.

"What has possessed you to tie yourself up?" Chadia demanded, utterly confused.

"Well, it's obvious you do not trust me, so I propose a game of wits. If you fail to answer correctly, one of the lengths gets cut. If you stump me, then you get to add a length. This way you feel secure and I have a fair advantage. What do you say?"

The charm and wit of the lad won her over and their epic battle commenced.

Most of the night, the two teenagers went from adversaries to fast friends. Isaak was amazed by the quick wit and sharp mind of his guard. Many a lass had tried to woo the handsome lad, but the air-headedness and haughty behavior was a very definitive turn off. For the first time in his life, he had found an equal in every sense of the word.

Chadia quickly fell under the Fire Brand soldier's spell. True, he was good looking, but his gentle nature and respect for her were like a cold drink of water after a long run in the wasteland. Most of her unit, the Leopards, saw her as either a girl to bed or Eirini's little sister. Only her fellow sisters in arms showed her the proper dues, but this intelligent, bright young man could be the male she had been looking for.

Together, they hatched a devious plan to not only win the battle, but to thumb their noses at the military system in general. Since all wounded had to be returned to the City of Tears for evaluations, Isaak volunteered to capture two horses, one from each camp, and they could escape to the south. It was the young lady that came up with the idea to steal both the battle standards, as protection from any retribution.

Like the intelligent hunters they were, the two teens stole into the chaos of battle and entered into history.

Smiling at the memory, Isaak almost walked face first into a horse's flanks. His shock and sudden movement caused the horse to kick back sharply. The Fire Brand leader danced out of the way and offered apologizes to the man guiding the horse. *"How can you be so stupid,"* he rebuked himself. He needed to focus on the task at hand if he were to make any headway with Ashur.

By the time he arrived at Ashur's tent, Isaak felt more in control of his faculties. He greeted two squatting guards on either side of the opening. The shorter of the two rose and blocked his path. With a short spear dancing between her fingers, she questioned the visitor.

"I know you, Fire Brand," she said, passing the twirling spear to her other hand. "You are the one we call Elem. How fares my Leopard sister?"

The question hung in the air, unanswered for a moment. Tears stung the visiting leader's eyes as his voiced cracked with emotion, allowing all the guarded feelings to burst forth.

"My Chadia died while blessing the world with light," he answered with shuddering breath.

There were other words uttered. Silent ripples shocked the middle-aged man. He had neither the strength nor the willpower to hold back the pain. Years of sorrow, guilt, love, and joy washed over him. All those private pains came to light in the middle of that makeshift camp.

The petite woman embraced the silently crying man and softly asked if the child had survived. A deep. saddening look was his only reply. She cupped his face in her hands and kissed each tearstained cheek.

"I will mourn with you, Elem, as will all the Leopards."

The grief and pain of losing a much beloved sister and wife became vocalized. The woman, joined by her fellow guard, rattled their spears against their shields and sent forth a pitiful grieving cry. Voice after voice joined the choir throughout the camp, as they all seemed to accept the loss and shoulder the burden. To Isaak, the cries were a rope that pulled the tremendous weight off his soul.

Ashur, hearing the cry, vacated his tent and saw Isaak amid a circle of Leopards, each placing a gentle hand on the grieving man's shoulders. Rearing his head back, his deep voice sounded with the others. For the Desert Lion was the leader of all the societies, but participated in none. Once his voice lost its power, he also shared an embrace with the man that had won his niece's heart.

Guiding the Fire Brand leader into his tent for some peace, Ashur poured them both a small glass cup full of grain liquor. The dark brown liquid had just enough burn to pull Isaak back to reality. The mourning husband, without thinking, downed the drink in a single swallow.

"My friend," the Tribesman stated, "have you truly mourned your wife and child? There is no shame in honoring the dead, but we men must allow the sorrow of lose to penetrate our souls, not just eat us alive. My niece was life personified. She could dance into a gathering like a sweet cool breeze and be as fierce as a raging fire. It would honor me, and all the Blessed Ones, if you would share a seat by my side this evening. A feast will be had in her honor as we celebrate the life she led."

Isaak was unsure on what to do. He had an obligation to his troops. That, coupled with the quite odd actions of Efrain, caused him to hesitate.

As if sensing the struggle within Isaak, Ashur offered an alternative.

"Your troops would also be invited to attend. I am sure many of them have heard tales of your exploits, but would like nothing more than to learn the truth, which I am sure none of us know for certain. Besides, many of us here, myself included, would rejoice in the man that tamed the wildest of the Leopards."

With an abrupt nod, Isaak replied that there was something the Desert Lion needed to know first. He began with the brutal beating of Harold and ended with the betrayal of Efrain. The younger of the two men in the tent felt responsible for both events, as if he were personally to blame for their actions. The elder tribesman listened as Isaak said that he saw his son, Zoreza, in the lads he was leading and had a duty to them all.

"Our elders could help your young man," the older man spoke kindly, "if he is indeed tainted by dark forces. Bring him to the white tent before the festivities and we shall see what we can do."

For the first time in what seemed like forever, Isaak felt a glimmer of hope.

———•———

Having regained his composure and returned to his tent, Isaak took a moment to breathe. For too long, the death of his family had haunted him. At first, he welcomed any feeling or impression of his dearly departed. It helped ease the pain of loss, but that desire soured to guilt and anger. Anger over losing them in childbirth, after failed attempts to get pregnant. Rage at the Gods from stealing them from him.

Mostly, it was self-loathing and hate for himself. Bandits and marauders fell before him. In designing battle plans, there were few better. But he was completely powerless to save them , and that ate at him most of all.

It had been six years to the day that he had buried them. And, in that small military-issued tent, Isaak finally came to terms with the death of Chadia and their son.

Just before the cooks began to gather ingredients for supper, Isaak emerged and announced that, in the spirit of brotherhood and peace, the Blessed Ones would be sharing their fires and food with the Fire Brands.

Confusion and apprehension mixed with odd fascination among the troop. On the one hand, almost all of them were curious to see what the desert nomads were like. On the other, if they were to engage in a battle with them, the march soldiers did not want to let slip any secrets that could be used later. As they lined up to leave the confines of the Temple, all were hesitant for the night's activities.

The impromptu gathering began with a rocky start. Both parties were ill at ease. Years of prejudice and ego were not simply cast aside in one day.

Ashur, seeing the awkwardness, signaled for music to come alive and drink to be dispersed. The sound of flutes and drums joined with cymbals and small horns to create a festive atmosphere.

That year, the number of female tribe members being tested outnumbered the male teens eight to one. Some of the desert Leopards were intrigued by the shy southerners who just awkwardly stood about. And so the young ladies pulled them along into a dance. Not long after, roasted meats, chilled fruits, and nuts were enjoyed by all.

Isaak, for the first time in what felt like forever, laughed joyfully as he witnessed an evening of peace and fun between the two warring nations. In his heart, he wanted to retire and live among the Blessed Ones, for their beliefs were more in line with his own. Their way of life afforded him a way to reconnect with his wife and son's memory. Sharing a glass of wine with the desert leader, he had little cause to worry.

———— ◆ ————

Senka grinned wolfishly. She had been resting in the shadow of the Desert leader's tent for the past day, listening to the comings and goings of the group. The Stranger, who had become their leader, sent her to find a way to widen the wedge between the societies. After all, the sheer strength of the storm he had conjured was enough to make Gareth and Senka kneel in allegiance.

As luck would have it, Isaak's brother-in-law was going to serve that purpose. She overheard his anger for the Southerner that "stole" his sister. A very loud and long argument had erupted between Eirini and Ashur about the gathering. The Water Seeker had no desire to make peace with the man that, in his mind at least, had kidnapped his only living family member. Senka knew his death would be the perfect lynch pin in her plan, and if not him, then the Desert Lion.

Patiently, she waited for sunset, often watching the patterns of people as they drank, ate, and danced. To amuse herself, she sent out tentacles of dark magic that caused people to fall or slip. Ironically, her interfering caused more of the tension to break. The sheepish grins of those falling were accepted with kind hearts and the celebration continued.

Her laughter was cut short by a force pulling her to the white tent, far to the east of her position. Senka's jade yellow eyes widened as she realized that the Blessed Ones could undo her magic. Knowing the Elders were trying to purge her Fire Brand puppet, Senka poured some Void magic into him, twisting his mind and damaging his soul. Fate was with her as night brought forth an amplification of the Shadow arts.

———◦———

The Elders of the Blessed Ones sat crossed-legged in a circle, slowly chanting. Efrain swayed with the subtle changes of the words and their pitch as the desert mages continued their purging of the dark energies.

The lad had been escorted from the Fire Temple to the white tent by a cluster of medics and herbalists. Certain concoctions and potions were needed to ease the young nobleman's mind and open his soul to the cleanse.

Such magic had not been performed since the Forsaken Ones tried to overpower the entire continent a thousand years ago. Although their skill was unmatched by most in the Shaman temple, the Elders had to constantly fight back the ever ending attack of dark emotions, lest they too became tainted.

Success seemed to be close, until the moon rose to its apex and a flash flood of dark magic spewed from the lad they were trying to cleanse.

———◦———

Eirini stood awkwardly outside the light of one of the larger campfires. Two groups of dancers were teaching the southern soldiers how to pass from one partner to the next without falling over. A sad smile became etched on the tall thirty-nine-year-old man's face. He wanted desperately to be included in the laughter and festivities, but was never good with strangers.

"Care for a drink," a voice called out behind the Water Seeker.

Turning, he was shocked to see Isaak holding two glasses and a clay jug of alcohol. The desert man's eyes tightened at the odd gesture of friendship. There was no love lost between them, and this was the first time since that fateful war game that they had actually seen each other face to face.

With a casual shrug, the military man tipped his head back and downed both drinks, to show there was no poison or ill intent from him. One of the servants passed and offered them both a tray of sugared nuts and dried meats. "Are you sure you will not join me," Isaak asked. He truly wanted to establish some form of peace between them, if not for them, then for the woman they both loved.

The noise around them stopped, as all eyes were on the two men. Everyone knew their story now and wanted them to bury the past.

With a gracious bow, the Water Seeker accepted the cup and drank a sip. "In memory of my beloved sister and her son," he shouted for all to hear. Since the Blessed Ones were hosting, Eirini could not afford to be the aggressor.

Cheers erupted around the fire, with more music and dancing following. Isaak, addressing Eirini by his true title of Master Seeker, offered the man a small folded bundle. "I know we have had our differences in the past," the Fire Brand officer said, "but please accept this as a peace offering. Chadia would have liked you to have it." His tears flowed with each word, as the bundle was a symbol of Isaak's desire for forgiveness. Once Eirini took the package, Isaak disappeared into the darkness, seeking the solitude of the night.

The Water Seeker, confused by the actions of Isaak, untied the red fabric cord and gasped with shock. Confusion and excitement swelled in his heart as he ran for his Uncle's tent, desperately holding the gift from Isaak.

———◆———

Senka smiled at her good fortune. Both of her targets were standing not eight feet from her, examining some cloth bundle with a red cord. Blood curdling screams from the white tent could be heard over the loud festive music as her spell finally activated. The dark mage knew that was indeed her signal to attack.

Conjuring all the hate and anger she was able to muster, sharp blades of darkness flew out of her shadow as her thin fingers pointed towards her targets. Time slowed as four things happened at once: Isaak, sensing the impending doom, jumped in front of Eirini, knocking him out of the way. Karniel, looking at the bundle, saw the blade heading for the Desert Lion and pulled the older man to the ground. Senka, sensing the flow of blood on one of her blades, smiled with delight. Lastly, Efrain's mind, becoming completely distorted by the dark magic, was forever lost, with no hope of recovery.

Cries for medics and help exploded throughout the camp. Everyone was utterly perplexed by the sudden attack. The dark shaman chose to leave amid the confused chaos and yells to find the assassin. She was sure they would be killing each other in no time, thus allowing little allies for the war to come.

Had she stayed a little longer, she would have realized her mistake. It was Isaak and not Eirini that took the blade deep into his stomach and out his spine. Gripping his brother-in-law tightly, two words were softly spoken just for the Water Seeker. Two words to bring about an epic change of heart for the desert tribesman: For family.

All the anger and abandonment over the last fifteen years melted away like the spring snow, leaving only regret and sorrow for Eirini. Mournful yelling filled the night sky so powerful that the Gods themselves surely heard it. And the one leading the mourning was Isaak's brother-in-law.

Ashur, with his eyes alight with rage, organized both camps to search for the killer. He wanted revenge for the death of Isaak, and no one, in either military group, dared to question his orders. Even the Blessed Ones' Elders were called in to help, as they felt dark, twisted magic was used as the murder weapon. Karniel, Liam, and Tomas led the Fire Brand Army's search, and, in turn, reported all their findings to the Desert Lion.

A pair of riders left not long after, heading straight for the City of Tears, each one bearing the banners that Isaak had captured long ago.

Within two weeks, the marching unit had returned to the Red Keep, still in a sober mood. With the loss of their leader to magical misdeeds, and the suicide of their comrade, Efrain, little could buoy their spirits.

18

The sunlight entering the library offered little warmth to the collected adults. The last part of the history caused many questions to come forth, but, for now, they kept their silence. Nursing a glass of chilled water, the Shaman rose fluidly and walked to the frost-covered window. The last part of the story had troubled her greatly. Few possessed the power to send that much dark energy through the Shadow realm. Touching a small charm around her wrist, she sent an inquiry to the Veritable Mother's abbey nearby. If that being was still alive, the Shamans had to be ready.

Rubbing the new stubble growing on his face, Mathis broke his silent reflection. "So why would Isaak return the banners," he asked kindly. Even though he knew the answer, any peaceful thought was needed to lighten the mood.

Yarmilla answered. "He wanted to make peace with his brother-in-law. War banners hold a special power all their own, and for him to willingly offer them up— it shows a respect that the Water Seeker did not understand." Turning to the Lord Commander, the young lady asked a pivotal question. "It is through the actions of Isaak and Karniel that we have had several years of peace, and even profitable trade with the Blessed Ones, yes?"

Smiling at her friend's cunning, the Shaman turned back towards the table and its occupants. She wanted to comment while Varg was thinking. "Even we have trained with the Elders of the Sky and Sand, and they with us. We all owe a debt of gratitude for the leaders of that particular March. And to their willingness to protect others, regardless of nation or creed," Asiza commented pointedly.

There was no doubt of the captured man's influence and skill, but one thing still pestered the Priest, like a buzzing fly: Why was he exiled from the Army? Straightening his robes, and plucking an apple from a bowl, Mathis asked the most important question of their discussion so far. "If Karniel was such a good soldier, why did your Inner Circle chose to strip him of rank and dishonorably discharge him forever?"

Rage burned brightly in Varg's eyes. He knew the question was coming, but still hated himself for being a part of it. It was a nasty business that brought shame on both the priesthood and the military. "That, *Priest*, is the final part of my time with the lad, and it is a very dark tale indeed. Your predecessor and mine were key to that particular fault, and it still eats at me, after all this time."

🔥19🔥

The northern section of the Red Keep was bathed in the golden light of the midday sun. Second only to the training arena in size, the eastern home of the Paladin Corp. enjoyed more peace than its martial neighbors of the rest Fire Brand Army. A fairly large-sized forge took up the entire eastern side of the area, which fed into the double wide stables, creating a continuous L shape. The heavy and powerful warhorses cantered and pawed at the dirt and straw floor, causing an almost permanent cloud of dust. A five-level barracks, and a quaint, blessed chapel completed the western wall, leaving the courtyard for practice and training.

The simplicity of this style of life was almost hermit in design, but no one could deny the power and strength of the warriors that called it home.

Karniel walked with stoic purpose through the red dirt courtyard from the armorer's forge to the barracks. It had been over four years since the death of Isaak and the beginning of Karniel's personal mission to bring the demonic murderer to justice. The fire that drove him still burned brightly.

Upon his return from the desert march, each of the four main branches of the military wanted to train the teenager responsible for saving the Desert Lion. They spent time trying to woo the lad in the hopes of gaining more prestige and influence among the political rings of government. Even though he had a solid dream of where he wanted to train, individual leaders did not have the decency to listen.

None of the regular divisions within the Fire Brand ranks could train him to fight a foe like the one witnessed on the night of the desert celebration. Only Pethio and his Corps were able to give him the skills necessary to combat the entity that still haunted the young man's dreams.

The Paladin Corps was not only tasked as warriors to combat creatures created from dark magics, unholy beings, and their twisted masters. Their main job was to bring justice to the outlying hamlets and farming towns. The small library, based in the Corps multi-level sleeping area, housed a multitude of volumes. Each was very specific on finding, tracking, and killing corrupt abominations, as well as tomes on common and noble laws. The armory contained a myriad of blessed or enchanted weapons and shields, and the students had to master each one before graduation.

Much to the shock and irritation of the Cathedral of the Faithful, Karniel opted not to be an ordained Paladin and further his training at their tower in the religious capital. He was the first to ever turn down such a promising invitation, but magic and spells did not appeal to the almost nineteen-year-old.

Spells served their purpose in peace and war. But, in all honesty, he felt a student of the arcane arts must dedicate himself fully to the mastery and he did not have the heart to do so. Much like the Priesthood, or the Military, the arcane arts were a lifelong calling. Karniel did not feel that magic could show him a way to self-mastery and discipline.

The new articulated plate armor felt comfortable on the young muscular man as he headed to meet Pethio. The armorer needed extra time to custom make each of the pieces, since Karniel was not an average-sized person. But, then again, none of the paladins were. None of the snaps or buckles hindered movement and even the gauntlets could fully close, allowing the wearer to make a fist. After four years of wearing similar armor on marches, while fighting and riding, the teenager felt almost naked whenever he had to remove it.

One final item was missing from the set of armor and that was a helmet. Most in the Corp chose not to wear one, as it tended to limit vision and head movement. The newly-minted Paladin, however, had one made, but not for himself. It was to be sent to Zuwl's grave, behind his house, as a testament to all he had done for the teen. The wide cylinder was made in a Master-of-Arms style, with eye slits and breathing holes. The sigil of two crossed cudgels was superimposed on either side as a tribute to the man that had raised him.

Ready for war, Karniel headed for Pethio's map room on the top floor of the five story bunk house. A special meeting of the Corp and the Rangers had been called, and the Grand Master wanted his prized pupil present. Climbing the last staircase to the fifth floor, a voice from the past called out from the shadows.

"Well now, don't you look ready for a parade and a dance?"

An inquisitive backward glance, and an arched eyebrow, was the large teen's only response to the teasing statement from the darkness.

The owner of the voice started up the staircase and came into view. His green leather scale armor and dark brown leather boots announced he was indeed a Ranger. But the dirk and crow's beak dangling off his belt advertised his skill in close quarter combat. The lean, muscled twenty-year-old smirked at Karniel, causing his goatee to twitch. "It has been a while, my Brother. How have you been?"

Walking to the speaker, Karniel returned the smile and felt his heart lighten a little bit. None of the friends he had made on the march into the desert opted to become Paladins. Instead, Liam joined the Heavy Cavaliers, quickly becoming a division leader and earning the title of Lanceman. Tomas joined the Archers. With his vast skill and speed, he was recruited into their elite Ranger unit, making Lieutenant in under three years.

It was he that stood before the youngest Paladin, and jovially laughed at the seriousness of it all. Tomas had been called in from the Western part of the country, near the southern marshes, to answer a threat to his southern homeland. He had requested that Karniel and a small detachment of Paladins accompany his unit. The citizens of Rogue's Bluff did not trust Fire Brand soldiers.

As the two friends embraced and walked up the steps, they knew this new adventure would become one spoken of for years to come.

Reaching the Grand Master's map room, Karniel opened the intricately-carved double doors. This allowed Tomas the chance to take in all the simplicity. A giant bookcase lined the right wall, reaching from ceiling to floor. A carved map of the entire island continent decorated the top of a polished ash table. Toy soldiers represented each faction of the army, lining the outer border. Every city, hamlet, inn, and crossroad was shown in vivid detail, as the church spared no expense creating the masterful work of art.

Twenty-four freshly oiled wooden chairs lined the left wall, most of which were occupied by the leaders of the Corps and the Archers. Pethio stood facing the Chief Ranger. Though half the giant Paladin's height and weight, he was rather imposing in his own right.

Having short-cropped black hair and stormy gray eyes, Jaecare had led the Fire Brand Army archers for the better part of twenty years. After almost forty years in service, the Chief Ranger's body had developed a powerful muscular force in his chest, back, and arms. Only a handful could match his skill and precision with the bow, but no one in the Archers was more respected and feared. Slow to anger, but quick to deal out punishment to the guilty, even the pirates in the southern seas wanted little to do with this man.

Snapping to a salute with two fingers over his heart, Tomas introduced Karniel to his commander and both men shook hands. Like most soldiers, they sized each other up. Not in a threatening way, but in the way two predators sharing the same field acknowledge a potential ally and foe.

"So this is the lad rumored to have so easily cast aside the gracious invitation of the Archers, Men at Arms, Cavaliers, and the Battle School," Jaecare inquired, still clasping Karniel's hand in a firm grip.

Tomas was shocked to hear that even his group had sought the giant of a teen out, as archers tended to be light and wiry, not built like bears.

Smirking with a dangerous twinkle, Karniel answered that he had little skill with a bow and would most likely break the precise and expensive instrument.

Heavy laughter rolled like thunder in the map room as the tension broke and respect was solidified.

Calling the meeting to order, Pethio explained that a great threat to the nation was festering in the south beyond the mountains. And it was the Corps duty to aid the Archers in any way. Casting his massive hand over the detailed table, the Grand Master activated a rune that sent ripples through the map. In under a few seconds, the entire southern region took up the whole table, showing Rogue's Bluff, the Fire Brand fort, and the Evermist Forest.

Completely surrounded by the sea to the south, and the Ghromheim Mountains creating an almost bow shape over the frontier of the region, it was a city-state to itself, instead of a loyal part of the county. Five clans had ruled the forest paradise for hundreds of generations, using the four rivers that cut through the land as natural divides for land and power.

The Stag Clan, known for their ranching and hunting skills, occupied the land in the southwest stretch between the mountains and the Aerie's Flow River. Rich lands for farming covered nearly the entirety of the region. The light rains coming off the mountains allowing the Stag family the ability to farm or ranch almost the entire year.

Next to them was the territory of the Bear Clan, a family rich in mining prowess and blacksmithing skills. The Castille at Shaman's Pass was under their control. But, using grace and understanding, they allowed the military a small home. Bear county, as the locals called it, was by far the largest area. It used Aerie's flow to the west, the mountains to the north, the rapids of Serpent's Tongue to the east, and the beach to the south for borders. Though most of it remained unused, small villages and fields dotted the land.

The smallest of all the clans was almost the wealthiest by far. Situated between the forked streams of the Serpent's Tongue, the Crossed Oars family studied enchanting and magic. They sent all their children to train in the academy at the Mystic Isles. Meanwhile, they offered small estates to those Islanders who wanted a place to hone their craft away from prying eyes.

The most heavy concentration of forest lay in the land of the Oak Clan. Masters of woodworking and sculpting, their artisan talents were second to none throughout all Dazmek. The eastern branch of the Serpent's Tongue river, and the Golden Vain river, created an odd wavy shape that contained the master carpenter family.

Lastly, and second in wealth and trade, was the Eagle Clan. They were the ones that founded the port city of Rogue's Bluff and still worked within her walls. A family of master sailors, traders, and navigators known the world over, the Brass Eagle had flown over more nautical miles of the great oceans than any other single group. Often at war with the pirate families of the Mystic Isles, this clan was always ready for a fight.

In whole, the entire southern region was roughly two hundred and fifty miles wide and one hundred and twenty miles long. It was by no means the smallest region on the continent, but the task Karniel and Tomas were about to face was daunting and long.

Focusing everyone's attention, Tomas explained that the latest intelligence reports stated the bandit tribes were clustering into small groups and raiding all the clan halls and villages throughout the forest. While this was normal, he assured, the attacking criminals were kidnapping women and children, but killing all the men old enough to fight. Tomas' own Oak Clan had suffered massive casualties. It was that clan's chief that demanded the involvement of the Paladins.

Pethio, sharing a look with his councilors, realized the implications of a bandit army in the forest. The sheer vastness of the woodland ran for miles. And, without the aid of the clans, no military force could find the hiding villains. Not only was it their duty as soldiers, but it was a direct call to the tenets they swore to uphold as Holy Paladins.

Every councilor in the Corps vocally agreed that something must be done. It was decided that an attachment of twenty paladins, ten ordained and ten not, would ride south under the leadership of the Rangers' banner. Once there, they would join with half the regiment in Rogue's Bluff. They did, however, have one condition: Karniel would lead the group.

Confusion and shock blazed on the new Paladin's face. There were other brothers and sisters of the order better trained, more experienced, and wiser than himself. He couldn't help but voice these points of concern. Surely they would be better suited for the task, whatever it may be.

All the leaders shared a hearty laugh at the teenager's expense as gold began to exchange from hand to hand. Even Tomas held out his hand and received three marks from Jaecare.

"You just made me a rich man," the knavish Tomas said to Karniel, flipping the coins in the air. "I told them you would not outright refuse the role, nor would you welcome it. You're too good-hearted that way."

In spite of himself, Karniel had to smile. It felt like they were back in the hot wastelands of the Desert and nothing had changed. Looking to his order's Grand Master, he asked what all the mission involved and to what latitude they were allowed to complete the objective. After all, he thought, if he was going to do the job he better do it right.

Pethio explained in a sober tone that such an uprising of lawless men could not be allowed to continue. Orders from the governing council of Four had been penned and sealed. Every single bandit, regardless of origin or reason, was to be put to death for crimes of murder, kidnapping, and civil unrest. The Grand Master looked sickened by the blanket death warrant. But he knew all the victims of the attacks were innocent and their blood cried from the grave for justice.

The Ghromheim Mountains stood majestically in wild and ferocious splendor. Eternally snow-capped, this impassable natural barrier protected both the Shamans to the southwest and the Evermist forest to the south. Few were able to traverse the dangerous passes and razor-sharp valleys. Many tales of ancient evils, and rivers of treasure, were connected to the perilous caverns and deep veins. But those who went looking inside the mountain range never returned.

Mines dotted the northern side of the range, where iron, copper, and other ores and gems were in abundance. Quite an industrial center thrived along the dry side of the natural barrier, with small, clay-tile homes and shops for the workers to sleep and sharpen tools. Larger homes were built to accommodate the shapers and crafters of the metal and precious stones. A skilled worker could make a small fortune in a few years of working there, but it was dangerous work.

Cave-ins and gas pockets were a rare occurrence. But bandits or thieves were always looking for ways to make a quick mark off of someone else's industry. Two master lock makers, and four chest masters, were kept busy trying to find new and elaborate ways of protecting the treasures found in the mines.

The younger children of the miners and skill masters had devised a game of echo they played every time a group larger than two wagons approached the community. And right in the middle of the hottest part of the day, the echoes started sounding throughout the outreaches. A dust cloud had been seen earlier in the morning, ten miles from the mines, and now it was quickly approaching.

Two lines of armed soldiers kicked up dust as they stomped rhythmically down the wide, red dirt road. Most were to relieve the stationed troops at the Forest garrison. The remainder were the elite force of Rangers and Paladins for use as a special taskforce to hunt down the growing menace of outlaws.

It was common knowledge that the military had but one small fort in the Ghromheim Mountain. This suited the clans and families of Rogue's Bluff just fine. The spirit of independence lived strongly in the South. They desired to keep their affairs out of military jurisdictions and squarely in the hands of the Paladin Corps.

It had been two weeks since the troop had begun their trek to the southern mountain range and the forests it protects. The rolling hills and rich plains of the middle country surrounding the Red Keep had given way to flat, grassy fields after a week of marching southward on the main road. Few trees dotted the landscape the closer the soldiers got to the natural stone wall. An almost barren land covered the last two days of their trip, with nothing but thorn bushes and briar patches filling the land.

Horses were left at the Miner's Waypoint, an inn and livery stable for the carrier services employed throughout the region. Hefty and plump, Aunt Tessie ran a clean and honest establishment, always welcoming traveling soldiers with a warm smile and a hot meal. She knew what lay in wait for the troop and her heart bled with a motherly sadness. Having lost her husband and sons to both war and sickness, she offered prayers on behalf of Karniel's group for a safe journey.

The idea of leaving their mounts and wagon drivers behind did not sit well with Karniel. Many of the supplies needed to be restocked at the old fort. Dried beef and chicken, salt, medicines, and tools were in short supply in the mountainous region. The teamsters just smiled at the expression of concern and took a western road. They knew their business and did not want to ruin the surprise for the newly arriving soldiers.

Karniel was about to voice his concerns to the Ranger leader, but stopped at the expression on his friend's face.

Tomas's face lit up like a bonfire on the winter solstice the moment they arrived at the mining base. The lad took a deep inhale and laughed. The scent of Pine, Maple, Cedar, and Oak filled his lungs, as the sweet smell of the great forest rolled off the mountainside. At last, he was finally home. After almost nine years in service to the Fire Brand Army, and eight years of daily training with weapons and tactics, he was ready to feel the sea air on his face and taste the ever present fog on his lips.

Tomas' mood became infectious to the others as laughter and roughhousing gained momentum. They were ready to protect and uphold the honor of the Fire Brand standard. More to the point, they were ready to reach their destination. Many tales had been told of the wonders in the South. And now these rather green soldiers would get their chance to see what was beyond the wild mountains. The squad leaders tried to rein in their soldiers, but to no avail. The energy had gained too much momentum and could not be stopped.

Elbowing Karniel, Tomas pointed at the old man in a gray leather jerkin standing at the end of the road. "That is one of the Silent Ones," he half whispered with awe. "They are odd ducks, but extremely powerful."

The borderline reverence in the twenty-year-old's voice caused Karniel to do a double take. Although not very religious, Tomas had never showed any particular awe or reverence towards the clergy before. Just a simple prayer, day and night, was all the belief he demonstrated. Seeing him talk about the Shaman in such a way was odd.

"Why is he here," Karniel asked, leaning close to Tomas. He had no knowledge of the Silent Ones or their powerful order. Staying mostly in the Shaman temple, the magically-fierce brotherhood never went to the Red Keep.

Tomas smiled like the cat that ate the canary. He did not want to spoil the wondrous event that was coming.

Sighing, Karniel barked a command that roared across the dust-filled air. Two hundred pairs of feet came to a halt, three steps shy of the mysterious Shaman. Corked canteens were opened and turned up while dry throats were bathing in the welcoming hydration. This side of the mountain range stayed fairly dry and warm, especially towards the early summer months. The dirt clung to the unit's sweaty bodies like a fine powder, turning normal skin into a leather-like toughness.

The Silent One, smiling at the troops, turned towards the base of a smooth, sixty-foot solid rock face, his bald head shining with sweat. Lightly pressing his right hand on the rock, a resonance vibrated through the mountain. A whorl in the stone appeared big enough to extend past the Shaman's fingers. The sound became a melody as the whorl became larger and deeper. Deep rumblings shook the ground, and yet the mute Shaman mage seemed unaffected.

The unit leaders had been warned, almost in passing, that magic was needed to enter the Mountains. Few took heed of the outlandish warning, as it seemed absurd. Surely it was a farce to scare the recently graduated soldier classes, they thought. As the ground shook, and small pebbles floated, the once laughable idea became a nightmarish reality.

Tomas yanked Karniel to the ground as they both ordered their men to get down. The pulsating force had caused temporary disorientation to the military force. More than a handful vomited violently or prayed for it to end.

As the magical music crescendoed, subtle rays of sun light shone through the rock face. Where solid rock once was, a hole about eight yards wide stood. It was tall enough to allow an armored rider astride a war mount to pass unaffected, and smooth to the touch. The Silent One glided around to face the slacked-jawed military men. His hand motioned for them to enter the path, a sly grin parting his face. Giving them a slight bow, he turned and walked away, leaving them to decide what to do.

Those able to stand helped their shield siblings to rise. The once arrow straight lines of military discipline became a haphazard jumble of bodies crashing into each other. Following the orders of their leaders to advance, no one spoke while they entered the cavernous opening. A spirit of caution took root in each of the soldiers. The Mountain felt more alive and awake with each step they took. Each soldier felt like a great deity was weighing their personal valor to see if they were worthy of passing through.

Desire for more than dim light forced the now cowering group to frantically ignite oil-drenched torches. Deeper and deeper they trekked, with no end in sight. Their torches were killing the very things that showed the way out. Soon, every step got lighter and each stride shorter.

"Hey, you lot!" An explosion of sudden words rang out in the dark reaches of the passage. Weapons were drawn to the ready and the company created a ring of steel as wide as the tunnel. "What's taking so long? I swear, didn't they warn you about this?"

An orb of bright blue light was conjured between the group of soldiers and the solitary figure. Shadows hid most of his features, but his bright orange eyes pierced the darkness. His voice left no room for argument as another command was issued. "Follow me and line up," the shadow-clad male snapped, turning back into the haunting darkness.

The orb of light bobbed in the air, almost as if it was alive and expecting the soldiers to follow its master. Being as whimsical as the conjurer was stern, the dancing light playfully teased those that trekked under the mountain.

With a combination of fear and courage, they followed in stunned silence. Karniel had Tomas and the other leaders passed word that all weapons should be put away for now, but kept close. None of this had been explained to them in the many briefings they had attended. But the leaders had to show courage or their soldiers would sink into a panic.

Living in the southern region, Tomas knew they were going to pass under a vast majority of the mountain's underbelly. But nothing could have prepared him for the sense of sheer power and pressure felt within. Years before, his father had told him that the rock barrier was a living being and only the pure of heart could pass through unscathed. The young Ranger finally understood what that meant.

It took the better part of the afternoon to cross the underground path. Normally such a trek would take days or weeks to complete, but, with the help from the Shamans and the mountain people, a straight line had been carved from north to south. This allowed those traveling underground to reach their destinations in record time, and without any interference from the elements. To the travelers, time ceased to exist and the feeling of unnatural weight bore down on each of the marchers.

The light conjurer, actually about four feet in height, kept glancing over his shoulder at the troops. Such tall folks had no reason to be in the mountain, the short man mused. Only his people truly understood the heart of the mountains and their secret ways. Using a mix of infrared and natural light spectrums, the guide was able to warn his fellow deep miners ahead of time via hand signals and had them seal up detours branching off the path. The last time he had lost a soldier down here, the poor fool was never found.

The natural light at the other opening began as a mere tickle on the mind. Ever so slowly, it clawed to the forefront of everyone's consciousness. With the celestial illumination, peace returned to the uninitiated military personnel. A freshness that had not been noticed before returned to the air.

The silhouette of the guide soon became distinct. Heavy fabric made up his grayish green hood and cloak. Leather scale mail protected his torso, while soft leather gloves and boots adorned his hands and feet. Strapped to his back, a full quiver and unstrung recurve bow sat with braided leather fasteners running across his chest and back. Closing his eyes, the small guide prepared himself for the full force of light about to assault their collective visions.

Abruptly, the tunnel opened to a lush green forest, with brush and leaves littering the moist ground. A fine mist hung low, covering everything and seeping into clothes and armor. This side of the colossal rock formation enjoyed regular rain and a humid yet cool climate. A mere one hundred and two miles of land separated the coast from the mountains, but the forest stretched for almost two-thirds of the region. This paradise was nearly untouched by mortal hands, as the inhabitants were taught to respect the natural laws.

The guide guilelessly chuckled at the momentary blindness of the troops. He figured, by their confused and spiritually wounded state, that their commanders wanted that feeling of being small to always reside with the arriving force. It was a good way to stay humble, he thought to himself. Far too many of the Army came from the haughty cosmopolitan areas and were very full of themselves. Those feeling led to nothing but disdain and ruined reputations.

An arrow sailed towards Karniel at lightning speed through the dense fog rolling towards the emerging crowd. Before he was able to register it, Tomas' iron buckler was there to block the arrow, sending the projectile into a bush of ivy. With a dangerous grin, the Ranger lieutenant returned the welcome with a thin, blackened blade he sent towards the shooter. A gruff curse sounded from the bushes as the blade slammed with a gratifying thud into a tree.

Like the forest ghosts in myth and song, a massive group of warriors, painted light blue and gray, rose from the bushes, ready for war.

Grey goose shafts, tipped with black iron points, presented an angry swarm as they enclosed the emerging group of Fire Brand military personnel. Soft leather boots adorned the arrow-wielding men, allowing silent movement even over crisp autumn leaves. Their garb was simple yet functional, with greenish brown pants and tunics, aiding in the ability to hide in plain sight. Each one carried a small axe or long knife, in the off chance they ran out of arrows. These elite foresters of the Bear Clan made the Army's Rangers look like children at play. Their training far outweighed any others. And, for this reason, any Southern that joined the Fire Brand Army was instantly given a commission as a Ranger.

The sound of bushes shattering pulled the Fire Brand members' eye line to the front. A bear-sized man, with broad shoulders and body, crashed through the last shrub before him as he headed towards the group. His sights were set on the one that had blocked his shot. A full head and shoulders taller than Karniel, the man stopped a mere inch from Tomas, towering his face over the youth. "Ya ruined me shot, *boy*," he bellowed like an ox. The two Southerners glared at each other, daring the other to blink.

Smack!

The large, bear-like man was sent reeling back as the heel of Karniel's gauntlet connected with the tender under jaw of his monsterishly large opponent. Light sparkled in the man's eyes as Karniel, using his right leg like a sweeping sickle, knocked the confused clansman off his feet and on his back. Ever since the death of Zuwl, Karniel felt a volcanic hatred for bullying, and this attack was too much to bear without action.

Sitting on the fallen man's chest, Karniel balled up his fist, preparing to pummel the offender into oblivion. It did not matter that over thirty trained foresters had armor-piercing arrows aimed at him, or the fact that the man on the ground was twice his size. Anger blinded him to everything but his target.

Deep, rich laughter shook loose the rage clouding Karniel's better judgment. His victim, rubbing the now tender part of his jaw, spoke. "That was a cheap shot, little paladin. I won't be forgetting that. By the by, the shot was for Tomas, not you. Get your heavy arse off me."

The Southern forester's voice was one of leadership and command, even if the sound was lighthearted. Easing himself to stand, Karniel looked to Tomas for conformation. A sheepish smirk, and an arched eyebrow, was all he got in return.

"He is my Uncle. Since my da passed, the leadership of our clan fell to him," Tomas explained as Karniel rose to his full height. "He just wanted to test my reflexes."

Tomas' uncle, somewhat playfully, took a swing at Karniel, but ended up crashing in the dirt once again. The large youth had caught his arm and flipped him over his strong back, with all the ease of a master. Dusting himself off, the bear-like Southern offered Karniel a hand in friendship. "My name is Arth. I am proud to be fighting beside you. Just don't take all the fun. We want some bandit blood too"

As they clasped hands, arrows returned to quivers and the battle frenzy mentality of both groups deflated. Arth waved a salute to the mountain guide as the short, stout man re-entered the hole. Within a few short minutes, solid rock replaced the one-time exit, protecting the forest and her inhabitants. With introductions concluded, an awkward easiness settled in as both groups headed for Rogue's Bluff, the only true port settlement in the Southern Region.

The trek down was one of slick ground and no real path to speak of, with gnarled tree roots and sink holes ready to trap the unsuspecting marcher. The clansmen were able to maneuver the landscape with ease, but they hung back, offering to help their new allies down the mountain. After an hour of bouncing like deer over gullies and pitfalls, a small trail became clear. The regular soldiers cheered, as they were already tired from the exercise.

Arth, rolled his eyes at the uselessness of the men "defending" the pass to the Shaman stronghold. These soldiers would not last a day traveling in my woods, the clan leader thought as he saw yet another infantryman step right into a rabbit's hole.

Speeding up to position himself next to his nephew and the Paladin, the bear-sized man tried to figure out the best way of finding out exactly what the plan was. Questions needed to be answered before such an enterprise this extensive could be undergone. The clan leader did not want his men to be used as bandit fodder.

"Paladin," the seven-foot-tall, bearded man called out. "I wanna know how you plan on fighting men who know this forest better than you and yours. It doesn't seem right to send such tender, green hammer wielders to lead this little hunt."

Tomas gave his uncle a disapproving look at the snide comments. He knew Arth was just trying to rate the measure of man Karniel was, but such insults would cost men their lives when battle plans were drawn up.

Calmly, and with a bit of cold feeling, Karniel responded to the statement. "I have no desire to play with your men's lives like toys." Looking Arth dead in the eye, he stopped walking. "I assume your people have family, loved ones, who want them to return, yes? Well, so do those under my command. It's true that I do not know this place, but Tomas does. So, if you have any real concerns, voice them now, please. Otherwise, we have a job to do and people to protect."

Nodding at the obvious emotion swimming behind the Paladin's green eyes, Arth had to give Karniel his due. He could tell the young Paladin had lost someone dear to him and did not want to repeat that trauma. Any life lost on this hunt would haunt the young man for life, as it tends to do with all commanders who care for their men. Clasping Karniel's right shoulder with his massive hand, the burly behemoth genuinely smiled.

"Your canter is rough, but appreciated. You will do well, me boy." Leaving his nephew and new ally to themselves, Arth hummed as he strolled to the head of the slow moving force. It was going to be a good hunt, the mammoth man thought happily.

About two hours of walking down from the exit they had used, stone replaced dirt. The path to the town widened so that two wagons could use the road and still have room. Gone were the pestering briars and bushes. Replacing them on either side of the road were two massive hedges, lush and green. Purple flowers dotted the plant wall and giggles were heard from hidden faces, almost teasing the soldiers to break rank.

Arth offhandedly commented that they should stop at the banks of the Serpent's Tongue River. The Oak Clan owned the land there and they needed permission to continue through the clan's territory. Karniel gave the giant man a confused look. The Paladin had thought all the clans were one huge family and no such accesses had to be granted.

Once they arrived at the rolling, frothy river, Karniel understood the warning.

Thirty-six hardened men and women stood on the far bank with bows at the ready. Fifty more, armed with swords, spears, and heavy axes, were behind the archers, working themselves into a battle madness. Each one had been supplied with dark brown-colored pants with long sleeved coats of the same hue. The rawhide coats, boiled for thickness and molded to the wearer, had iron rings sown into the front and back of the stiff animal hide. A great golden Oak tree had been branded into the armor. These house militia were not there to welcome a wanted ally.

Stopping a pace from the rope-and-timber bridge swinging in the light breeze, Karniel shouted over the churning river crashing over the rocks below. "Hail, sons of the Oak Clan. We simply wish to pass through your lands for Rogue's Bluff. If you wish to escort us, welcome."

Typically, such a party would have no problem crossing clan lands, but with the bandit raids growing with alarm, no one was safe.

A clan pikeman, with a surly look and ill-tempered manners, replied from his side of the bridge with equal gusto and some curtness. "Where were you pretty northern boys when we needed ya, huh? Every man in these parts has suffered greatly by those lawless bastards. What do yas plan to do, *boy?*"

His demands were as wounded as his clan's mentality. The Oak Clan had been the hardest hit and the most devastated by far. Ancestral homes were burnt to the ground and sacred places were ransacked for plunder.

Such bloodshed and senseless violence had not been seen for over a thousand years. But many in the South were already prepared for the worst, deeming the event The Heretic's Return.

Hearing the grumblings from those sent to be stationed at Shaman's Pass, the Paladin Captain turned to the unit leaders and barked a single command for silence. Such bellyaching would serve no one and might even cause more damage. Returning to the task at hand, the young leader offered to meet the militia leader halfway down the bridge to secure passage to cross the land unharmed.

River mist shot up over the crossing as both commanders agreed to meet and make terms. It took all of ten minutes to obtain allowances to pass through, but in such a short time Karniel became soaked to the bone. With the arrival of the Fire Brand soldiers on the eastern bank of the river, the young Paladin officer thanked all the clan sentries, offering each a small flask of fire brandy as a token of friendship.

Pethio had given Karniel the small containers with a wink, telling him they would come in handy.

Out of ear shot of the Oak Clansmen by several yards, Tomas let loose a thunderous chuckle. "Had you started with the brandy, we could have gotten free passage in a caravan to the City instead of walking the whole way. Oh my dear friend, one of these days you *will* learn."

Karniel smiled at his friend's joke. He had secretly wanted to walk the country and see the faces of the people who lived within the natural boundaries. It was almost impossible to aid a region without knowing the terrain. But the young officer wanted to see if the reports were accurate, not some power grab by a noble house.

Over the course of the next three days, the marching group stopped off at each and every hamlet, village, or trading post along the Miner's Trail that led to the port. Village chiefs and tradesmen all spoke the same abusive tale of being extorted for money, women, and anything else a militant band would need.

Those from the North had never seen such a sight of utter destruction before. Animals lay dead in fields and farm homes were scorched to the stone foundations. Blank, hopeless stares greeted the visiting troop and a subdued mood crept into each of the soldiers. With each stop, more and more of them offered to help clear out barns or move heavy timbers for the victims. Some even left behind coins to aid in the rebuilding effort.

By noon on the third day, Miner's Trail joined with Heartbreak Path to form the Port Road, a smooth mosaic of large granite slabs from the nearby rock quarry. Arth and the others in his group were quite surprised with the youthful Paladin leader and his continuous offers of aid to all those they met along the way. The general feeling among the clans was that the Red Keep, along with the Cathedral of the Faith, cared little for the affairs beyond the Mountains. And yet there was a leader and an officer proving all that wrong. His calm, caring actions would forever be remembered by those who had lost everything.

Within an hour, from the beginning of the Port Road, stone ramparts were visible over the horizon. Steel gray, and equally imposing, the walls were seventy feet tall and a warning to all who entered: do not break the law here. Almost nine miles long, and two wide, Rogue's Bluff rivaled both the Cathedral and Red Keep in size and power.

Many of the northern soldiers had heard of the sheer size of the port town. But no one could have prepared them for its realistic combination of power and danger.

Built on an existing rock island formation, the port housed two tavern districts, a traditional chapel, four industrial sections, a wharf, and a mile-and-a-half long port with forty stone docks. Each part of the city was utilized and planned with careful consideration. As luck would have it, several fresh water wells had been found and walled up, thus allowing a constant supply of the life-giving liquid. Three major roads divided the enclosed city into six clusters, with the Port Lord's manor built right in the middle of town.

The municipal leader's personal house guards yelled from atop the wall to the gatehouse below as the marching group drew close to the far bank of the forty foot watery drop that surrounded the city. Chains jingled and gears squeaked, easing the massive drawbridge down across a rather deep, natural moat. A hearty thud sounded with power as the twenty foot bridge landed and a lithe young Paladin stepped forward to meet the arriving military personnel.

"State your name, rank, and affiliation," she yelled for all to hear. For five years, the lightly-tanned, short, blonde-haired woman had controlled the north gatehouse in a stern yet fair manner. There were not many female Paladins in the Order, but most of them ended up at the port city. They seemed to hold their own a lot better against the sweet, sweet temptations of the flesh that were so readily found within.

"Oh, Kayth, darling, loosen your tightly-strapped armor and relax," the clan leader spoke, winking at Tomas. "My nephew has come from the far north to visit and maybe share a dance with you, lass."

Laughter broke out among Arth's group, and a few snickers from the Fire Brand soldiers as well. Many men in the city had tried to woo the pretty Paladin with soft purple eyes, but most were knocked on their butts for the effort. She had no desire to marry, nor was she ever comfortable being romanced. On top of that, none of these men were even attractive at all to her.

"I seem to recall the last time you got drunk, Arth. You tried to dance at the Beehive and nearly broke the floor." Her snide remark was rewarded with even more laughter. It was common knowledge that the Clan leader drank like a fish and was not light-footed.

Seeing the only option for his pride was a dignified retreat, the boorish man bowed, stated his name, and waited for the lass to check her records. With an arched brow, Kayth performed her sworn duty and waved him in, shaking her head as he passed. The rest of the Foresters followed suit and soon were allowed entry into the port city.

Tomas, blushing, was the first soldier to step up to the waiting Paladin. "Hi," he hoarsely spoke, shocking Karniel. The Southerner was never at a loss for words, but seeing the athletically-built woman somehow turned his silver tongue to lead.

"Well, handsome, do you have a name?" the female Paladin asked, choosing a bit more provocative stance, with her head cocked to the side and a hand on her hip. She enjoyed the bumbling shyness of the Ranger. His cheeks blushed a shade of red so bright she thought they would burn the city to ash.

The sound of someone clearing their throat pulled Kayth away from Tomas and into the eye line of Karniel's emotionless expression. The sight of his massive frame in the traditional armor of the Order reminded her of Pethio. Her former instructor would never put up with that kind of foolishness. Mentally shaking herself, she checked in the arriving Fire Brand soldiers, each one glaring at Tomas for holding up the line.

Karniel, choosing to be last, handed Kayth a small, sealed letter from Pethio. It contained the orders for the unit, and instructed every Paladin in the city to be under Karniel's command. The young campaign leader did not like the last part of the message, but he wisely did not mention it. No one liked a whinny leader. And, if they were to succeed, he needed to gain the respect of those stationed with the blonde-haired young woman.

Kayth's eyes brightened at the message as she read it. Many traveling caravans had been attacked over the past several weeks. The criminals barely left anyone alive to tell the tale, but a single image was drawn in blood at each scene. The fishing villages along the southwest coast were refusing to send any more aid or trade until the raids were put under heel. Having lost friends to the murderous bandits, Kayth wanted payback and now she was getting it. Signaling for Tomas and Karniel to follow her, she entered the city ready to get started.

A handful of Arth's men guided the regular troops to several inns near the northern gate. The Army had prepaid for their rooms and meals, but other festivities were to be covered by the soldiers alone. The taverns of Rogue's Bluff were legendary for their fine drink and beautiful women. Most military men waited their whole careers to get the chance to partake in the lush entertainment of the port city, and none are left unsatisfied.

The detachment of bandit hunters had another destination in mind, so they bid their travel companions a fond farewell. Along the southern wall of the city, facing the forty deep sea docks, there stood several large warehouses. Each was able to hold eight frigate-loads a piece. One of these massive structures served as a makeshift headquarters for the Paladins stationed in the city. Being situated by the southwest watchtower, it was by far not the largest of the stone structures. But it was more than adequate for the needs of the armored enforcers.

Being three levels high, each floor had a purpose and a goal. The top level housed the bunks and two wash rooms. As it rained quite a bit there, rain basins were added for a constant supply of both cooking and washing water. The middle floor housed the library and chapel. Both rooms were not as detailed or extravagant as the Church in the center of town. But, in their simplicity, there was a calming peace that each Paladin enjoyed. The most spacious of floors was the lowest. Housing weapons, practice dummies, a small stable, and even three medium-sized storerooms, this area was ideal for planning and executing an offensive.

The combined special military unit made their way across town, passing every tavern, inn, and shop along the main stone road. The sun, drying out the cloud cover, poured its mighty light upon the force, as if to announce that the God of Fire and Righteous Cleansing personally blessed the arriving unit. Throngs of people stopped and stared at the might of men and women sent to rid the south of the deadly plague. A group of small children ran forward and wove their way between each soldier, offering prayer beads and amulets for luck.

Karniel smirked as he felt the light touch of several pickpockets and cut-purses ply their silent trade. A bit of sad nostalgia flickered in the Paladin leader's heart. He knew what they were doing and how most of them would not see a single coin of the goods they were pilfering. Gently, he guided the young fingers away from his prayer beads and money bag. Even though the bag was empty, it was a gift from Liam and he wanted to keep it.

Having finally arrived at their destination, Kayth pushed open one of the massive warehouse sliding doors and welcomed them to their new base of operations. Fifteen Paladins, in varying stages of removing armor, greeted the arriving mix of Rangers and fellow Paladins with tired expressions. Seeing this, Karniel asked if they could save the introductions until after everyone had time to find a bunk and settle in. The prospect of sleeping on a cot, instead of the hard earth, was so enticing that the whole group agreed.

The young leader had to smile as he watched his troop be guided upstairs. Already, they had a spirit of friendship that would serve them well in the days to come. Turning back to his second in command, Karniel asked Tomas what he thought they should do for joint training and preparation.

Both groups were accustomed to fighting in their own signature styles and strengths. But being independent warriors would not aid them in the hunting of such a cunning foe.

Rangers could pick a specific target from two to three hundred yards away and send an arrow within an inch of where they wanted it to land. This made fighting bandits ideal, as the raiders did not have a true chain of command. If the fighting ever came in close, the elite archers were masters of knife and hand-to-hand combat, making quick work of those encumbered by bulky armor.

The Paladins were the masters of field and siege combat. Using their plate armor as weapons, they were trained to take out any and all leaders of the opposition, especially dark mages or shadow priests. While only the ordained holy warriors could use healing or protection magic, all were trained to use sword, spear, axe, and hammer to bring righteous judgment to all.

Karniel's biggest concern was how to make them work as a cohesive unit.

Noticing Kayth hovering in the background, sizing up them both up, the Paladin leader called her over and the three of them devised a series of drills and strategies to try and use. They would be leaving in four days, and, for the life of them, it needed to work.

❦21❦

An old man in raggedy attire and greasy hair looked just beyond the hedgerow to see the Fire Brand troops and the Bear foresters arriving in the city. He had been following them since their arrival on the southern side of the mountains. Each soldier was carefully counted and remembered, on the off chance he needed that information later. Most folks called him Ashith, or the hermit, but few truly understood his mission.

A subtle grin creased his lips. With the arrival of the Fire Brand's special unit, his plans were in full swing. As he hobbled out of sight, his pace took on power and vitality and his back straightened. The hermit melted away and a middle-aged man appeared in sailor's travel garb. With a spring in his step, the man pretending to be a sailor mounted a horse that had been secreted away beyond the hedgerow. With a final glance, the costumed man yanked on the reins, spurring the horse towards the north road. If everything went according to plan, he and his allies would control the region in a week's time.

It took the better part of the night, and a fresh horse, for the man to reach his destination at the farthest point on Heartbreak Path, the old keep. To outside eyes, the abandoned ancestral home of the Oak Clan looked run down and in disrepair, but it was very much alive with activity. Torches were already lit, and the overnight sentries were fresh at their posts. Crisp salutes welcomed the arriving rider as he crossed over the bridge and into the cylindrical keep that was built flush against the mountains. Tossing his reins to a stable man, the middle-aged rider marched up the stone stairs to the awaiting war room.

Four sets of eyes looked up as he entered the once magnificent banquet hall. The leader of the keep, Harold, smiled grimly. "I take it your little trip was profitable, Gareth," the former Fire Brand leader asked.

Arrogance filled the former soldier's voice as the Bandit King Gareth poured himself a drink. For over five years, Harold's dream of besting

Tomas and reigning fire and destruction upon the Southern Province fueled the out of control spiral he had once had into a typhoon of madness. The Stranger had sent Gareth to guide the once respected soldier, and hopefully cripple the southern region in the process.

Pulling from a well of composure he had gained under the Stranger's tutelage, the cunning Gareth answered to the affirmative, only giving specific answers and not volunteering any extra information. Returning to the map table, he conveyed what had transpired at the mountain opening and the city gate. To the bandit's joy, Harold took the news somewhat bitterly.

"So Arth has returned from the Mystic Islands," Harold asked to no one in particular. "I will *end* their bloodline," he swore, driving his fist into the table. Barking for more wine, the enraged Fire Brand traitor demanded his lieutenants stay and formulate a new plan.

Gareth, knowing this would take at least two hours, settled into a chair and waited with anticipation. He knew Harold was not skilled enough to launch a full scale war against the mighty walls of Rogue's Bluff. What they needed was to wait for the hunters to leave their defenses and then attack in force, but Gareth knew it would never happen without a little luck.

Any time a solid idea or strategy was offered, the drunken idiot, Harold, roared it down. He wanted scorched earth and razed settlements, but that was not the way to win these types of campaigns. Hit and run tactics had always been the bandits' way of life, with speed as an ally. Combining several bandit units was hard enough, but adding the idiocies of Harold was making it nigh on impossible.

Harold had lost his nerve over the defeat in the Desert, and what was left of his respect when he was released from the army in dishonor. The thirst for blood, and his "good name", had driven the man to madness and utter stupidity.

Choosing to stay in the war room until Harold screamed himself hoarse, Gareth dismissed the rest of the men. He told them to get some rest as he, too, left the former soldier to wallow in self pity and wine. Casting one last look at the self-proclaimed king of the south, Gareth wondered if that was how he looked all those years ago.

With the arrival of the early morning sentries on the outer walls of the keep, the former desert bandit was in his room on the top floor, pondering over an old tome he had salvaged from the Oak Clan's library. He had changed greatly over the last four years. Gone was the blind rage and weak ambition. Now, only cold calculation and thinking several moves ahead dominated his mind. It disgusted him that he was once like Harold, easily manipulated and controlled by the more baser prides and pitfalls that so easily beset fools.

The Stranger had kept his word and forged him into a leader of men.

Placing the tome on the dresser near his bed, Gareth laid down, placing his hands behind his head. Sleep slowly relaxed the man, with dreams of strategies and contingency plans for what lay ahead.

———◆———

The irritating screaming of gulls woke Karniel long before he needed to be up. Regular sleep schedules were hard to come by, as the port and her docks never closed. Fishing vessels were out and about long before the sun, as well as food vendors tempting sailors and dock workers alike with their wares. The smell of fish always drove the gulls into a frenzy, thus the never ending cries. Cursing the birds for their disturbance, the leader of the special unit balled up his pillow and buried his head in the soft fabric, hoping for a couple more hours of sleep. Such dreams were forgotten with Kayth entering the small store room that he had slept in.

The upper level of the building was filled to capacity so Karniel had found a room small enough to sleep in and had crashed for the night. His troops, however, stayed up talking with the Paladins assigned to the city, getting a layout of the locals and how they felt about the attacks and the military in general.

"Rise and shine, lazy bones," Kayth quipped as she opened the storage room door. Housing two shelves lined with dry food, it had enough room for a sleeping roll and the man trying to fall back asleep. The death glare she received only made her chuckle more. "Not a morning person, I see. Well, your friend Tomas has already eaten and is chomping at the bit to start the day."

Yanking the blanket off Karniel, she gasped and blushed at what she saw. In Kayth's mind, if there was ever a mortal that personified the God of War and Fire, it was the male specimen laying before her.

Karniel wore a pair of pants, but no shirt, and his corded, strong muscles tightened as he rose with a growl. Several battle scars were evident against his powerful, tan torso. And the whipping marks from his childhood still discolored his arms and back.

"Wait outside, Paladin." Such simple words, but the manner of conveying them caused Kayth to spin on her heels in a flash and run out of the room. She slammed the door shut and pressed herself against it. Her frantic breathing was so loud she did not hear Tomas approaching.

Shaking his head scandalously, the Ranger poked fun at the awkward situation as he leaned against his long bow. "I warned you it was a bad idea. Even Pethio was not foolish enough to try and wake him." His laughter compounded into a full, all-out fit of giggles as she was lightly pushed by the door.

Karniel had gotten dressed in a light boiled leather tunic in a flash, but he could not leave, as the door seemed to be barred shut. All he could hear was Tomas' laughing, and the half awake Paladin was in no mood for games. Leaning his right shoulder against the wooden surface, he shoved the door open with little resistance.

Kayth's eyes dropped as she spun on her heal and back-stepped from the door. Her new senior officer stepped out of the doorway, anger boiling in his eyes. This was not how she wanted to start the day, especially since she was up for promotion. Her brain and mouth seemed to fail. All she could do was fumble through a disheartened attempt to apologize.

Cutting a death glare at Tomas, who was rolling on the floor giggling, Karniel went straight out of the warehouse and into the nearest tavern. He wanted to hide from his friend's laughter and Kayth's apologies. The last thing he wanted to do was lose his temper their first full day in the city, and he was dangerously close to doing exactly that.

———◆———

The Golden Whale, rather by luck or divine providence, found itself directly in front of the Paladins' southern headquarters. With a steady stream of law enforcers as customers, the tavern was free from the typical rowdiness that usually populated such establishments. That suited the owner just fine. The ale stayed cold, the hearth warm, and the food good, thus allowing a better class of patrons.

There were only a small handful of dock workers in the tavern, as the morning meal had already been served and lunch had yet to be cooked. The bouncer at the bar inclined his head to the entering Paladin, signaling for a tavern maid to tend to the arriving guest. Electing for a back table deep in the far corner, the rather large, green-eyed young man sat fuming over the morning's events.

Why Kayth had decided to wake him so early was beyond Karniel's comprehension. The sun had not yet risen so he could have still slept for at least another hour, he mused in anger. His brooding was such that a rather attractive red-haired bar maid dropped off a plate of warm, crisp bread and eggs and gave him a wink without his notice. Normally such attention would cause the Paladin Captain to blush, but all his lack of regard managed was to hurt the server's feelings.

The sound of wood screaming under the strain of a heavy body broke Karniel out of his headspace. Arth groaned, and, helping himself to the bounty, tore Karniel's bread in half. With a grin, he nodded at the freshness of the loaf. Turning his attention to the young man, the clan leader spoke from the heart.

"Me nephew is the last living heir of our clan, and a damn fine Ranger. His father would be proud of what Tomas has made of himself. I owe you a debt of gratitude for helping him on the March. Gods alone know why anyone would want to go to such a hot place."

Thumping his chest, the robust clansman continued. "Proud we are of our heritage, ancestors, and always having strong chiefs to lead, like my brother and I. It keeps the clan protected and whole. All I have are silly daughters, who all married weak husbands incapable of leadership. Tomas must survive," he grunted, using his bread to point.

"I want your word as a man, and a Paladin, that you will do everything in your power to help Tomas survive or kill the fool who ends his life."

Karniel understood the concern of his company. Hunting bandits, especially organized ones, was particularly nasty and dangerous work. Only the best were handpicked by the Inner Circle to eradicate the menace. Tomas was the best archer and knife fighter his division had seen in decades. Karniel reluctantly swore the oath, but explained that he was not able to stay with his friend every minute of every day.

Rich laughter caused the other patrons to look at Karniel's table with irritable surprise. "I don't expect you to share his bed, lad," Arth commented with a hearty chuckle. "Just keep him safe in battle, son, and we will be even." A smile broke through the Paladin's perplexed mood and the two shared a good meal, exchanging stories of past glories.

———◆———

Tomas, now in a serious mood, ran his archers through the drill again. Only five were able to get their arrows into the helmet slits at one hundred feet away. Their leader wanted at least half of them to be able do it. Fifteen longbow strings hummed in the ground level of the Paladin-owned warehouse. An extra three penetrated the armored head gear, with two more making it into the slit. Smiling with excitement, the Ranger leader praised those that had hit the mark. Soon, he thought, they would be out hunting bandits and everyone needed to be their best.

As the morning continued, Tomas incorporated the Paladins into the mix. He had the bowmen hit specific targets while the mace-wielding warriors stemmed off attacks from some of the foot soldiers that were assigned to the fort. Each group performed their respective dance moves with ease and grace, ready to test their worth against the allotted foe.

Karniel and Kayth entered the warehouse, after spending time with the visiting clans' leadership, and called all to attention. Local intelligence claimed a large and dangerous cluster of raiders was seen coming towards the port city. It was time to act.

Looking at the gathering with a sense of pride and caution, the Paladin leader told them to prepare themselves. In the morning they would go hunting. With the aid of the clan foresters, they hoped to have a handle on the situation by a fortnight, if not earlier.

As cheers erupted and echoed off the warehouse walls, Tomas felt a foreboding chill run down his spine. They were suppose to have more time to train and work out a solid battle plan. The dark feeling refused to dissipate from his mind. He just hoped it was not like the night his father had died.

———◆———

The Golden Whale and her sister taverns were busy that night with drinks flowing into the wee hours of the morning. In fact, the whole city seemed to come alive and be in quite the festive mood with the destruction of the bandits on the horizon. As the ale and mead loosened the soldiers' lips, dancing girls and tavern maids took interest. The women knew a particular man that would pay handsomely for information, especially when it came to the Fire Brand soldiers.

One extremely drunk unit leader climbed atop a table and proclaimed that he would kill every single law breaker in the country. Disruptive cheers joined his exclamation. No one noticed the patroness of the Golden Whale slipping out the back.

Gareth, in the guise of Ashith the beggar, waited in a side alley near the taverns, smiling at the voluptuous brunette before him. She ran his eyes and ears in the taverns and the port. Her deep eyes and attractive figure trapped every soldier and sailor for fifty miles.

"They leave tomorrow," she purred with a grin. "Most are heading to the fort to the west of us, but a handful are hunting you and yours. Arth and his clan mean to join this little game. Be ready. As usual, none of those goody Paladins decided to join in the fun."

Smiling wickedly, he tossed the tavern owner a small sack of coins. "My thanks, dear one. Keep us informed of any changes and we will make sure you and the girls stay well-funded."

Returning the smile, the patroness giggled and bowed. "Anything for the Bandit King." Her hips swayed in a tempting way, hoping to entice the man she knew was under the rags and powder. Pausing at the inn's rear entrance, she blew the former desert bandit a kiss before returning to her drunken customers.

Ashith's brain raced to find a way to cripple the arriving force before they even reached the fort. An ambush would be ideal, he thought, as his character leaned against an empty ale barrel. But where could he get the much needed numbers in time? Then a truly wicked idea came to him like a strike of lightning and he disappeared into the night.

———◆———

Pounding heads and queasy stomachs controlled the troop the next morning as they marched away from the Inn District and out the main gatehouse. Almost the entire replacement troop was sporting hangovers, with a few still mildly drunk. Kayth called for a quick-step speed to make up for the lost time of finding all the wayward soldiers. She personally had to find three of the Master-at-Arms sergeants in a wine cellar and had to rouse them from the beds of bar wenches. Morale was dismal at best as a faint mist rolled in and cloud cover blanketed the sky with a steel gray color.

Right outside the Northern Gate, the hung-over soldiers bid farewell to their fellows and proceeded down the bank to a brick road that led to the Castille of Shaman's Pass. It would take the company a total of five days to reach the wondrous mountain fortress. But, with as slow as they were moving, Karniel would be surprised if they showed up within two weeks.

Twenty miles from the port city's outer wall, the Port Road forked back into the Miner's Road and Heartbreak Path. There, in the green, Arth's clansmen waited in all their glory.

Gone were the camouflaged cloaks and clothing. This hunt begged them to present the clan colors and banner. A rich ocean blue sash, checkered with a gold design, was worn as a belt by the lower ranks. Those with more experience and hunts sported the same colors, but in tunic form. This was not to be a covert operation, but open season on a swarm of pests that had overstayed its welcome.

Arth's son-in-law, a tall, sickly man nicknamed Temoer, clutched the standard for dear life. Its arrangement was simple yet inspiring, with a golden honey bear on two legs, backed by a blue field. No bandit, having seen this flag in battle, had lived to tell the tale.

Nodding to the clan, Karniel called his company to a halt. He had noticed some of the Southerners were sporting bandages streaked in red.

A haunted gaze of death controlled those native sons, especially the ones that had lost family. No illusions of a romantic nature clouded their idea of war. This was to be payback. Pure and simple.

"We have bloodied ourselves already," Arth barked with a sinister sparkle. "The fishing hamlet along the banks of the Golden Vain Creek was razed to the ground, and there were no survivors. Those foolish enough to stay behind were given a one way trip to the Parthenon. The tracks for the rest of them head west towards Shaman's Highway and Council Plains."

Spurring his massive warhorse, the giant of a man towered over Karniel. The metallic scent of blood and fear oozed from his double-bellied axe. "It's time to put you pups though your hops, lad. There be folks that need to die."

The last words were whispered as a prayer of thanks. Yanking on the reins, Arth rallied his troops and charged towards the land of the Crossed Oars Clan. He intended to kill everything in sight. Karniel followed suit, albeit begrudgingly. As they thundered down the hunting trail, and over the rolling grasslands, the Paladin could not help but wonder if the regular soldiers heading to the western border were under attack.

22

The fearful shrills of horses dying, mixed with death rattles, filled the smoky, dust-filled air. Gareth sat ramrod straight astride his gray stallion on the hill top and watched the carnage unfold on the road leading to Shaman's Pass. It was he that had sent those few raiders to the fishing village. He needed to do something to keep Arth busy while other plans were made.

Gareth's group of fifty mounted marauders and twenty archers were turning the dirt road and the lush emerald grass red with blood and body parts. Despite being outnumbered and outmatched, the bandits were making easy work . This was due to the sheer amount of alcohol these Fire Brand men-at-arms had consumed the night before. It was truly a pathetic sight.

Normally, such a devastating lose could not have happened. But the former desert bandit had told his network of working girls to keep the soldiers drinking well into the night. Laughing at his own genius, Gareth remembered the last words his father had imparted before the young man left home: never trust a beautiful woman. Oh well, the reformed bandit thought, as he surveyed the scene, they should have known better.

The ragtag raider force was comprised of criminals from the jail cells of Rogue's Bluff. Most were rapists, thieves, or murderers, while some were just petty fools who got caught disrespecting the Port Lord. Luckily, all wanted out, and a handful of gold leaf coins. Equipping them was a far simpler matter. Weapons and armor were in great supply in the jail storeroom, so they liberated the necessary instruments of death.

One of the scouts raced towards Gareth, out of breath and sawing the reins of his stolen horse. "It's completed, my Lord," the young man said through gasps for air. Blood was spattered across the lad's face and torso, but none of it his. The attacking leader was about to thank the scout for the news, but spurred his mount forward as the messenger vomited from shock and fear.

"Was this your first time to kill a man, son," Gareth asked, while circling the mounted rider. A pale, sweaty face gave a confirming answer to the question as another wave of gut-wrenching nausea engulfed the young man. "It will be alright, my boy," Gareth commented, handing the lad a flask of grain alcohol. "Just breath and the shock will pass. Everyone pukes their first time."

With the utter defeat of the replacement troop, and the pilfering of the dead that followed, finished, Gareth blew a loud, solid note on his bugle, calling his men to regroup and hunt for another target. They would lead the combined hunting force on a merry chase, giving Harold the much needed time to finish the siege preparations.

In less than an hour and a half of hard riding over hills and crossing the Golden Vain Creek's delta, the combined forces of the Paladins, Rangers, and clansmen arrived at the scene of a bloody massacre.

Mangled limbs were tossed this way and that, as wild animals and birds feasted on the discarded remains. Some bodies were stripped of armor, weapons, or boots. But, down to the last man, each one had been ravaged for coin, jewels, or precious items. Even the horses and mules had been disemboweled in an effort to find anything hidden away.

Tied to a sign post was the leader of the replacement troops, the same one that had boasted the night before of ridding the south of all law breakers. He had been positioned as if to embrace the wooden post, with his arms wrapping around the sign. Braided rawhide lashings joined both hands, as it ran across his back, showing off a symbol that had been carved into the man. To all present, it was a familiar image, one that was chosen to bring forth feelings of strength, honor, and duty. But seeing the seal of the army so disgustingly displayed, the only feeling was that of uncontrollable rage and fury.

Feral, barbaric cries for revenge and blood erupted out of the small valley, flowing up and down the road with the power of churning rapids. Nothing would stop these men from avenging their fallen comrades. Nothing.

———— ◆ ————

Relentless drizzle streamed down the wall of the map tent. Overcast skies matched the mood of the troops in the forest. It had been two weeks and they had not seen hide or hair of a single bandit troop they were chasing. Even with the added men from the Stag, Crossed Oars, and Oak Clans, this ordeal was beginning to feel like chasing a gang of ghosts. Morale was dangerously low in the camp. The fire and rage from the valley massacre had begun to grow cold under the never-ending rain and cold nights.

Karniel, Tomas, Kayth, Arth, and the other clan leaders stared at the map of the great forest. In the last three days, the hunters had begun to cast a wide net, sending out small groups of fighters to box in the prey they so desperately sought. Only two miles were left unmarked on the provided map. All eyes went to the old keep deep within the Oak Clan's territory.

"If they *are* there, it will be a tough nut to crack," Arth commented in a gravelly voice. Long had he suspected that bandits had a spy somewhere in the camp feeding them information. All the leaders felt the same way. How else was it possible for the bandits to vanished into thin air? None of the scout reports had been accurate since this hunt started.

An alarm rippled through the camp as a rider in full military armor approached. All the leaders walked out of the tent to face the new arrival, only to have that murderous flame reignite in their hearts.

Harold smiled disdainfully. None of the troops he saw in the camp worried him greatly. Their morale was down and many looked ready to abandon the campaign. Sitting straighter in the saddle, he reveled in their misery. Too many campaigns had taught the traitor that such feelings would soon fester mutiny and death. He loved it.

His blood lust tripled as Tomas walked towards him. But what truly irked Harold was how all the leaders had weapons drawn, except for the whelp. Astride his cream-colored horse, Harold addressed the company, but his eyes kept returning to the young Ranger.

"Mighty warriors," he began with arms stretched out, "your effort has been a valiant one. Let us dispense with false ideas and foolishness. My associates and I just want to live in peace with our neighbors. You came to our land seeking war and violence." His powerful words caused a flicker of worry among the Fire Brand troops. Was it possible they were sent under false pretenses?

"I have called my friends to run from you in the hope your leaders would see the honesty of our ways. I pray to each of the thirteen saints that we can reach some form of peace."

A deep commanding voice broke through the rehearsed presentation, questioning the validity of the rote speech. "Do you fear us, old man?"

Harold turned towards the voice, seeing a parting of the troops and the leaders approaching.

"The last time we faced each other, you lost spectacularly, and then got your arse whooped by Isaak, our March Commander." Tomas stood defiantly, with his typical roguish grin plastered on his face, leaning against his long bow. "You looking for a rematch? And as for wanting to live in peace, what do you have to say for all those women , children, and old men you carted off? What of our fallen brethren you butchered like cattle two weeks ago? Either stand and fight or leave, *coward!*"

The challenge struck a chord with the troops as anger and pride filled their souls for their fallen comrades once again.

False pride and arrogance fueled the return statement. "Meet us at the Keep, *Boy*, for my spear thirsts for your blood!" His facade quickly faded away with every word. Wrapping the reins in his gauntleted hand, Harold yanked hard to the left, causing the animal to circle wildly. He spurred the horse into control and galloped towards the stone edifice, ready to end the game once and for all.

———◆———

Life was again pulsating in the combined camp as each weapon was sharpened and every piece of armor was checked. Years of drilling and training guided the preparatory actions. Meanwhile, the leaders returned to the tent to plan a lengthy siege. Now that the target was clear, true preparations had to be made.

By nightfall, a plan had been formulated and every unit was prepared for the battle ahead. With the added numbers of all the local clans, Karniel's force grew four-fold, allowing for auxiliaries to the Bear clan militias. Siege warfare was a risky business for both parties. If food stocks or water became tainted, or sickness caught hold of either group, the battle was over.

Egos and long-time rivalries were forgotten during this momentous occasion. Each clan had a clear objective that would allow for revenge without being blinded by anger. All eyes looked to the Keep. It was time to end the fight, once and for all.

———◆———

For all Harold's drunken tirades and outbursts, he needed victory to crush the spirit of the southern region, thus creating his own little kingdom. None of his followers were with him on principle or heart. Each one of them was promised a section of land and slaves to work it. If he couldn't deliver that, the army amassing outside would be the least of his worries.

Being built into the mountain, the Keep was protected from normal siege tactics. With a solid rock outer wall, fully equipped with a drawbridge and portcullis, this operation would not be an easy walk for Harold's enemies. The former ancestral home had four internal water supplies, and a network of caves that ran deep into the mountains.

Harold had training dummies built to be placed along the wall to give the illusion of greater numbers. If the attacking archers wasted their munitions on the false troops, all the better. Smugness settled in the former soldier's attitude as he walked throughout the Keep, double-checking all the preparations. He knew he would win, no matter what. It was his destiny.

Gareth charged into the barracks like a whirlwind, causing the door to slam and crack against the stone wall. "Where is he," the lithe predator demanded, eyes alight with fury.

The command caused every member of the ragtag marauders to jump with shock. A dark cloud of violence and mayhem festered around the reformed bandit king. They all had heard stories of his spectacular displays of ire and bloodletting, and they wanted none of it.

"Answer me, you worthless lot of milk drinkers! Where is Harold!?!"

Thirty-four fingers quickly pointed at the door leading to the war room. Harold might be their leader, but Gareth held the real power and the reins on everyone's fears.

"You short-minded idiot," Gareth roared at the man studying the battle plan. "We were to wait another week, until they were almost broken, and then destroy their camp. What stupor possessed you to do this?"

Crushing a clay-molded soldier, Harold declared he wanted revenge for his slighted name. Chunking the clay remains at Gareth, he commanded his personal guard to remove the man from the Keep. "I have no further need of your false help," Harold growled at Gareth's retreating figure. It would be his victory, his alone.

Through the Keep, Gareth was guided under armed guard. He knew where they were leading him, and oddly enough, it actually suited his purposes. Even though Harold's map room was on the first floor of the tall keep, several sub levels had been added by the slaves captured in each raid. Coming from strong stock, the southerners were able to carve out numerous alcoves and install iron walls with a door.

Now that an attack had become a reality, just about every alcove in the sad, gray-colored rock was full of the same workers that created the makeshift prison. Seeing each of the kidnapped victims, Gareth almost felt a pitch of pity for them. If they were killed off, who would till the ground and harvest the crops? Harold's lust for blood had made him forget the first principle of warfare: never kill the populace unless it was needed.

Soldiers were trained to kill, not farm. If the army had to become farmers, then who would be the army? Such ideas had to be planned for and understood. Despite all his efforts, Gareth knew this was a lost cause. The patchwork force of armed bullies would never be enough to stem the flow of trained Paladins, Rangers, and people who wanted their land back.

As luck would have it, one of the younger caged people threw a chamber pot at the guards escorting Gareth. This gave the broad-shouldered prisoner the much needed chance to liberate a dagger from the guard on his right. Plunging the sharp, six inch steel blade deep into the former owner's throat, the desert bandit made quick work of the last three men sent by Harold.

Hearing the jailer attempting to warn the others, Gareth flipped the blood-soaked instrument of death over. Gripping the tip, he sent the knife sailing through the air with deadly accuracy. A loud grunt and gurgling was all that sounded in the stone hallway. The jailer, who had regularly abused and raped his prisoners, died, drowning in his own blood.

Freeing the keys from the abusive dead man's belt, Gareth unlocked each of the cells containing locals, and told them that an attack was about to happen. He led them through a back passage that emptied into a small cave three miles to the west. The jail breaker was shocked to hear a chorus of praises and thanks from the escapees. Never had he been thanked before, and the feeling felt as foreign to him as a fish trying to swim in the sky.

Casting a final glance down the prison passage, Gareth sighed with defeat. It was a good plan, he thought as he ran down the natural path towards freedom. He knew the Master would not see it that way, but then again, he should not be surprised that the rabid dog had turned on his caretakers.

23

Hushed whispers passed from unit to unit as they fanned out along the tree line twenty yards in front of the Keep. Excitement buzzed as the hour grew close for the attack. The plan was simple and everyone had a role to play. The time for the romantic side of warfare was gone. This was dirty, nasty, bloody work and only those mentally prepared would survive the night.

Tomas, facing the front gate, notched a heavy metal arrow. Its purpose was simple: drive into the portcullis chain and dislodge it. Lean, powerful muscles drew the bowstring to his chin while he took aim. Seeing the chain gear box, the young archer changed targets and released. His arrow soared true, striking the gear and knocking the chain and gears loose.

Furious yells from inside the courtyard soon followed as the heavy wooden portcullis slammed into the ground, locking in place. A handful of Harold's men tried to get the barrier to rise, but to no avail. They were stuck within the walls, with no known way out. More bandits rushed to the outer wall, running along the upper passages, trying to figure out what to do.

Fire arrows lit up the night sky as they sailed into the Keep, striking the mock soldiers, criminals, and wooden barrels. Harold's army scattered like rats, looking for water and praying their leader had a plan. Nightmarish chaos continued while the almost endless downpour of arrows littered anyone that dared to come out of hiding.

This madness allowed Arth and his clan to fire hooked arrows over the wall, with ropes trailing behind them. With Tomas' archers sending another volley, the clansmen were able to spider crawl up the thirty foot wall, over the ramparts, and engage the enemy.

Step one complete, Karniel thought as he called the Paladins to him. With four thick cables secured to the stone ramparts of the wall by the clansmen, his group made their way up to fulfill their sworn duty.

Arrows, shot from the far end of the wall by a handful of Harold's men, struck a few of the armored fighters climbing. Their plated armor protected the more vital areas. The initial shock had worn off and order returned to the bandits, under the leadership of the more seasoned raiders. A fresh unit arrived on the wall, just as Karniel and Kayth crested, and they wanted blood.

The blonde rushed forward and slid across the stone floor at the last minute, cutting the first three off at the knees. Their comrades, knowing no brotherhood, tossed the fallen fighters off the wall and met Karniel in full force.

The male Paladin did not bother to pull his weapon. Armored gauntlets crushed jaw bones and broke ribs with each overwhelming blow. A pure, white hot fire raged in the former street urchin. These men were not fighting for duty or honor, but some fool's idea of power.

With the last of his attackers down, and the wall clear, Karniel blew on a horn. This signal sent a group of fighters down each of the steps, leading into the courtyard of the Keep, in a pincer movement. It was time for justice to finally have its due

———◆———

Tomas called his Rangers to the walls. Bows were unstrung and left behind, as they would provide little in the way of close quarter fighting. Long dirks and small throwing axes were the weapons of choice for these men. Each had endured years of training, and hours of practice, in the bloody art of knife and axe warfare. Up the wall they climbed, like ants, refusing to break their speed. Loyal to a fault, Fire Brand Rangers never left a soldier defenseless.

The pandemonium that had erupted in the courtyard began to spill into the front halls and rooms of the Keep. The bandits had no exit in place and they could not stem the tide of never-ending clansmen or Fire Brand fighters. Falling back to the main hall, the bandits needed room and time to launch a counter offensive.

Harold was in the map room, discussing a plan with four lieutenants, when a handful of bandits poured in, screaming out of fear and pain. Grey goose shafts had turned those would-be soldiers into a seamstress' pincushion. All they wanted was the pain to stop, and they got their wish. Grinning like a mad man, the former Master-at-Arms crushed the heads of each bleeding man with a spiked mace that he had snatched up from the table. Gleaming in gore, the crazed leader demanded more men run towards the outer wall and kill all who dared oppose them. He was back in his element, commanding soldiers and controlling missions.

The mad bandit leader, hearing the clash of steel raging within his castle, rallied his personal guards and headed for the main hall. They knew the last of the fighting would culminate there, and he did not want to miss the chance to cut down the filthy clansmen. Serrated boar spear in hand, Harold cried out for challengers as he entered the hurricane of violence.

Relishing the bloodshed, Harold became drunken with blood lust. Forcing the ripple-edged spear into the stomach of a clansman, he laughed wickedly. Delusions of victory blinded the bandits to the reality of the moment.

With the Rangers joining their Paladin brothers, a well-practiced death machine sliced through all newcomers, like reapers in a wheat field. The Goddess of Death, and her minions, were extremely busy dragging the souls of the damned sent to her kingdom to reluctantly serve her as penance for sinful lives.

The bandit leader's vision narrowed as he spied Tomas entering the fray. A devious plan concocted quickly in his mind, with Harold yelling for Tomas to look his way. The middle-aged man ran up the stairway, pausing just long enough to issue the young bowman a deadly challenge. He wanted to get the lad alone, away from the protection of his friends.

———•———

Tomas, fighting side by side with Kayth, saw Harold running up the stone steps. The words that Harold had shouted were drowned in the noise of men dying, but the intent was clear: he wanted Tomas to duel him. Knowing this could all end with the death of Harold, the Ranger opted to grant the challenge. Turning to the stairs, the southerner flicked his dirk, sending it right into a charging bandit's throat that blocked the path.

Kayth, who had been guarding Tomas' back, grabbed the departing Ranger and planted a kiss on his lips.

"Return to me and I will dance with you," she said, blushing. Her feelings were young and tender but true. His gentle, playful nature had gradually won her over during their campaign. And, despite her never wanting to marry, Tomas respected her and every bit of her rather interesting personality.

Swooning from the power of her kiss, Tomas smiled his most roguish grin and retrieved his dagger. His ma always told him to find a woman worth living for, and by the Gods, he had. Caution guided his steps as he followed the deranged leader up the spiral staircase. The Ranger only hoped the battle would end soon.

———•———

From the middle of the room, Karniel and Arth made quick work of Harold's personal guard. The massive clan leader used a torn tunic to wipe the gore from his ax as he surveyed the damage. Not seeing Tomas, rage engulfed the bear of a man.

"Find me nephew, Paladin," he growled, before cleaving another bandit in half. Karniel watched as the God of Battles possessed Arth so completely that friend and foe gave way to the hellish demon swinging the double-headed weapon.

Seeing Kayth, the male Paladin rushed into the fray straight towards her. He drove his war hammer into the spine of a marauder at her side. His death scream caused the blonde to turn, ready to send a foe into eternity. "Where's Tomas," Karniel yelled over the sound of crashing steel and death. Rapid hand signals told the story of Harold's retreat and Tomas' pursuit. Quickly acknowledging his counterpart, and cutting his way through the enemy ranks, Karniel's mind centered on his oath as a Paladin and a friend.

———◆———

Cresting the last step, Tomas' mind could not comprehend the scene before him. Gems sparkled in the blanket of black that covered the sky. Normally, the Ranger would have enjoyed such an artistic view, but his prey was nowhere to be seen. Just a wooden chair and a bow propped on the seat populated the ramparted roof. As the young archer walked over to the lone seat, a crazed cackling caused the young man to turn back from whence he came. Seeing Harold rushing towards him, spear in hand, Tomas had little time to react as the serrated edge of the spear ripped through his abdomen and out his back.

A soul-splitting scream echoed down the stairway so loud that those in the main hall paused upon hearing the unearthly sound.

Taking the last few steps two at a time, Karniel burst onto the tower roof. Tears filled his eyes as he saw Harold slam both Tomas and the head of the spear into the back of the wooden seat, pinning the younger man in place.

"I've won," Harold proclaimed with nefarious purpose. His arms reached towards the heavens, as if to offer thanks to some heinous deity. Slowly pulling a dagger from its leather home, the fanatical man pressed it against the dying archer's throat as he leaned forward to whisper in Tomas' ear.

"You were never good enough to stop me, dirt digger," Harold spat, with all the hatred in his heart filling each and every word. "Now that you are dead, I will reign down fire and death upon this miserable speck of land and make a new kingdom. Then no one will dare disrespect me again!"

Seeing the pain and anguish that blazed on his friend's face, pure unadulterated hate exploded in Karniel. A singular purpose moved him now, and the Goddess of Death guided his actions. With six sprinting steps, the Paladin leapt into the air, double gripping the deadly weapon overhead, like the killing machine he needed to be.

Pethio had warned him about the finality of this crushing maneuver years ago. Every muscle had to be ready, and one's mind at peace, for this killing blow to work. There was no turning back from it, and no way for the attacker to defend, if the strike failed to miss the mark.

Harold's fighting instinct turned his head to face the heavily-enraged entity soaring towards him. Fear seized his heart, stopping it for a beat. His ears never heard the Paladin's battle cry, or the sickening crush of steel and bone, as the war hammer successfully completed the onslaught known as Driving the Nail. A quick flash of pain and blackness was all his degenerate mind registered before it was completely destroyed.

Stone gray rain clouds parted and columns of sunlight brightened the forest and the Keep. Arth and Kayth celebrated the hard won victory with a joke and a handshake. The portcullis was cut down, and medics, accompanied by shaman healers, poured into the Keep. All the bandits had fallen in the battle, save one, and Arth's ax loosed his tongue. He named people they used as informants at every tavern and brothel in town. The clansmen went on a hunt for the hermit, but he was long gone, through a long forgotten passage.

A lone shaman, the same Silent One that had opened the mountain those weeks past, walked up to Karniel, taking in the scene of absolute heartache. The young man, cradling Tomas' head, had wrapped Harold's cape around the wound, hoping to stem the flow of blood. The Paladin looked up to the shaman with a silent plea, praying for a miracle of magic and hope.

Bowing his head in complete reverence, the Silent One knelt beside Karniel and placed a hand over Tomas' heart. Even in an extremely weakened state, organs could be restored and blood returned to the body. Feverishly, the Shaman went about his work, trying everything in his mighty power to return life to such a deserving hero.

A well of sadness, anger, and confusion struck the Silent One as he looked into Karniel's eyes. The giant of a Paladin knew his friend was gone, and there was nothing that could return him. The Silent One rose and felt the pain of everyone in the Keep, but none more than the young man who ran out of tears.

———— ♦ ————

A week had passed since reports were written and funerals arranged. Tomas, being the only one of his clan to perish, had the largest funeral procession ever recorded in the history of the region. Stories of his greatness and honor were shared by all in the City, for there was never a more favored Son.

Kayth, and the other Paladins, returned to normal service right after the funerals, but none truly wanted to stay in the area. Four of their siblings-in-arms had died in the assault, as well as many clansmen they had come to respect. A depressing cloud hovered over the region as the task force was broken up and orders were given for new assignments.

Arth, true to his nature, went to see his nephew's best friend, who had yet to return to the Paladin warehouse. Bearing a red satin bag, he knocked on the wooden door before entering. Karniel sat on his bed in his rented room at the Golden Whale, nursing a cup of mead, seemingly lost in thought.

"Got somethin' for ya," the gruff man said, half choking with tears. True friends were rare in the military life, and Arth saw Karniel like a son.

The seated young man received the gift for what it was: a peace offering. Untying the thin cord, Karniel was at a loss for words. Tomas' bow, the one he won in the Desert, stood unstrung and freshly oiled. A note from Tomas fell out of the cloth container.

"Read the note, lad, and know that if you ever need a place to live or family, you have one here with us."

Before Karniel could answer, a heavy knock pounded on the door. Jerking the door open, the clan leader glared at two officers in shiny Fire Brand armor. His anger caused them to step back several paces, but his outburst truly set them on edge.

"How do you Northerners expect us to mourn in peace, if you fools keep banging on every table, wall, and door?"

Normally, his mountain-size fury was kept on a tight rein, but his grief was getting the better of him.

"We seek the Paladin Captain Karniel of the Red Keep," the taller officer said, quite distraught at the sight of the clan leader's hand dropping towards his ax.

Sighing, Karniel set down the cup and bow, heading out into the hallway to meet them. He wanted to laugh as eight more clansmen, Arth's personal honor guard and best fighters, encircled the officers. They left no exit down the hall to the left or up the stairs to the right.

"I am the Paladin you seek. What can the Corps do for you?"

His question was understood as a warning. He did not work for the Army alone, but for the Church, and any requests had to be issued by both.

"We are to detain you on suspicion of killing a senior officer. Your trial will be two weeks hence at the Council Room of the Fire Brand Castle."

Angry protests from the surrounding southerners caused more to pour out the tavern' common room and up the stairs, preventing any way of escape. Soon, fifty clansmen were in the building and the street, wielding blades and demanding their friend's release.

Remembering Pethio's orders to heed any calling to return, Karniel quieted the outrage of the clan and agreed, on the condition that he could bestow command on a fellow Paladin before leaving. Not seeing much in the way of a choice, the Army officers agreed.

Carrying the letter and the bow, the young Paladin headed straight for the warehouse and Kayth. He knew she would be there, in her usual spot on the roof, looking out to sea.

Dressed in a green tunic and leggings, the blonde sat on the edge of the roof, basking in the afternoon ocean breeze. Her thoughts of late had been troubling and dark, especially her dreams. Ever since the battle, images of Tomas haunted her: his smirk, the way he blushed, how he leaned against his bow right before saying something. Most of all, she kept seeing his body atop the pyre, while she screamed that all was lost.

Heavy, purposeful steps broke her reflecting and Karniel appeared by her side. Had she not been so pained by the memories of Tomas, she would have seen the sadness in Karniel's heart.

"Kayth of the City of Tears, I hereby pass to you the mantle of Paladin Captain, with all the authorities, powers and responsibilities thereto."

Shock, fear, anger, and loss collided in marvelous chaos in the female's heart the moment she realized what he had said. There was only one time when a Paladin chose to relinquish command, and that was by the order of the Military and the Church.

Following Karniel out of the building and into the street, tears obscured Kayth's vision. She wailed in heartbreak the moment her beloved and respected Captain was put in irons like some common criminal.

Every single living member of the attack force still in Rogue's Bluff lined the main avenue. They held weapons drawn and ready for the command to free the chained warrior. None came, however, as Karniel put his faith in the system that he was so willing to die for.

Casting a final smile to his friends and allies, he waved farewell from the caged wagon and began the journey northward.

24

Karniel's jailers forcefully removed all his armor and weapons the moment they had him secured in the southern gatehouse of the Red Keep. Even the golden hammer medallion Pethio had given him to show his rank was brutishly taken and stored in a secure location.

After that embarrassing ordeal, chain shackles and woolen prison clothes were added to ensure insult to injury. No one spoke as he was marched, under the armed guard of ten men, through the Keep's courtyard in plain view. His former unit members were commanded not to witness the spectacle, as the Inner Circle feared a riot within their halls.

Never had such an ostentatious display presented itself within the walls of the Red Keep. Half the reports from the battle claimed Karniel to be a hero, a savior even, to the southern region. Under his leadership, a great victory was won. Yet, there were a small number of conflicting stories. The loss of an entire replacement division, a spy ring set up to deface the Fire Brand's foothold in the city, and the death of a former high ranking officer all appeared to condemn the Paladin Captain. The only option left to truly find the truth was a trial.

Thus, Karniel found himself escorted to the bowels of Fire Brand Castle, like a common thug.

Positioned in the sub levels of the Castle, hidden away from the world, was the cold and dangerous world of the Mine. Although the name was something of a misdirect, prisoners worked day and night to open up new tunnels for water flow and waste movement. They were the ones that actually maintain the foundations of the Keep and her cellars positioned deep into the bedrock.

Taskmasters walked about with clubs or staves, waiting for the slightest pause or misdeed. Sadistic and abusive, these men cared little for those in their charge, nor in any ideas of justice.

The cells, located in an abandoned section of the Mine, were a mere four feet across and eight feet deep. Sacks of straw or saw dust were used to keep the inmates from getting cold or sick. But, more often than not, the pathetic excuse for a mattress was never changed out. Fleas, ticks, and lice covered everyone, and the dust from the mining gave each worker a persistent hacking cough.

A single guard would unlock the heavy iron door to the cell chamber every day as the prisoners were herded to the work areas. The same action was used at night to lock them all up at the end of their twelve hour shift. Thus, escape was nigh on impossible for anyone sentenced to the forgotten realm beneath the Keep.

If Karniel could survive this environment for seven days, his official trial in front of the military tribunal would begin.

By the third night in the stone underbelly, a string of disgruntled and angry visitors began to stop by, cussing and spitting on the caged man. None of his fellow prisoners came to Karniel's aid, nor did the guard stop them. It was all part of the plan to break him mentally, emotionally, and spiritually. The sad irony was that none of these men actually served with the dead traitor Harold. They just could not stomach the fact that a Paladin bested one of their own.

The morning of day four brought different visitors to the imprisoned Paladin. The guard did not unlock Karniel's cell door, like the previous days. Instead, an evil, toothless smile was plastered to his face as the rest of the condemned were corralled away. The former Paladin figured they were just trying to starve him or attempting to play some form of mind game. So he sat on his mattress and meditated in the utter darkness.

Torch light flickered down the hall as wooden batons clanked on the iron bars. Both the light and the noise pulled Karniel back to reality and into a battle calm. Emotionless eyes watched as six drunken men staggered against the pig iron bars, yelling for vengeance.

Each one wore a tattered version of the Master-at-Arms uniform, complete with stains and tears. Gone was the air and prowess of a soldier. All these men were a lifeless dried husk of what they had been. The leader, a task master from another of the Mine's sections, produced an old iron key with an evil grin. Rusty gears turned under the key's influence as Karniel realized what the game was: they wanted him to fight back, or possibly to kill. That way there would be cause to sentence him to a lifetime of working in that nightmare.

Rising to meet his oppressors, the giant of a man calmly accepted the stupidity of the situation. Karniel knew these were mere pawns, worthless fools sent to bring about an end to political theatrics. What he did not count on was the extent they would go to achieve their objective. They wanted blood, and by the Gods, they would have it.

Over the next two days, the beatings were a regular occurrence. No bones or vital organs were damaged or injured, but such brutality and violence left a different type of mark. Any illusions of a fair or just trial were gone like the dew of last season. He knew they were going to kill him in order to save face. His faith in the military had finally crumbled to dust.

Such underhanded politics did not deserve to be embedded in the fabric of the military. The next fools that came to his cell would understand how poorly they had judged the situation.

A massive explosion rocked Jaldo's tower to its very foundation. Stone dust and wood splinters created a dense fog as the shards from the handcrafted wooden doors shattering like glass. The fragments lodged in the opposite wall. The room's occupants did not even have time to register the attack before the Grand Master of the Paladin Corp entered with all his wrath and glory.

Divine Light radiated off his body, creating a halo that engulfed his person. His eyes glowed with a rich, earthy color as he called upon his power and magic. The full extension of his office burned with each measured step. He came for answers, and not even Death herself would stop him from getting them.

"Have you lost your mind," Varg demanded of Pethio as he rose to his feet, sword drawn and at the ready.

Such actions were in direct violation of the charter all four guilds had signed over a thousand years ago. The Lord Protector placed himself between the intruder and his leader, ready to defend the Lord Commander with his life, if need be.

The Grand Master respected Varg's willingness to place himself in harm's way. Such loyalty was to be commended, but this was neither the time nor the place. Raw emotions clouded sound judgment, and Pethio had no desire to stroke egos.

With a slight flick of his left wrist, the enormous Paladin sent Varg flying through the air and on to one of the newly added benches. Landing with a loud grunt, the military leader was shocked, but in no way injured.

"Release Paladin Captain Karniel. You have no right to hold him by common or spiritual law." His tone, while flat and nonthreatening, demanded action from the listeners.

An uneasiness settled deep into the room. Jaldo shared a knowing look with his fellow leaders. Standing, the Lord Commander retrieved a single leaf of parchment from his desk. He had a feeling it would come to this, but he did not relish the fact.

"This was not my idea, old friend," the Lord Commander commented with sadness, handing the giant man the piece of thick paper. "Your orders are to return to the Paladin tower at the Cathedral until further notice. By decree of the Council of Bishops, you and yours are not to interfere with the trial or testify on the behalf of the young man. I am truly sorry."

Any affection or sympathies were lost in the soul-splitting, gut-wrenching despair that controlled Pethio.

Never hah such an order been issued. The Corps was trained, even indoctrinated, with the ideal of never leaving a brother or sister of the Order behind. Yet, here was a command from the Holy Bishopric demanding just that.

The Grand Master left in stunned silence as the faith he carried in his beliefs and ideals fell to the ground with his tears.

———◆———

Liam glared at each of the Inner Circle, in turn, while easing his dagger in its sheath.

His father, the Heavy Cavalier Commander, had called for this particular meeting of all the Inner Circle. He felt they needed to discuss the growing hostility within the ranks. Each of the five leaders had hoped to keep the trial a private matter. The hero status Karniel had earned throughout his career, and at Battle School, made that next to impossible.

Slamming his goblet on the table, the Master-at-Arms Commander made his intentions known. Harold was a good friend. They were even thinking of naming him the next successor in leadership, before the whole incident in the Desert. The insult of claiming that he had turned traitor, and, worse, that he had killed a fellow soldier, was too much to bear. Not since the White Raven cleansing had the Army had such a turncoat.

The list of Harold's victories was weighed and measured against the prejudice towards Karniel's bloodline. With each snide comment, Liam's blood boiled even hotter. These old men had grown fat and lazy in their leadership, the young man thought as he watched the foolish theatrics. How were they able to lead an army, to bring honor and justice to the country, if politics and lies were all they cared for?

Standing to straighten his tunic, Liam calmly walked across the room and sharply backhanded the arrogant commander defending Harold's actions.

Deafening silence commanded the room as the stunned leader reeled back. Turning to the rest of the Inner Circle, the enraged young man berated all present like wayward children. None of them had had the opportunity to serve with the prisoner, and yet, they felt qualified to pass judgment.

The scolding continued for almost two hours, with the youthful cavalier tearing down every false testimony and foolish thought. Slamming his gauntlet down, he dared anyone to condemn an innocent man. As muttering and grunting were the only sounds coming from the collection of aged soldiers, Liam cast a murderous glare at his father. And, before leaving the old men to their politics and foolish laziness, issued a challenge to the entire Inner Circle.

———◆———

Eight heavily-armored sentinels beckoned Karniel to wake. The day of his trial had come and his escort had arrived to ensure he would not be late. Calmly, they attached a heavy leather belt around the prisoner's waist, running chains through the iron rings. His hands and feet were secured, allowing just enough slack for a full stride.

The confidence of the guards caused all but Karniel to worry as they trekked throughout the Mine and up to the Keep. They had their orders, and no one but the Lord Commander could stop them. Four more guards, in ruby red chamberlain armor, awaited the group at the council room doors. Pushing the thick metal doors open, the chamberlain guards escorted the prisoner into the cavernous chamber. The eight waited in the foyer.

Karniel felt his shackles become hooked to the heart of the Fire Brand mosaic in the center of the floor. Soft muttering buzzed in the air as all five of the military branches and their leadership found their seats. Only Commanders, Aide-de-camps, and unit leaders were allowed in the raised benches this day. The chained Paladin refused to look at anyone but the man that claimed to be his father's friend.

A familiar itch between his shoulders caused Jaldo to turn from speaking with his councilors. Someone was boring holes into the Army leader with deep intent.

Studying the chained young man, Jaldo felt saddened by the person staring before him. Gone was the youth who showed love and honor for his departed father. Vanished was the lad who showed courage and loyalty to all that he helped. Only one thing resided in his young eyes, and that was death. Pure, unrefined Death.

The Lord Commander tilted his head as he saw the yellow and purple bruises on the prisoner's body. He knew what had happened to Karniel, and those responsible would pay with their lives.

Krakula, the Chief Chamberlain, struck his black-wood staff against the tile floor, calling the trial to order. Producing a page of parchment, the Chamberlain read aloud the charges against the accused by both the Fire Brand Army and the Cathedral of the Faithful.

Eadala and Varg shared looks at the odd development. Official charges were a serious matter, but, in the listing, Jaldo only accused Karniel of beating twelve taskmasters into a coma. The rest of the charges were issued by the Council of Bishops.

A maelstrom of fire burned in the accused eyes while the Master-at-Arms and the Archer Corps shouted at the charges being read. Their voices were so loud they were drowned in the echo. One side wanted the young man hung like a horse thief, while the other wanted him released with a full pardon.

Jaldo sat back and swallowed. He expected the outburst, but not the inconsolable rage that was occurring. There was no way to stem the flow of emotions festering under the surface of military order. Everyone was aware of the young man's parentage, his record of service, and all the lives saved in the Desert and the southern Keep. The very fabric of their cultural beliefs was on trial with the White Raven that had yet to utter a sound.

Blinding yellow lightening forked off Krakula's staff, silencing the outrageous yelling. The Chamberlain's staff glowed dangerously with a crystalline blue hue as his gaze passed over all present.

"If you cannot keep any opinions to an appropriate octave, gentlemen, then the Ruby Guard *will* escort you out."

The four powerful guards looked around the room, as if to prove their leader's point. They only reported to the Chamberlain and the Lord Commander, so their power was absolute. Grumblings were heard from both parties, but no one dared cross the Chamberlain or his handpicked group of elite fighters.

The Lord Justice Eadala stood with a sigh. It did not bode well for Karniel that the Ruling Council of Bishops had recalled the Paladins. How were they able to have a just trial without their testimonies, he wondered. The law demanded both sides be heard, but a dark feeling gripped his heart. Signaling for the advocates to begin, Eadala watched the defendant.

The military advocates, men chosen for their understanding of the law, gave their respective beginning statements. Each swore their cause was just, and the other was wrong. Their words were flowery to be sure, but were ignored by Karniel. The chained young man scanned the faces of those present. Most were not sympathetic to him. Closing his eyes, the Paladin Captain prayed to every deity he knew to aid him.

———◆———

Liam bounced on the balls of his feet. Choosing light leather armor, the young man mentality prepared himself for the coming offensive. Only one of the Inner Circle dared to accept the challenge he had issued while berating them earlier, and that person entered the arena. The sound of metal rubbing against boiled leather grew as Liam's opponent neared. A smile settled on the young man's face. He had been trained by the best sword masters in the country, but he had a trump card as well.

The Commander of the Heavy Cavaliers, Lord Polini, neared his son.

He felt uneasy fighting his own blood, but such a challenge could not be refused. Memories of his precious son flooded into view. The boy's first step, the first time he held a sword, his first hunt, among others played a disturbing symphony in the older man's mind.

Mentality shaking himself loose from the nostalgic chains, Lord Polini adjusted his armor. "We don't have to do this, Son," the father commented, hoping to save them both from embarrassment. "I know he is your friend, but there are forces beyond your understanding wanting this."

The pleading of an earnest father was not lost on Liam. Loyalty, not politics, drove the young man and his conviction for the truth. Opening his eyes, the younger Polini saw not his father, but an opponent. He was just another obstacle to overcome. Sinking into an attack position, the youth signaled for the judge to begin the duel.

------ ◆ ------

Striker delivered his testimony to the courts, with stern conviction. In his mind, this was a farce, a foolish mockery of *his* military code of conduct. Neither advocate dared to truly cross-examine the Commander of the Battle School, for he still carried his whip. Krakula thanked the trainer with a bit of a chuckle. They were old friends and, oddly enough, both liked the defendant.

Sounds of fighting in the foyer caused every eye to attentively look at the door. Karniel shook his head in disbelief. Hoping that was not Liam, the chained Paladin looked irritated at the prospect of another friend losing his life for a military that did not care about the code it swore to uphold. Gone was his desire for living a life full of heartache and pain. Everything he ever fought for, bled for, and killed for was a lie.

Liam pushed the doors opened with a grunt. Looking very worse for wear, the younger Polini sported a black eye, swollen lips, and a gash in his right arm. Blood trickled on the floor as he limped towards his friend. The duel with his father and the guards had been hard fought and justly won.

With a flick of his thumb, the wounded lad sent a signet ring sailing towards the Chamberlain. A sharp snap of movement heralded the Chamberlain catching the ring, shock registering for all to see.

"The court recognizes Lord Liam Polini, Master Horseman of the Heavy Cavaliers. What say you to this gathering?"

Liam had a hard time standing, as he could not breathe properly and had to use his sword as a cane to steady his wounded body. Pausing to give Karniel a winning grin, he began his speech.

"I have defeated my father in righteous combat, and now, by law and blood, I stand before you all, having full command of the Heavy Cavaliers. You fools present an innocent man to the slaughter to hide the sins of a traitor. Harold assaulted Isaak in the Desert, killed Tomas, and became confederates with our sworn enemies just to rebuild his dark pride.

"How can any of you be allowed to lead? I was raised here, played in these very halls, trained within the grounds with your children. Is this how we *act?* Why are none of the Paladins here? None of you sad, pathetic men, if you can be called men, dared to stand up and fight an obvious scapegoat. My vote is innocent. What says my fellow leaders?"

The lithe-built leader of the Archer Corps yelled innocent. Master-at-Arms screamed guilty. Striker stood for the Battle School and proclaimed innocent. The Scouts Division chose not to vote, stating they did not have a dog in this fight. All eyes turned to the three leaders. By default, Karniel should be released and reinstated, but, without the Church's blessing, such desires were a pipe dream.

"Paladin Karniel," the Lord Justice began, "without the backing of the Cathedral and the Paladin Corp, we cannot allow you to stay in the army in your current rank and position. For your crimes against the military code of conduct, we hereby banish you from all military service pertaining to the Order of the Paladins. Ruby Guard, step to!"

Three of the Chamberlain guards held Karniel in place while a fourth used a white hot knife to burn the wings from the brand that he wore so proudly. Pain tore through the prisoner as his soul was scarred far worse than his arm. A well of sadness sank deep into the young White Raven. He knew they would always see him and his clan as a scourge upon the land, and it broke his heart.

———◆———

Katril and Striker accompanied Liam as they escorted Karniel from the Red Keep. The Veritable Mother provided the former soldier with several vials of balms for his burned arm.

Silence controlled the group as they reached the outer wall of the same arena he'd first stepped into as a twelve-year-old boy, with all the hopes and dreams of becoming a member of the illustrious Fire Brand family.

Karniel had not said a word since they had removed his brand, despite his friends offering jobs or places for him to go. His mind, still broken by the complete and utter betrayal, did not even register the aid or their apologies.

Liam handed his friend a rucksack and a long, green velvet bag. "It's not much, but I made sure to get you clothes you could actually wear."

A sad smile creased the young man's face as he opened the green bag and found Tomas' bow. A simple nod was all Karniel could manage without breaking into tears. Katril cried as she gave her former charge a hug. Striker, with tears streaming down his face, clasped Karniel on the shoulder.

"Don't worry, Son," he spoke softly, almost sounding like Zuwl. "You will find your way, and when you do, not even the Gods will be able to stop you."

Pulling away, Karniel glanced one final time on the place he had once called home before disappeared into the traffic just beyond the gate.

EPILOGUE

The Ocean Snake pitched hard with the western wind finally catching its sails. It had been three weeks since the battle of the southern Keep and Gareth finally had to explain himself and the epic failure he had partaken in to his leader. The man he knew only as Master sat comfortably, resting in a full-backed red oak chair. His right hand held a goblet full of wine, and nary had a drop hit the deck.

Senka lounged easily on the ship captain's bed, basking in Gareth's discomfort. Their master looked on failure with no acceptance or mercy. Years had not eased the memory of her failure in the desert and the spectacular punish she had received. Gareth had stood silent then, and now she would enjoy watching him squirm.

"What did you learn," the goateed man asked, joining his fingers like a steeple after setting down his drink.

Another pitch of the waves slammed into the ship, hitting the former bandit with an urge to vomit. "He was so focused on his revenge, he could not see reason. I lost control of him, Master." He knew better than to ask for a pardon, for there was none to be had from those cold eyes.

"That is true. No general can control all his soldiers, which is why strong and wise leaders are needed." A single finger pointed at the anxiously standing man and he writhed in pain. "You did not stop me when I punished Senka those years ago. In return, you will be punished in a similar nature for your failure."

Their master stood, focusing his disappointment and anger into the man vomiting and convulsing on the cabin floor. He cared little if the ship's crew heard, for they would not live to see the harbor. One piece of information did peak his interest: the young, powerful Paladin. The Master wondered if that young man could indeed be the one he had been searching for all these years.

———◆———

Asiza only half listened to Varg and Mathis during the discussion over who was the most at fault over the trial. Her main concern was Yarmilla, who had become increasingly silent over the course of Varg's testimony. The young lady's mood had progressively gotten dark and angry. Why was she like this, the Shaman wondered, with slanted lids.

Mathis, leaning back in his chair, seemed content with the information he was hearing. It appeared that the White Raven was not a danger, but a victim of circumstance.

"So he was the reason why all the Paladins left the Tower," the Priest asked, almost laughing as he remember that day. Many in the Priesthood marveled at the mass exodus of the warriors and their personal belongings.

"Yes, I was the one that sent the carrier bird," the Fire Brand leader responded in a quiet voice. Jaldo and Eadala had retired not long after the trial and the scandal it produced. Each man returned to a quiet life, far away from the burden of leading. Both had recently passed away, Jaldo in his sleep and Eadala on a hunting trip.

Yarmilla's patience had finally come to its breaking point. Her time with the man in question was not common knowledge, but she felt it relevant to his salvation. "He told me of the trial and what transpired." All eyes were on her now. Varg's eyes were pools of shame and Mathis looked almost hungry for information. Asiza, however, seemed calm, as if the final pieces of a puzzle had come together.

Pain and fury streamed from the Harvester with the flood of memories flowing down her cheeks.

"You and your *precious* army would not allow the public to know that a man being groomed for the Inner Circle became a filthy twisted husk of a man. You excommunicated the perfect scapegoat. Who would question the combined *wisdom* of the Fire Brand Army, and the Cathedral, when they weighed it against the prejudice of the White Raven clan?"

Her testimony and questions were ablaze with a passion none of her fellow leaders had seen before. "Three of his most beloved family members lost their lives for your cause. He led, won, and honored your pathetic "code", and for what? To be cast aside at the earliest convenience. The Gods have a special place for cowards and fools, Varg. I pray you keep that in mind."

Her outburst astonished everyone. Such intimate knowledge of his trial stirred remorse in the Lord Commander. He knew they had condemned an innocent man, and yet he was the only one still alive to bear the burden. Not even Mathis was party to the decision to abandon the young man to his fate.

"You loved him." Such simple words uttered by Varg, and yet, they hit

Yarmilla like a typhoon. "When I learned he was found alive, I prayed it was true. No God would give me peace, child, but maybe he can grant me forgiveness. What happened to him after we abandoned him?"

The state of emotional and spiritual desolation that controlled the Lord Commander was not lost on Yarmilla. "Let me tell you the tale of how he won my heart and saved my life."

———◆———

Conjuring up a foot stool, the Lord of Chaos eased back in his throne, thinking over the events he had just witnessed. The treatment of one such as Karniel was not uncommon in that world. Instead of praising the young man for his valiant choices, the power-hungry fools of that so called religion made him a cautionary tale of what happens to those that oppose the ways of the abusive elite who used religion to fuel their desires.

Fawdake's laughter vibrated through the throne room. He did not need acolytes or disciples to gain power. All he needed was people foolish enough to use a scapegoat and those gullible enough to belief the Lord of Chaos was involved. This fear fueled the Deity to action.

Sniffing the air, and turning to the right, the laughing God called out to his visitor. "Oh, do come out, Brother. It seems such a waste to hide your pretty flames in the darkness."

A tornado of heat and light whipped around between the looking glass and the throne. Angry tongues of fire flickered out to the seated God, but could not touch him. It was eternal law that the Parthenon members were not allowed to kill each other. The God of Flame and Purity would never cross such a commandment.

Corded, toned muscle, etched around a chiseled frame, manifested itself in pure glory. For most of the mortals, he was the epitome of divine perfection. Square-jawed and broad-shouldered, Kogien feared nothing, celestial or mortal. Tipping his lance in a half salute, the majestic being spoke, his voice booming off the vaulted ceiling.

"You disappoint me, Brother," he confessed, driving the butt of his weapon into the shimmering floor. "Your champion was so easily captured by my followers. It almost seems like you had forgotten your place in this grand plan."

Leaning forward, and resting his elbows on his thighs, Fawdake eyed his counterpart with a gleeful stare. "Little sibling, I am afraid *you* are confused. That young man was not *my* follower. In fact, he was one of *yours*." Rising off the throne, he continued. "The mortal holds no special purpose for me, but your disciples just condemned an *innocent* man. A true believer in Order, Law, and Military Faith. Feel his anger, little flame, and realize his faith in you is dead."

The shock of his arrogance and pride came crashing down as Kogien felt the resonance of Karniel's soul. Blind anger and overpowering hate for the Fire Brand Army burned so brightly that not even the Fire God was able to withstand its strength.

Panting at the sheer power of being cast out, the visiting Deity from the Halls of Eternal Victory did not register his brother's voice whispering in his ear a simple yet powerful thought. "Now you understand the folly of casting aside one of your own. He will never pray to you again, little one. Never."

Watching his fellow deity wallow in shock and realization, the Lord of Chaos mused over the true nature of the fire element. "Thus is the price of fire. Life must be destroyed for the fire to exist."

Daniel Lucas

GLOSSARY

Karniel – kar-nel (karnɛl) - raised on the streets of the Red Keep as an orphan, Karniel has suffered persecution and abused for his family legacy. Adopted son of Zuwl, he is considered the last of the White Raven clan

Yarmilla – Yar-mil-ah (yarmmɪlæ) - Short and petite, she is sharp tongued and highly intelligent. The Current leader of the Harvesters.

Harvesters – the Trade and Banking clan set up to maintain trade and coin throughout the realm.

Asiza – Ah-cee-zah (æsizæ) - Leader of the Shaman's Temple and Master Mage

Shamans – The Mages guild whose sole purpose is to preserve, train, and create magics.

Varg – V'arg (vɑrg) - Leader of the Fire Brand Army

Fire Brand Army – Patroned by the Fire God, the military is broken down into the Battle School, Rangers, Cavaliers, Masters at Arms, and

Mathis – Mah-thus (maθaɪs) - High Priest of the Cathedral of the Faithful Cathedral of the Faithful – Once worshippers of the Wood God, the religion grew into doctrine of oaths, covenants, and rites.

Fawdake – Fal-dah-kee (fɔdɒki) - Lord of Chaos, God of Eternal Change

Striker – strahyk-er (straɪkər) - Chief trainer for the Battle School

Finley – Fin-lee (fɪnli) - Army soldier

Katril – Kah-trel (kɒˈtrɛl) - Veritable Mother attached to the Red Keep

Veritable Mothers – A mix of nun and mage, this all female order care for all with faith and magic

Pethio – Pa-thee-oh (pɛθiˈɒ) - Grand Master of the Paladins

Paladins – Seen as the law enforcement of the country, these armored monks use magic and war hammers to ensure justice is enforced.

Jaldo – Jal-doh (dʒældoʊ) - Former head of the Fire Brand Army before

Varg – V'arg (vɑrg) - Leader of the Fire Brand Army

Deston – des-stuhn (dɛstʌn) - Army recruit

Zuwl – Zuh-al (zuɔl) - Former leader of the Red Keep watch, Karniel's adopted father

Kevah – Key-vah (kehva) - Aide-de-Camp to Jaldo

Burgess – bur-jis (ˈbɜr dʒɪs) - Innkeeper in the Rut

Isaac – Ee-sak (isæk) - Leader of the March into the Desert of Mirrors

Liam – Lee-uhm (liʌm) - Army soldier and son of the Cavaliers

Tomas – Toh-mas (toʊmas) - friend of Karniel, member of the Ranger Corp, and clansman from Rogue's Bluff

Ashur – Ash-ur (æʃər) - Leader of the Desert tribes, often called the Desert Lion

Eirini – Ee-ree-nee (ireɪni) - Leader of the Water Seekers, a society in the Desert tribes

Arth – Ahr-th (ɑrθ) - Clan leader in the Rogue's Bluff region

Kayth – Kay-th (keɪθ) - Female Paladin

Ashith – Ash-eeth (ashiθ) - Often called the Beggar, a disguise used by Gareth

Zoloto – Zoh-loh-toh (zoʊloʊtoʊ) - Owner of the Golden Honeycomb Inn

Gareth – Gahr-eth (gærɛθ) - Former soldier, he gained the monitor of Bandit King.

Senka – Dark Mage, Acolyte of Volshebec

Questioner – torturer used by the Cathedral of the Faithful

Volshebec – Vohl-she-bek (voʊlʃɛbɛk) - Powerful mage, Enigmatic leader of Senka and, later, Gareth

Chadia – Chah-dia (ˈtʃædiɑ) - Isaac's former wife

Zoreza – Zoh-rey-zah (zoʊreɪzɑ) - Isaac and Chadia's son

Mokolot – Moh-Koh-Lot (moʊkoʊlɒt) - Field General of the Master at Arms

Jaecare – Jey-kahr-eh (dʒeɪkɑrɛ) - Chief Ranger of the Ranger Corp

Efrain – Ee-freyn (ifreɪn) - Fire Brand Army soldier

Harold – Har-uhld (ˈhærəld) - former leader in the Fire Brand Army

MAPS

Daniel Lucas

THE FIRE BRAND ARMY CASTLE AND RED KEEP

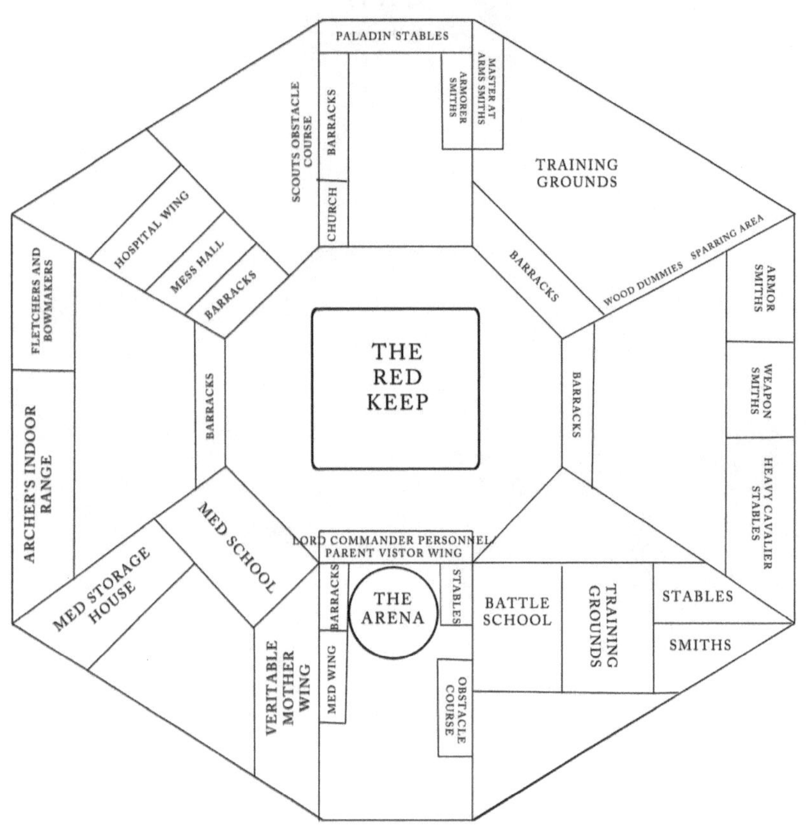

Dazmek

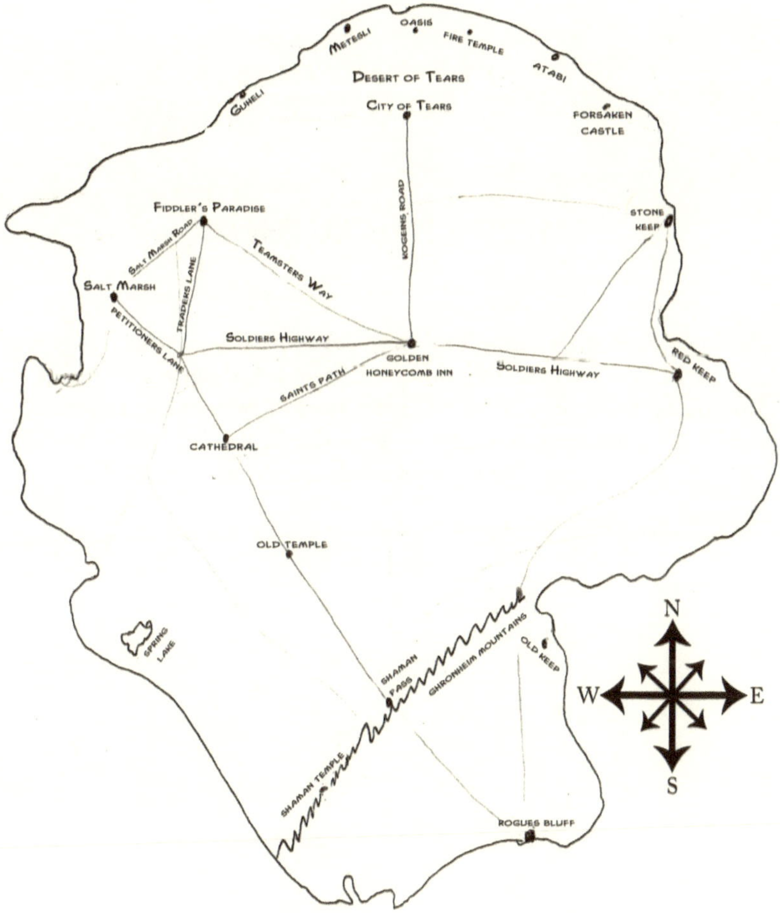

METEGLI
OASIS
FIRE TEMPLE
ATABI
DESERT OF TEARS
GUHELI
CITY OF TEARS
FORSAKEN CASTLE
FIDDLER'S PARADISE
STONE KEEP
SALT MARSH ROAD
TEAMSTERS WAY
MOGERNS ROAD
SALT MARSH
TRADERS LANE
PETITIONERS LANE
SOLDIERS HIGHWAY
GOLDEN HONEYCOMB INN
SOLDIERS HIGHWAY
RED KEEP
SAINTS PATH
CATHEDRAL
OLD TEMPLE
SPRING LANE
SHAMAN PASS
GHRONHEIM MOUNTAINS
OLD KEEP
SHAMAN TEMPLE
N
W
E
S
ROGUES BLUFF

ABOUT THE AUTHOR

Daniel Lucas considers himself a storyteller more than a writer. A graduate of his wife's intense course in writing, he has worked hard to hone his skills in putting his stories down on paper for others to enjoy. His usual occupation is as a financial educator, where he helps the middle class figure out how to improve their incomes.